You've Got Male

You've Got Male

New York Times Bestselling Author
Marina Adair

Entangled Publishing, LLC
644 Shrewsbury Commons Ave., STE 181
Shrewsbury, PA 17361
rights@entangledpublishing.com

Amara is an imprint of Entangled Publishing, LLC.

Visit our website at www.entangledpublishing.com.

Edited by Molly Majumder
Cover illustration and design by Elizabeth Turner Stokes
Interior design by Britt Marczak

Trade Paperback ISBN 978-1-64937-648-0
Ebook ISBN 978-1-64937-485-1

Manufactured in the United States of America

First Edition June 2024

10 9 8 7 6 5 4 3 2 1

To
My father-in-law, John.
Thank you for sharing your stories,
which were the inspiration
for Lenard.

Love is love is love.

At Entangled, we want our readers to be well-informed. If you would like to know if this book contains any elements that might be of concern for you, please check the back of the book for details.

Chapter One

Evie

Evelyn Granger knew from experience what it looked like when life was about to attack—and this attack was going to be Shark Week worthy.

The minute Evie saw her ghost of exes past, her already complicated day set itself on fire. She closed her eyes for a moment and manifested herself being anywhere but there in her parents' coffee shop, wearing the same uniform she wore in high school, working the same job she worked in high school. But upward job mobility wasn't an option when one's dad was diagnosed with kidney disease and could no longer run the family business, Grinder. In fact, doctors' appointments and dialysis meant giving up her dream job to come back to her teenage job as a glorified barista.

What had she done to piss off the gods? Because this could not be happening. Not when she was wearing coffee-cup themed leggings, a tank that read "Get Your Grind On", and holding a TOASTY BAGEL BALLS sign. Unfortunately, when one's husband catches an acute case of Slippery Dick Syndrome and leaves you to raise a child alone, passing out toasty bagel balls can become the new norm.

"Yo. Babe," her ex-husband, Mateo, said in that bro-tone he used that made her stomach curdle. Dressed in ankle-hugging jeans, checkered Vans, and a stone-washed shirt, he looked like he was headed to the skate park instead of being a dad to their sixteen-year-old daughter.

Then there was the sparkly, pretty, plus-one on his arm, whose coed smile, designer leggings, and yoga top did little to conceal her barely there baby bump—nor the extremely recent addition that was winking from her ring finger. A diamond that cost way more than their daughter's private school tuition Mateo harped on and on about. *Are you serious right now?*

"When are you due?" Evie asked, trying to keep the status quo in their relationship going. Surface questions, polite smiles at kid-swap, and flipping him the bird when no one was looking.

Heather curved her perfectly manicured fingers around her belly and gave a dreamy smile. "I'm sixteen weeks along."

"Does Camila know?" she asked.

Mateo and Heather exchanged a look that made Evie's skin itch. And there was her answer. A resounding *no*. Not that she was surprised. Had Camila known her dad, who saw her only every other weekend, was going to become a full-time parent to another kid, there would have been heartbreak. Dramatic, over-the-top, soul-crushing heartbreak.

Evie considered getting mad, but she'd wasted so much mad on her ex over the years it would take a lot to muster up even a "Screw you." If she wasn't so tired, she might have even had a good belly laugh at the situation. The kind that brought tears to her eyes. But the tears threatening to break through her fortress of *everything's fine* were humorless. And unexpected.

Mateo walked out sixteen years ago, right before Camila was even born. Oh, he'd always paid child support and came around most weekends, but for the day-to-day he'd been absent, especially in the beginning when he'd been finishing up law school.

When it came to dating, all the Granger women were crazy. Her mother dated men who were too young—*"They work harder to impress,"* she'd say—her daughter dated men who were too old—*"Boys my age have the emotional maturity of frappuccino!"*—and Evie, well—to the disappointment of her family and coworkers—didn't date at all.

A prime example of why was standing right in front of her.

"When are you going to tell her?" Evie asked. And again she was met with silence.

Having an absent co-parent had been especially hard in the earlier years. Evie's parents stepped in, giving Evie the love and support she desperately needed. But having an absent dad who wandered in and out like the changing of tides had been devastating for Camila. And no amount of love and support could make up for the missing hole an absent parent blasted through a child's heart.

"We were going to tell her at the wedding," Mateo said, running a hand through his straight black hair.

"And when is that?"

Another look was exchanged, and that turned those itches into hives. "We're getting married at the end of the month. In Hawaii." Mateo said the last part as if it didn't affect their aerophobic daughter, who couldn't walk onto a plane and not hyperventilate.

"Hawaii?" Evie nearly knocked the toasty bagel balls over. She couldn't afford a trip for two to Hawaii. She could barely afford the car insurance for a teenager. And in a month? It just wasn't possible. Mom couldn't work both shifts, Dad had dialysis, and Camila—

Shit!

"Camila has overnight cheer camp that weekend. It's mandatory and gives them a chance to win an early bid to Nationals." It was the most important week of the year for Camila and her teammates. It's where they got to know each other, made inside jokes, bonded. If she didn't participate, she ran the risk of being left out of the fun. For the entire year. "You're supposed to be on carpool duty and drive the kids to Grand Junction."

"I'm sure she'll understand," Heather said with the confidence of a woman whose kid had never suffered disappointment. "Plus, if she can't make it, we can always FaceTime with her."

"FaceTime?" *No way.* Heather might not care if her soon-to-be stepdaughter was there but Camila would. So much so that just thinking about it made Evie's heart hitch. "I'll find a way for us to go. Maybe I can call her coach, explain the situation. I can ask Julie to pull extra shifts at the shop," she said, referring to her closest friend and the shop's part-time assistant manager. "Mom can handle the dialysis appointments. And..." She trailed off because the energy of the room had shifted.

Oh God!

"You don't actually want her there, do you?" she asked.

"It's not that. It's just a kid-free wedding," Mateo explained as if she were the one not grasping the enormity of what would transpire in the next few moments. But Evie knew. She knew her kid's relationship with her father, how she viewed her self-worth, and what her relationships with men would look like were on the line.

Evie set the tray down and lowered her voice, praying she got through to him. He might be a self-focused philanderer, but he wasn't cruel. And this was cruel. "She isn't just any kid, Mateo.

She's *your* kid. And she'll be heartbroken if she isn't there. You don't want me there, fine. We can figure something out. I'll figure something out."

Wasn't that what Evie had spent the past year doing? Figuring out other people's shit?

Despite what people thought, she always felt one step away from completely losing her own shit. Even more so now, as she watched the self-involved lovebirds saunter away with their orders, hand-in-hand, as if they hadn't just left her in yet another bucket of poop.

She remembered the moment when she realized that she was in it alone. When she realized that she couldn't be all things to all people. No matter how hard she tried, she was going to fail at something: parenting, her career, her personal life—or maybe all three. She knew why people talked about the sandwich generation. After Mateo walked out, she was forced to move back to her childhood home, sleep in her childhood bed, and raise her child on her own.

But three generations under one roof meant three generations of opinions. From arguing about what show to stream, to how to modernize the coffee house, to who was the cuter Hemsworth brother—it was a constant challenge for Evie to meet the needs of her mom and her daughter, and she often felt like the referee of the family.

But then there was also three generations of love all shoved into one house. Evie loved her neighbors, and she loved her childhood home, but lately it was as if they were living on top of each other. Lately, it felt as if Evie was using her parents as a crutch—and she was ready to walk on her own.

If you'd asked her friends, they'd say Evie slayed at life. Unknown to them, Evie's life was one Xanax away from falling apart.

• • •

"Don't let that man take up one more cell of energy," Moira, her mother, said while placing a fresh batch of toasty bagel balls on the tray. "And don't you dare use him as an excuse to stop dating. You've made so much progress lately."

"I've gone out on two dates." Evie placed each ball in its own paper liner. "One wanted to measure my neck for a collar and the other didn't believe in deodorant. That's what happens when you swipe right on life. It's time to admit that I have the worst picker ever. All the Granger women do. Look at you and Dad." She pointed to the mustached man behind the counter wearing a pink flamingo shirt, pressed white skinny jeans that were cuffed at the ankle, and a pair of Coach slip-on sneakers with the classic logo in rainbow colors.

"Yes, look at us. I was married to my best friend for sixteen years. Had a beautiful daughter and a beautiful life."

"Mom, when I was twelve, he announced to the world that he was gay." The world announced back that they already knew. Well, the world minus Moira and Evie. In a blink, Moira's life went full circle, going from best friend to lovers and back to best friends.

Her mom gave a casual shrug. "So he likes men? So do I. In all shapes, sizes, and ages it seems. In fact, last night I met up with this personal trainer from Boulder who can crush a melon with his—"

"Remember when you used to say, 'I'm not your friend, I'm your mother'? Well, I need you to be my mother right now."

"You're right." Moira took Evie's hand. "And this mother notices how much her daughter always takes care of everyone and everything else, leaving no time for herself. It's time for you to take care of you. And I want you to know that you can count on me to be there for you."

It took a moment for Evie to form a response through the emotion clogging her throat. "Thanks, Mom."

With a motherly pat to the cheek, Moira walked behind the bar top to help with the never-ending line. Grinder wasn't just a local coffee shop; it was an institution in the Denver area. People had been coming there for thirty years.

This place meant everything to her dad, and her dad meant everything to her, which was why she plastered on a smile for the next customer and said, "Toasty bagel ball?"

Her gaze locked on to a pair of familiar blue eyes and a strange unfurling happened in her stomach. Warm and tingly and pheromone induced. It was as surprising as it was unwanted.

"Toasty balls?" her neighbor, car-pool buddy, almost-one-night stand, and arch nemesis, who always managed to swarm when there was chum in the waters of her life, said. "I didn't know that was a service you provided."

"Are you offering yourself up for scientific study?" she asked.

"I like my balls just the way they are." A challenging look entered Jonah's eyes and more parts, inappropriate parts, tingled, igniting a heat that zigged then zagged, colliding in the dead center of her chest. A clear sign that her anger was starting to rise. A usual occurrence when in his presence.

He was dressed in a faded University of Colorado tee, which had a coffee stain on the hem, day-old sweats, and a five o'clock shadow from summers past. Like Evie, his life was a complete shit show. Unlike Evie, he didn't try to hide it, instead wearing it loud and proud.

"Why are you here?" she asked.

He picked up a bagel ball and popped it into his mouth. "I heard that you were throwing a shindig tomorrow night and I was wondering where my invite was."

With a beaming smile, Evie dug through her apron pocket and pulled out an envelope. "Consider yourself Cinderellaed."

He eyeballed the letter suspiciously before accepting it. She couldn't help the victorious grin that overtook her when he opened it. He met her gaze, then smiled.

"Congratulations! I didn't know you were going back to school."

"What?" Panic hit like a sledgehammer. She grabbed it back, glanced at the acceptance letter to CU Denver's business school, then hastily shoved it back in her apron. "Whoops. Wrong one." A big whoops, since that letter was a secret—even from her family. Especially from her family. She'd had so many decisions made for her, she was taking her life back. If she went back to school it would be because she decided to, not because her family guilted her into it. This was her life, her decision. Just like writing out this invite for her neighbor. "Here."

She handed him the proper letter. He took it, and she remained silent as he read it and knew when he got to the good part.

"What the hell is this?" He held up the letter and jabbed a finger at the bolded paragraph in the middle of the missive.

"That is a summons for you to appear in front of the Beautification Board to discuss the current state of your yard."

"*You* are the Beautification Board."

"I'm *part* of the board." She softened her voice and took a small step forward.

"You could have just come to me."

"I did. Three times and there has been zero change. Your lawn resembles a wheat field. To be fair, I asked the board to give you a chance to explain your landscape plan of action before they fine you."

She left off the *again*, but it hung in the air.

His wife passed away two years ago, leaving behind a teenage son, an infant daughter, and a distraught husband, who went from being a big player at a prestigious investment bank to an at-home day-trader who wore T-shirts with holes in the armpit. He also wore his grief like a familiar old blanket that wrapped around him and everything he touched.

Jonah crumpled up the letter and stuffed it into his pocket. "Is this about my pomegranate tree?"

He was referring to the pomegranate tree that had launched a neighbor-war equivalent to Hatfield and McCoy.

"No. This is about our neighbors, who call, show up at my house, at my work, all to bitch about your yard. As if somehow, because your tree hangs over my property line and drops concrete-staining fruit onto *my* pathway and the sidewalk and attracts rodents, I'm the responsible party. I've held them off as long as I can."

"I just need a little more time. Plus, what's the big deal, it's a yard. There are more important things in life than a fucking yard."

Evie knew he was talking about his deceased wife, Amber, and what it must be like to raise two kids alone. She felt for him, she really did, but she couldn't handle one more thing on her plate. She had so many plates spinning that one more distraction would have them crashing down like a Greek wedding.

"I've held them off as long as I could. But you're on your own, buddy. Plus, your landscaping skills need work."

He stepped closer and a whiff of his dreamy cologne engulfed her, awakening her senses. Or maybe it was the stiff Denver breeze coming in from a customer who forgot to close the front door.

"I don't comment on your *ladyscaping* skills."

"You've never seen my ladyscaping."

"Is that the story you're sticking with?"

"Fine. You saw it once, but that didn't count."

"I know I've said it before, but I'm sorry for how that night ended," he said quietly, reaching out to brush the back of his knuckles against hers. She jerked away like she'd connected with the end of a live wire.

"And like I said before, I get it." But did she? Because while her mind knew Jonah was still struggling with the way things had transpired in the last few months of his wife's life, Evie's gut was screaming that he'd stopped for an entirely different reason. A reason she desperately wanted to understand. Because now there was this awkward strain between them, and she didn't know how to fix it.

Didn't want to fix it. It was safer being enemies than friends at this point. At the moment she couldn't think of another person who grated on her nerves more than her messy neighbor. Just the way he took care of his appearance was enough to send her off the edge.

Then there was that familiar feeling that pinballed in her chest, banging against each rib, growing to the size of a sledgehammer by the time it reached her confidence. Rejection.

The burn added to her already scorched heart.

Chapter Two

Jonah

September was flexing her muscles. The air was so hot that with one breath Jonah felt his lungs ignite into flames. And the high altitude wasn't helping. He'd grown up in the Mile High City, but he'd never acclimated to the dry heat of summer.

Jonah pulled into the drive and took in the gray-and-white 1912 Tudor he and his late wife spent six years renovating into their dream home. With the steeply pitched roof, narrow leaded-glass windows, and large brick front patio, it was the gem of the neighborhood. Or it had been. Gone were the sprawling gardens and manicured trees. Left to their own devices, the grass had taken over the flowerbeds and the trees now encroached on the easement. It was just another aftereffect of what happened when one's wife was three months pregnant and diagnosed with cancer.

Encroachment.

Jonah's therapist would say that the condition of his house was a metaphor for the anger and disillusionment he'd adopted as his natural state of being. He didn't used to be the cynical prick who purposefully went out of his way to piss off the neighborhood, but he wanted them to feel even an ounce of what his life had become. A complete shit show.

For example, after dropping Waverly at preschool—where he sweet-talked some of the moms into siding with him at the Beautification Board meeting—and making some headway on chores, he'd spent the day sending out resumes and calling every contact he had in his past life praying for a job. Or at least the chance to get his foot in the door and prove he was the man for the job.

Evie may have thrown fire on this next-door-war by calling tonight's Beautification Board meeting, but it didn't mean Jonah wasn't going in with some serious ammo in his back pocket.

He was just finishing up his community campaign when the high school called, requesting his appearance. Which was how he'd spent the past hour with his stepson's principal, football coach, and Spanish teacher discussing the finer points of Ryan's shit-tacular progress report—which was the first Jonah was hearing of it.

Ryan was a straight-A student, always had been. Until his mom passed. Then everything changed. He'd become moody, distant, secretive, and unmotivated.

Four things Jonah could relate to.

One look at his wife and his entire world had changed. Jonah had changed. Being loved by a woman like Amber had that kind of effect. Every day he was embracing the fact that she was gone, but how did he move past his wife's death without leaving her memories behind? Especially when there had been so much discord right up until the end. Discord that could have been avoided if he'd supported her decision to forgo treatment and spend her last few months around her kids and not hooked up to an IV.

Slowly he was coming to terms with the loss. He only hoped he could change fast enough to be the kind of dad his kids deserved.

Brushing the sweat from his forehead, which had nothing to do with the spiking temperatures, Jonah grabbed the takeout from the front seat and walked up the brick pathway to the front porch. He opened the front door and let out a sigh that came from the depths of his soul. Ryan's school things were strewn in the entry, his cleats haphazardly lying in the center of the floor— at least he'd bothered to take them off this time.

"Ryan?" he called out.

A grunt of acknowledgment came from the family room.

"I got takeout." Jonah had to look for a clean space of countertop just to set the bag down. Jesus, it looked like an episode of *Master Chef* had exploded in his kitchen. Dirty dishes were stacked on the counter right above the dishwasher, frozen pizza wrappers were lying around like carcasses, and dirty mixing bowls were filling the sink.

"There's this thing called a dishwasher. It actually does all the work for you," Jonah called out.

"It's full."

"Then run it."

Jonah inhaled for eight, held it for four, and then exhaled. A trick his grief counselor had taught him and the only reason he hadn't killed his stepson. Then he walked in and saw a first-person shooter game on the television and all that breathing ramped back up. Ryan was sunken back into the couch, barely visible, his socked feet up on the coffee table, and snuggled upnext to him was his baby sister, Waverly.

The room smelled like a post-football practice that took place on the surface of the sun and stale Fritos. There were more wrappers and plates on the coffee table and dirty football pads hanging off the armchair.

Jonah picked up the remote and turned off the television.

"Dude, I was streaming that," Ryan said.

"And your baby sister is watching you blow off the heads of people."

"She's watching *Paw Patrol*." Ryan pointed to the tablet in Waverly's sticky little hands. She was in a cute green dress that matched her eyes, white bows that were about to stage a coup with her hair, and bare feet, with a red frosting stain above her lip.

"What happened to no sugar after lunch?"

"I didn't think it was a big deal, since it's Mom's birthday and all."

Which explained the dirty cake pan and red food coloring on the slate countertop.

Jonah dropped his head and pressed his palms to his eye sockets. He'd been so focused on this meeting with the principal and the Beautification Board meeting tonight that he'd completely spaced.

"I'm sorry, bud. I forgot."

"No big deal. Wave and I had our own little party."

"Maybe we can do something this weekend."

"Maybe." Ryan shrugged, but the weight shoving his son's shoulders down caused Jonah's heart to contract like it was being strangled by the strength of a thousand gods.

"Your mom would have loved that," he said, then looked at his daughter, who wouldn't remember her mom's face or voice or life-changing hugs. "How long did she nap?"

"She didn't. I tried. She wasn't into it," Ryan said, and Jonah didn't bother with a lecture. Waverly got her mom's red hair, her big green eyes, and her tenacity. When she set her mind to something, no one could dissuade her.

On the other hand, Ryan was quiet, thoughtful, and emotionally mature. That was until Amber died. Now he was just sullen and angry, testing every boundary Jonah set. It didn't help that his birth-dad was out of the picture. Jonah had adopted Ryan when he was ten, but that kid was his through and through. He loved his son so much it hurt to see him struggle with the immense amount of grief his mom's sickness and death caused.

"I tried to put her down twice and both times she crawled out of her crib and right over the baby gate. I laid down with her for about an hour but she just cried. So here we are."

Jonah knew that pain. It had been the routine for the past few weeks—ever since he'd enrolled her in preschool. He'd tried every parenting tip he could find online and none had worked. He was at a complete loss. And exhausted. And ready to hire a professional parenting coach.

"Uppie."

Jonah lifted Waverly and she locked her little arms around his neck, resting her head on his shoulder. He held her tightly and breathed her in. She smelled of baby powder, vanilla frosting, and heartbreaking memories.

"Hey, bug," he whispered.

Her answer was a little puff of exhausted breath against his skin. He could feel the weariness seeping through her body and guilt came on swiftly. A little yawn tickled his neck.

Shit, if she slept now, she'd never go down tonight.

He held her for a long moment, but when he went to set her down she clung to his neck and started to cry. He knew he should be strong, do some of that tough love he'd read about, but he couldn't. He hadn't seen her since this morning and last night's bedtime was a complete clusterfuck with tears and hysterics, where he sat outside the door listening to her howls and nearly cried himself.

She might not remember her mom, but she seemed to crave her touch all the same. He pulled her back into him. "Daddy's got you."

This was why he was here at four in the afternoon, instead of making million-dollar trades in a million-dollar office downtown. To be with his kids.

His coworkers thought he'd lost it when he'd quit months before making partner, and maybe he had. But when Amber passed he knew his kids needed him here more than his ego needed him in a thousand-dollar suit playing big man on campus.

A memory of Ryan holding his mom's hand as she took her last breath gripped him by surprise. A war of emotions had been battling inside him that day: sadness, helplessness, and a lot of anger. At the world, at the doctors, but a small portion was also aimed at Amber herself. She'd died while he'd been angry at her. And that was something he didn't think he could ever get over. Just like he knew Ryan was having a hard time getting over the loss. Which was why Jonah had given him a wide berth and the space he needed to come to terms with losing yet another parent.

But he'd clearly given him too much leeway.

From the moment Jonah met Amber, standing in line at the grocery store, he'd had one goal. Marry her. Have a family. Work hard to give them the life they deserved. That she came with a son only sweetened the pot. Then they found out she was pregnant with Waverly and he thought life was perfect. Until the diagnosis and the fear of losing the best thing in his life set in. Then came the helplessness and finally the arguments over how they should proceed.

She was asked to be part of a groundbreaking trial that could have prolonged her life for up to five years. But it was brutal on the body. Six-hour treatments three days a week. Never-ending tests. In hindsight, he understood her decision, but at the time all he felt was that she was yet another person to leave him behind when she had a shot at staying.

He knew Ryan carried the same questions and insecurities about why his mom wouldn't want to fight for him. But Jonah was fighting to keep his family above water, only he was afraid he was doing a crap job at it.

"You want to talk about your grades?" he said, sitting gently next to Ryan on the couch so as not to jostle Waverly, who was now fast asleep on his shoulder.

"What's the point? Since it seems like you already know."

"I met with your principal, and she is threatening that if you don't pull up your grades they'll put you on academic probation."

Ryan shrugged as if he hadn't a care in the world.

"That happens and you're benched until they come up."

That got his attention.

"They can't do that. I'm their starting running back. Scouts from CU Boulder are supposed to be there in two weeks."

"They can and they will if you don't pass your upcoming tests. Coach and I got them to give you two weeks to pull them up to passing. But I expect them to be stellar. You're also a scholarship student. So no football, no scholarship. Do you have any idea how much Saint Ignatius costs?"

Not that Jonah didn't have the money. He'd invested his wife's life insurance policy wisely, nearly doubling its value over the past year. But that was meant for college and weddings and retirement.

"Have you considered asking Camila for help?" he said, referring to Evie's teenage daughter.

"She's too busy with Monty. Or is it Arlo this week?"

Jonah had to bite back a smile. Ryan and Camila were best friends, had been since they were in diapers, but ever since

Camila grew curves Ryan had been more brooding than normal. That she was dating his older teammates only added to the kid's frustration.

And her mom wasn't dating at all—at least, she wasn't open to dating him. Which was probably for the best. Jonah needed to extinguish the dumpster fire that had become his life. And admiring Evie's ladyscaping skills would only further complicate things.

"Well, you might want to get on her dance card and soon, because you're going to need help if you want to clean up this mess."

Jonah wondered if that was part of *his* problem. That he needed outside help to gain a new perspective on his life. He felt like he was running a race with no sense of where the finish line was.

Chapter Three

Evie

"Don't you dare move," Evie said to the about-to-topple stack of garbage bags full of clothes that she had purged from her closet for Goodwill during spring cleaning. It was now September.

Between helping with the store, being a mom, and running a household of four, things were falling through the cracks. Something she'd come to terms with the moment she discovered she'd be a single mom. Up until that point, her life was as organized as Marie Kondo's closet. It was what had made her, at one time, such a great CPO: Certified Professional Organizer.

Evie loved the feeling of accomplishment that came with letting go of the old to make way for the new. It was how she managed to get through the most challenging years of her life, by letting go of the hurt and sadness. Most importantly, it was the ability to let go of the dreams that could have been. But that was an important part of the healing process. And that's what she had helped her clients do. Organize the grief and sorrow, the joy and happy times, and hold on to what mattered and give away what was holding them back.

Oh, if her former clients could see her now.

Evie's life was such a mess she'd had to quit that last thing that was truly hers—her being a CPO—to bail her parents out of a bind. Help them let go of what wasn't working so they could implement things that would grow their coffee shop.

For years, she'd managed to balance being a mom and running her own CPO division at the company she worked for. She'd even come to terms with being in her thirties and still living with her parents. Her divorced parents, who shared a home and a business and a plethora of dating tips for Evie. They doled out unsolicited advice on just about everything. From parenting, to finances, to how to relax her pelvic floor.

Evie might not be sure what her pelvic floor was doing, but her mom hadn't needed to give her a gift card for a ten-session pelvic floor massage for Christmas—which Evie did not redeem.

She grabbed a basket of clothes, which were rolled but still not in their drawers, and shoved it under the bed.

"Mr. Karlson just pulled up," Lenard called out.

"Tell that lemon thief he can wait on the porch until seven. Doesn't he know it's rude to arrive at an event early?" her mother snapped.

Moira didn't have a mean bone in her body unless it came to Mr. Karlson. They made Jonah and Evie's bickering look like a playground squabble.

Evie looked at her watch and panic set in. More people would start arriving at any moment and she hadn't even had a chance to change her clothes. She was still in her barista uniform, smelled like a pumpkin spiced latte, and she didn't have a speck of makeup on.

Hefting a gigantic pile of bills and receipts that her father had strewn around the office that she'd brought home to sort, she walked to her corner desk—the same desk that had Nick Carter covering it—and set it next to her idea book—which was more of a stack of clippings—for her mom's surprise sixtieth birthday party.

It was going to be a garden party glamorous enough to knock her mom's socks off and she couldn't accomplish that with Jonah's yard in such discord, or rats on the guest list. She needed this meeting to go her way.

On her nightstand, in its own stack, was the most important thing in the room. A letter stating that Grinder was nominated for *Denver's Best Coffee Shop*. The winner would be decided by the public and Evie wanted to be that winner. No, she needed a win—and so did the shop. The kind of publicity that came with the honor could singlehandedly pull them out of the red.

Another knock sounded and Evie heard the front door open and shut.

"Mom, light the cookie dough candle," she hollered down the hallway. "It will make people think the cookies we bought are homemade."

Moira peeked her head in. Dressed in a teal pantsuit, with her highlighted, choppy hair spilling over her shoulders, she looked like one of Charlie's angels.

"They *are* homemade. Their former home just happens to be the market," Moira said, looking down at the pile of Goodwill bags that, three minutes ago, had been lining the front hallway. "No one will care."

"I'll care."

"Clutter makes a home look lived in."

"Your kind of clutter makes a home look like a yard sale. And I can't preach beautification and have our house be one bag away from starring in *Hoarders*."

"You mean, you can't lecture our sexy neighbor on community guidelines and have him see that you're human and sometimes forget to make your bed?"

"This has nothing to do with our neighbor," she said, and Moira sent her a knowing smile. "It doesn't. The meeting that is cutting into my weekly bubble bath, that is all about him and his yard. I caught another rat in our trap today."

"That is becoming a problem. They're nibbling on the roots of the rose bed." The roses her own grandmother had planted fifty years ago when they bought the house. No gang of needle-teethed, tail-whipping rats were going to take her down. She had singlehandedly raised her daughter, cared for her parents, was bringing a café back from the dead, and was throwing her mom the best garden party ever. Not to mention she'd decided to take accountability for her future and at least send in the acceptance letter for the placement exam for classes any day now.

And she wasn't about to let her neighbor's incompetence ruin her plans!

"Which is why this meeting is so important!" She stomped her foot and her mother lifted a brow at the usually calm-in-the-middle-of-the-storm Evie. Well, she was stepping out of the eye of Hurricane Granger spinning around her and taking some of the power back. If she wanted her life back on track then she needed to venture into unknown territory and find some damn tracks. "He either cleans it up himself or the board sends in a demolition team and landscaper at his expense."

"If you're so bent on besting him, then why do you have your favorite blue dress out?"

Evie stood in front of said dress, blocking her mom's view. "I'm not trying to best him. And I just picked the dress up from the dry cleaners."

"Well, you should wear it. People underestimate the power

of a good dress. I still remember the dress I wore the day your father asked me to marry him," Moira said, her voice thick with nostalgia. "I knew he was going to propose."

"You never told me that," Evie said. Her mom rarely talked about her life before the closet had been thrown open on her marriage. "How did you know?"

"I can read your father like a book. He can't hide anything from me."

"Mom, he's gay," Evie pointed out.

Moira took in a deep, trembling breath. It didn't sound like heartbreak or sadness, more of an *If I could turn back time.* She walked to the bed and sat on the edge of the mattress. "I think deep down I knew that, too. But I'd found my soulmate and love can blur the truth until all you see is color. And your father is the most colorful person I know. Bright, brilliant, and so warm he felt like home. He's still my home."

Evie sat next to her mom and took her hand. "I'm sorry, Mom."

Moira patted Evie's hand. "Lenard is my soulmate. I have no doubt about that. No matter how he came to be in my life, all that matters is that he is."

"Why do you think he proposed when he knew it was a lie?"

"When Lenard was younger, maybe sixteen, he fell in love with a boy from his neighborhood. They kept their relationship a secret, then Ken was drafted and he and your dad would send love letters to each other," Moira said. "One day, his mom was putting away his laundry and found the letters. Your grandparents confronted him and said, 'This ends now.' That was it. No conversation, no acceptance, no trying to understand. Then they stood there and made him rip up the letters."

Evie could barely speak through the enormity of the conversation. "I can't even imagine a parent turning away from their child when they needed them the most."

Moira cupped Evie's face. "That's because you're a good mother. Now you know why it's so important to your dad that the heart of his business doesn't get cut with budgets and minimizing overhead. He built the safe place that he dreamed about having as a child. A place where all people are welcomed and can come together to celebrate love and friendship. Some of our regulars have been coming since we opened thirty years ago. And my answer as to why he proposed, he said if he could make it work with anyone it would be his best friend."

Evie couldn't tell whose eyes were mistier, hers or her mom's. Her parents might not have the most traditional of love stories, but it was a love story nonetheless. When Evie was ready to start looking for a partner, and that was a questionable *when*, she hoped to find the kind of loving and supportive partnership her parents shared as the foundation for more. Only one that was more than platonic.

"Now, about that blue dress," Moira said conspiratorially.

"Tonight isn't a blue dress kind of night."

Moira didn't look convinced as she patted Evie's knee and stood. "You'll know when it is. Now, I think I'd better light that candle and let you get ready. Is there anything else I can do to help you, honey?"

"I'm good. But thanks."

Moira blew her a kiss, then closed the door behind her. Evie didn't waste time. She yanked off her uniform and, in nothing but her cotton boy-cut undies with gnomes on it and "Gnope" written across the butt and her weekend bra, fumbled through her closet, dismissing one outfit after another. None of them were the blue dress, but if her mom caught on that she was dressing up more than usual, then Jonah would certainly notice—and he'd say something. Then she'd be forced to lie—again.

Gah. She was a terrible liar. It's why she still hadn't told Camila about the wedding.

"White pencil skirt?" She pulled it on and looked at her butt in the mirror. "Looking nice, but it's too late in the year to wear white."

Next came a yellow romper. "Shows off your legs but does nothing for the girls." She cupped her breasts and lifted them to where they sat before childbirth, and with a sigh tossed the romper onto the bed.

Next came a flowered sundress. "Too soccer mom."

How hard was it? She just wanted one take-charge, boss-girl outfit that didn't betray the fact that she'd stayed up all night trying to figure out how to save her dad's shop and all day with her head under a frother.

The panic had nothing to do with Jonah coming to the meeting. Not a single thing. She was just thrown by seeing Mateo and his new fiancée, that was all. It was perfectly natural to want to feel a little sexy after bumping into your ex while holding toasty balls.

She draped a silky pink top across her chest and imagined herself in a pair of dark fitted jeans and swayed back and forth. It was sophisticated without looking like she'd tried too hard and had this sweeping neckline that bordered between sensual and sensible.

"How many more outfits can you possibly try on, Evie?" she asked her reflection.

"I'm hoping the entire closet," a familiar male voice said from the doorway and her heart flip-flopped.

A lump of horror materialized in her throat as she rewound the last five minutes, wondering just how much Jonah had heard—and seen.

Grabbing the first thing she could find—her robe, luckily—

she held it to her body and spun around. Thankfully, he had his back turned her way. She slipped on her robe, heart still pounding away in her chest. "You can turn around now." As he started to, she asked, "What are *you* doing here? Come to bring me another fruit basket?"

He put a finger to his lips to shush her and that's when she realized, sitting in the crook of his arm, was a pissed-off Waverly, eyes red, cheeks flushed, and dressed in a duckie-covered footed pajama set, with already shed tears streaking her face. Jonah on the other hand wore a pair of faded jeans, a blue T-shirt, and his hair looked as if he hadn't slept in a week.

"What are you doing here?" she hissed in a bare whisper.

"You invited me, remember?"

"To my house, not to my bedroom."

"Your mom directed me to Camila's room so I could try to put Waverly down, but I like this view better. Your mom did say third room on the right."

She was going to kill her mom. She just couldn't help inserting herself in Evie's life. Especially her dating life. Well, there would be no dating because she'd adopted a man-free diet. And unlike her five-years-running New Year's vow to give up doughnuts, she was going to stick to this diet.

"Well, show's over," she snapped. After the day she'd had, there was nothing in the world she wanted less than to be stuck in her bedroom with a man who drove her crazy.

"Too bad, I was just about ready to pull out some twenties and make it rain."

"Make it wain," Waverly repeated.

"Seriously? You have a toddler in your arms."

"Before you start throwing stones, just know that your daughter showed up at my house for a tutoring session dressed like a go-go dancer."

Evie gestured him away and quickly put on the top and the jeans, and fastened everything up tight. Making sure it was all on the right way—she didn't need any more embarrassment—she walked over and tapped Jonah on the shoulder.

"Don't say it," she warned as he turned around, and he made a big deal of zipping his lips and throwing away the key. Then her eyes fell to Waverly, leaning against a wrinkled shirt that said "Sorry I'm Late I Didn't Want to Come". "Is this some kind of ploy to get sympathy votes?"

He smiled. "Is it working?"

"The shirt sends mixed messages. Your daughter isn't a golden retriever you bring to the beach to attract women."

"Sunshine, are you asking if there's a woman in my life?"

She snorted. "You wish."

"I wish for a lot of things." His eyes went to the neckline of the silk top. "Seems the Wish Fairy is on my side tonight."

She rolled her eyes. "Shouldn't she be in bed?"

"She and Ryan had a party and mainlined sugar and red food coloring. It's like he gave her an IV of Red Bull. I couldn't get her to stop crying. Every time I put her to bed, she lost it."

At the word bed, Waverly's little face puckered up in defiance. "No bed!"

"You have to go to sleep sometime, bug."

"No sleep!" she said more forcefully, that little quivering lip sticking out. Then Waverly curved her body in, her pudgy legs and arms going ramrod straight, waist bent as if doing downward-facing dog on Jonah's chest. "No. Bed!" she wailed at a pitch that only bats could hear. "Down!"

"No deal, bug. You stay in my arms, that was the agreement."

It took everything Evie had not to laugh, but he looked so miserable she held it in. "You're trying to make a deal with a tired toddler?"

"Down! Down!"

"I see your point." If Jonah had looked resigned before, now he just looked defeated. "I made the crucial error of letting her take a twenty-minute powernap right before dinner."

"That will do it."

"Her sleep schedule's been off ever since I put her in preschool and they have her napping twice a day," he said over Waverly's grunts and attempts to free herself. "So she's wired at night."

"Sometimes they have to cry it out."

"Yeah, well sometimes this dad can't handle her tears and wails." Jonah collapsed on the edge of the bed and propped his daughter on his knee, giving her a little bounce. As if on cue, Waverly changed position, pulling her body into child's pose before exploding her limbs out in every direction like a pissed-off starfish. Then came the wailing and flailing.

"Sorry about the noise." Jonah shook his head helplessly. "I don't know what to do when she gets like this."

Evie opened her mouth to tell Jonah this was the universe's way of punishing him for the "hilarious" basket of rotten pomegranates he had left on her front porch and other shenanigans he'd pulled on her over the past few months. Like after she asked him to clean up the fallen leaves and he had put them in a tidy pile in the center of her driveway. Or how, on his side yard that faced her bedroom, he'd put in a light bright enough to be seen from space. But instead she heard herself offer, "Here. Let me try something."

"Are you sure?" he asked, but he was already holding her out. "She's built like a brick and has a wicked left hook."

Evie wasn't intimidated. She'd suffered enough forehead to the chin action in Camila's younger years to know how to bob and weave. She gripped Waverly under the armpits and the kid stopped squirming until she realized she wasn't going to be put down, then it was like trying to hold a slicked pig at the county fair.

"I," *gasp*, "want," *gasp*, "downie!" And then came the sobbing crescendo.

Ignoring the tantrum, Evie walked into the bathroom and turned the water to cold. With the confidence that comes from years of dealing with tantrums, she bounced the toddler on her hip, wet her hand and then rested it on Waverly's cheek.

The cool touch shocked Waverly and broke her next sob midway. Waverly opened her mouth again, a cry right there waiting to be released, when Evie did it again to her other cheek, gently cupping it. They played this game a few times before the little girl's sputtering slowed, breathing regulated, and her body started to sag, her little palms unfisting and going flat against Evie's chest.

"You're just sleepy is all," she said quietly, swaying back and forth. "I'm pretty sleepy, too."

She rested her cheek on the top of Waverly's head and took a deep breath. God, she loved the smell of babies. Loved how they felt and how they sounded. Even when they were fussy, Evie couldn't get enough.

She gave a few more shushing sounds and ran a cool hand down Waverly's neck. Evie opened her eyes and found that they weren't alone. Jonah was leaning a shoulder against the doorframe, one ankle crossed over the other, arms folded, a gentle look on his face Evie had never seen before.

One she didn't want to investigate too much. Only she couldn't seem to look away. A problem, since neither did he. Holding her gaze, he slowly approached and rested his palm on his daughter's back and made comforting little circles. And that was how they ended up sharing the same five-foot-square space with a sleepy toddler tying them together.

The longer they stood there, the more intense this feeling in her stomach grew, the more at ease they became with each other, until it felt as if the clock had turned back to a time when there was comfort between them. The connection was the same, yet somehow different.

Deeper.

"How did you do that?" he asked quietly.

"When Camila was this age, sometimes she'd get fussy just from being fussy. A cool hand can be a little reboot."

"Does it work on adults?" he said lowly, and even though she knew he wasn't flirting, the air between them felt heavy.

"Do you need a reboot?"

"I think I need more than a reboot. My whole life is a constant 404 Error."

Evie connected with this on such an elemental level that when he held his arms out, she nearly walked right into them. The urge and need to close the distance gradually built until her heart was thumping hard against her ribs. His gaze met hers and something deep and tangible passed between them.

He opened his mouth just as Waverly let out a big yawn, breaking the moment and reminding Evie of why this could never happen. He might not want to acknowledge that their lives and obligations and external expectations were between them, but there they were.

They were both in different stages of life. He was at the start of fatherhood. College was becoming more of a reality every day for herself and Camila. Her world was messy enough without adding another person to her to-do list.

Although her hormones said he'd be a great to-do addition.

His eyes went soft with disappointed understanding as he took Waverly and cradled her to his chest.

"I know you weren't around when Ryan was this age, but

I promise it gets easier." Evie soaked a hand towel in the cool water and put it on the back of Waverly's neck.

"Ryan's grades are bottoming out and he spends more time at home playing video games than with his friends."

Her heart cried for Ryan. The teen years were already hard, but to wake up one morning to discover your mom's time on Earth had an early expiration date would be devastating and confusing. Camila's shattered family unit was enough to affect her views on relationships and self-worth; Evie couldn't fathom the scars Ryan would carry for the rest of his life.

When his daughter was relaxed, her head resting lazily against his shoulder, Jonah backed out of the bathroom and slowly paced from one end of the bedroom to the next, stepping around the bags and laundry baskets, rubbing Waverly's back the entire time.

"Today is Amber's birthday," he said softly.

"I am so sorry. I didn't know." Or she never would have summoned Jonah to a meeting that, in the grand scheme of things, didn't matter.

"Me neither, until Ryan locked himself in his bedroom earlier, after he'd made a cake with Waverly. I completely forgot."

"And now it's all you can think about," she said knowingly. "Shit happens, Jonah. Things fall through the cracks. It's called being a parent."

"Do things slip through your cracks?"

She snorted. "All the time. In fact, I forgot to pay the electric bill for the shop and they shut it off midday, I nearly missed pickup today because I fell asleep in the lunch room at work, Mateo doesn't want Camila at his wedding, and I haven't even told her there *is* a wedding."

"Why not?"

"Because it will crush her."

"No, why doesn't he want her there?"

She shrugged. "Because his girlfriend is pregnant and he doesn't want to deal with how that's going to affect Camila. He wasn't there for her but now he's all-in on another kid? That's going to crush her. Plus, Mateo's a coward," she said. "So I'm trying to figure out a way to blame it on a conflict in scheduling, rather than have her think her dad doesn't want her there. And don't even get me started on the stacks of invoices and bags of donations. My life is one fire after another, but if you tell anyone what a hot mess I am, I will deny, deny, deny."

"Your secret is safe with me. The wedding and *those* 'Gnope' panties. Doesn't mean I won't be thinking about them all night."

A flutter took flight in her belly. When was the last time a man had looked at her the way Jonah was looking at her now?

Remember his overgrown yard. The basket of "ha-ha" pome-granates he left on your porch as a joke—not funny. The complete lack of consideration for his neighbors. Those flutters were nothing more than heartburn, plain and simple.

She pushed past him and opened the bedroom door. "Maybe you should stick to thinking about how you're going to convince the board to let you keep that tree."

"I will abide by whatever the board decides," he said as if he'd been waiting all day for this meeting to begin.

Something was up. Her mom-dar was sounding the alarm. Then there was the arrogant grin he sent her way. A wash of unease trickled down her spine like drops of sweat.

He brushed past her, his shoulders purposefully grazing hers, and the air seemed to *snap, crackle,* and *pop. With anger,* she told herself. Then a wave of spicy testosterone smacked her in the face so she held her breath until he exited. Only right before she thought she was safe, he turned to face her and all that swagger had vanished, leaving behind a vulnerability that she felt all the way to her core.

"Thanks, sunshine," he said.

"For what?"

He lifted a heavy shoulder and let it fall. "Not making me feel like a shit dad."

Shock had her at a loss for words. She'd never imagined that Jonah would write himself off as a bad dad. From what she'd seen he'd always been attentive and present, a parent whose love for his kids was tangible. All-encompassing.

"You're a good dad, Jonah. This is just a rough age."

He gave a single nod and headed across the hall to put Waverly down in Camila's room.

"And Jonah, let her cry it out for a little bit. She's just tired and moody. If she knows you'll rescue her whenever she makes a peep she'll just keep playing you."

"How do you know?"

"Because Camila played me for five years. She still does. Tears are a parent's kryptonite."

He winked and she felt her toes curl. Maybe she'd stumbled onto another unwanted kryptonite.

Chapter Four

Jonah

Jonah watched Evie work the crowd like a pro. She'd managed to greet every guest with a warm, personable hug, asking about their family, their hobbies, how their garden or home projects were coming along. The woman knew everything about everyone. Not in a busybody way like her parents, but like she genuinely cared about each and every guest in her house.

Him, on the other hand, she was avoiding. Well, as much as one could avoid when stuck in a tight space where they could smell one another's shampoo. By the time he'd joined the meeting, there was only one vacant chair—way in the back. Since she'd practically ushered everyone to their seats, he knew she'd left the one farthest from the podium for him.

Without ceremony, Jonah picked up the chair, dragged it to the front of the room, and placed it directly in front of the podium, creating his own row. She narrowed her eyes, and those full lips went into a full-on pissed-off line.

He smiled.

She did not smile back. In fact, she made a big show of looking over his head and ignoring him, which he found amusing.

Sunshine indeed.

"Did everyone get a copy of the agenda?" Evie asked, all prim and proper from her makeshift podium, which looked more music-stand-from-the-local-middle-school than presidential.

No one listened. Not even Jonah. He was too busy taking her all in. She'd opted for the pink top and ass-hugging jeans and she looked lickable. The silky pink number cupped her breasts to perfection. Then there were her legs. Covered in denim so tight, the fabric hid nothing. Long and toned and the kind of legs a man could spend hours exploring—yoga legs. He knew this because he'd caught glimpses of her from his back window doing downward-facing dog.

Not that he should be thinking about her in spandex while sitting so close he could hear her breathe. Besides, he was still unnerved about how his heart had reacted to seeing her hold Waverly. The simple act of the moment had jumpstarted it.

There hadn't been a lot of simplicity in Jonah's life recently. He'd been so connected with Amber that when she had passed his world unraveled. He was through the worst of the grief and finally in a place where moving forward didn't feel like a complete betrayal. Only he didn't know which direction to go. His GPS had gone dead at the funeral. Now it was flickering back to life, but he didn't want the chaos left behind to overflow onto the people around him.

Evie cleared her throat. "Let's bring this meeting to order."

"Good," Mr. Karlson said. Karlson was in his later sixties with a white crop of hair and grew petunias like he was one of the King's botanists. "I would like to talk about ethical choices when it comes to the community garden."

The community garden was three lots down from Jonah's and looked like something out of a Disney movie. Apple and cherry trees, lamp-lined walkways, and a bunch of vegetables and bright flowers that changed with the season. This community took their gardening seriously.

"The key word there is 'community,'" Moira said, those usually friendly eyes hot enough to scorch. "I live in this community."

"You're growing marijuana," Mr. Karlson pointed out.

"Which is completely legal." Moira stood and addressed the crowd. "As a Colorado resident, I am allowed to have six personal plants."

"At your house, not where the neighborhood teens can make a doobie."

Moira rolled her eyes. "Kids don't call it 'doobie' anymore. It's hemp. And it's medicinal."

Evie shot her mom a look that could fry an egg. "And it's not on tonight's agenda."

Mr. Karlson stood. "It's offensive and against community policy. Which is why I'm starting this petition to have the plants torn from the garden."

"You do that and I'll have Lenard pour bleach on your precious petunias."

"Enough," Evie said in her mom voice, and everyone fell silent except Jonah, who took the moment to chuckle at her stern expression. She was in boss mode. And damn if that wasn't attractive. "We're only here to talk about the 452 Spring Street situation."

Jonah arched a brow because that was news to the owner of 452 Spring Street. "I thought that my house was *on* the agenda, not *the* agenda."

"Didn't she tell you?" Mrs. Gomez asked. "This is a special

hearing. Had to miss my *Jeopardy!* to make it."

Jonah had spoken to Mrs. Gomez that morning about just this issue, and while she said she'd come in support of him, she'd never mentioned that Evie had called a special hearing. So much for giving him a chance.

He met Evie's gaze and her cheeks pinkened. "So I'm special, huh?" he whispered for her ears only.

She leaned over the podium and whispered back, "You wish."

The position did amazing things to her cleavage so he took the moment to enjoy the view, then wiggled a brow.

She glanced down at her chest and then snapped upright, pressing her hand to the gaping neckline. Then she pushed her shoulders back and chin up, her tone dialed to President of the United States about to give the State of the Union. "Spring Hill Community Beautification Board meeting, September ninth, is now in session. If you'll all turn to the agenda, we can get started."

Jonah's hand shot up.

"Yes?" she said overly brightly.

"Back to this special agenda. Why was I only given twenty-four hours to prepare?"

"The agenda was posted on the community website last week, as per regulations."

"I didn't see the posting."

"Not my fault. You've had a total of three warnings about the state of your yard. You've ignored each one."

"That's not true. I did pick all the rotten pomegranates up off the sidewalk." Then he'd put them in a gift basket on Evie's porch step as a little joke. The fury in her eyes told him he was the only one who found the humor in it.

"And it brought the rats that are feasting on the fermented pomegranates to my house. I can hear them in my walls, Jonah. This has become a health hazard."

"I'll hire an exterminator."

"Which only works if you cut back the fruit trees in your yard or maybe, I don't know, actually eat the fruit? Or they'll just come back and continue to devour my grandmother's rose garden. Some of those roses are fifty years old and the rats are gnawing at the roots."

Wow, he didn't know it had gotten so bad. "I'll fix it. I just need time. I'm sure you all understand I've been a little busy," he said. "Swinging single parenthood and being my own boss keeps me on my toes."

The brackets around Evie's mouth became more prominent as she fought to keep her professional smile in place. "Which is why we are considering giving you a one-week extension to get your yard in order before we send in a team to relandscape your yard. And maybe get rid of those fruit trees."

Anger like none other mixed with panic. "Anyone who touches those trees will be sued. Understood?"

The whole group went silent at his threat. But he intended to be clear. Nobody but him would ever touch his wife's orchard.

"And seriously, one week?" How the hell was he supposed to clean up nearly two years of neglect in one week? Especially with Waverly still potty training and Ryan's pressing school and football schedule? Not to mention his son's grades. He needed to be on top of things *inside* his house. He didn't have the extra bandwidth to deal with hedges and sod.

"That does seem a little excessive," Mr. Karlson, Moira's nemesis, chimed in.

Mrs. Lichfield, community dictator when it came to beautification, put on her usual scowl. "He has been given three warnings. We need to send in the landscapers, and he's paying for it!"

"All I'm asking for is a little more time," Jonah said.

Moira elbowed Lenard in the ribs and whisper-yelled. "You

remember how hard it was when Camila was going through the terrible twos."

Great, so the entire house heard him trying to get his kid asleep.

"Which is why we've been talking and we think a week is asking a lot," Mr. Karlson said with authority.

Evie looked around the room. "Who's been talking?"

"We all have," Mr. Jamieson said.

"Not me," Mrs. Lichfield said. "I say we fine the man now. Hell, let's bring in the bulldozers and landscapers Monday morning."

Jonah stood. "One person sets foot on my property, and I'll weed-whack your hedges to the ground," he said to Mrs. Lichfield, who gasped like she was a lady on *Downton Abbey*.

"No need for all of that," Mr. Jamieson said and motioned for Jonah to sit, which he did. "The majority have decided to give you and your family another six weeks to bring your yard up to code."

"Six weeks?" There was a hint of panic in Evie's voice that piqued Jonah's interest. It was gone as quickly as it had come. She nervously smoothed her hands down her jeans. "That doesn't work for me. And since when do we discuss board matters outside of board meetings?"

"Seeing as Jonah didn't have a babysitter for the evening, he took it upon himself to come and chat with us individually to explain his situation," Mrs. Gomez said sweetly.

"You did." It wasn't a question. It was an accusation.

"I didn't want any more neighbors calling you on my behalf," he said steadily.

He could tell she wanted to argue but couldn't because he was only repeating what she'd told him—instead she ground her teeth.

"Well, if we're all in agreement, then why don't we call this meeting to a close and enjoy some of the cookies. They smell delicious," Moira said.

"If anyone has a different opinion, please feel free to voice it," Jonah said, daring Evie to go against the majority.

She looked at Mrs. Lichfield, seeking support, but she let out a sigh and said, "Six weeks, but not a day more."

"Snickerdoodles it is," Moira said, standing and surprising Jonah. He hadn't spoken with either of Evie's parents and had expected the most pushback from them.

He looked at her father, waiting for the lecture, but Lenard just shook his head disappointedly at Jonah, who now felt like a class-A jerk.

Moira led the way to the kitchen, where the rest of the group followed. Except Evie, who was gathering up the abandoned agendas off the seats and, for a brief moment, Jonah thought he saw her hands shake as she stacked them together, and something didn't settle right in his gut.

Then her gaze met his and it was hot enough to nuke his nuts. "You blindsided me."

"I took responsibility for my yard and apologized to each and every neighbor."

"A fun fact you could have explained when we were in my room."

Yes. He could have. He should have. But he thought it would be funny to see the look on her face when she realized that her whole plan to screw with his life backfired. Only he wasn't laughing now. "I was going to tell you but then Waverly went ballistic." *And I saw you in nothing but panties and my mind was scrambled.* "I should have told you."

"It wouldn't have mattered. You already rigged the vote. You used that single-dad charm and won them over."

"So you think I'm charming?"

"I think you are a gigantic asshole."

"You said you wanted everyone off your back. That's what I did."

She stepped into him, toe to toe. "What you did was go charm everyone into getting"—she poked his pec—"your"—poke—"way." *Poke. Poke.*

He trapped her hand beneath his. "Just like you went around riling everyone up about my yard. Well, checkmate, sunshine."

Unexpected hurt flickered through her anger. She jerked her hand back and crossed her arms around her belly. "I didn't ask for this meeting, Jonah. Mrs. Lichfield did. I'm guessing she left that out during your morning coffee."

"I didn't meet with Lichfield. Knew it wouldn't make a difference."

"So you admit the point of your surprise neighborhood visits was to get people on your side?" she asked quietly.

"There aren't sides here," he said, watching emotions play across her normally schooled face. "What are you not telling me?"

Evie stared at him for a long moment, and he could see the exhaustion and a hint of vulnerability seep in. She brought one arm across her chest and defiantly gripped the bicep of her other arm, then gave a tired shake of her head. "Nothing I can't work out. Good night, Jonah."

He watched her walk down the hallway, away from the party, a party he knew she'd never pass up. For one, she was a people person. And secondly, she lived and breathed party etiquette and leaving her guests to fend for themselves went against every host-rule she possessed.

Jonah was about to go after her when Mrs. Gomez approached. She was dressed in mourning black, pink orthopedic shoes, and a cloak of grief. She clutched a stack of documents to her chest.

Gloria had lost her husband a few months back to a heart attack and was having a hard time bouncing back. In fact, tonight was the first time he'd seen her outside of her yard since the funeral.

"I know you need to get your little one home, but I need a minute."

"What can I do for you?"

"It's about my Raoul's life insurance. Those little pricks at the insurance company are giving me the runaround about my payout, and I know that you gave them hell when they tried to deny your claim after Amber passed. I can't even make heads or tails of what it says. It's like trying to understand the inner workings of the male brain. I swear they write it that way on purpose to confuse people."

Unfortunately, that was the truth. Jonah only knew his way around a policy because when he'd been a broker at the firm, he'd specialized in investing and growing insurance payouts.

"If you want, I can take a look at it."

Mrs. Gomez's eyes took on a grateful sheen, as if she finally felt like she had an ally in the fight. It made Jonah wonder if Evie had any allies and who they were, because tonight she'd been on her own. Even though her parents clearly loved and adored her, her mom didn't hesitate to question her stance on the vote.

"Moving on is just so hard," she said with a sniffle.

Jonah put a supportive hand on the older woman's shoulder. "I know."

Chapter Five

Evie

"He literally said 'checkmate.'"

"Weren't you the one who served him papers?" Julie asked.

Julie's hair was pink with blue streaks today. Her tattoos were from shoulder to wrist and her piercings were too many to count. She was an up-and-coming photographer, who worked part-time as an assistant manager at Grinder to supplement her income until her career took off. She was also Evie's ride or die.

The two had met when their kids were in diapers at Fam Jam, an organization for new parents. They immediately bonded over being the only single parents in a herd of happily married mommies. Whereas Evie had been single by circumstance, Julie had gone the route of a sperm donor.

The two immediately jelled and began supporting each other through the trials and limitations that came with single parenting. Swapping babysitting hours, recipes, and forming their own carpool crew. Then Amber came around, another single mother, and joined their carpool crew—although they were never besties like their kids, they were neighborly.

It was at one of Evie's garden parties that Evie had introduced Amber to her neighbor, Jonah, and the rest was history. Within months the two had fallen in love and married, and shortly on their heels Julie met her soulmate and tied the knot, leaving Evie a little bit of the odd girl out. But two years ago everything changed.

"I didn't serve him," Evie defended over the whirl of the steamer. Julie was making a latte while Evie was placing fresh bagel balls on a tray to serve to the customers, the hot vapors sending her curls into corkscrews. "I simply handed him an invitation to the next board meeting."

"It looked like official business to me. You had that look."

"What look?"

"That chick energy you get whenever you're around him. Like you want to eat him alive."

Julie took the latte from Evie and with a toothpick made a chain of three hearts. Sheesh, being married had turned her once cynical friend into an ooey-gooey, Team Cupid, hopeless romantic.

"Or kill him slowly."

Julie lifted a challenging brow. "Hey, if you're into that, who am I to judge." She looked around the shop, which was busier than usual, and shouted over the chatter of morning greetings, "Adam. Latte for Adam."

"He actually collected every rotten pomegranate off the ground and placed them on my front porch. In a gift basket. All wrapped up with cellophane and a matching pomegranate-red bow."

"So his love language is presents. Sexy."

Evie picked up the next cup, read the order, and began

making an extra-dry cappuccino. "He did it to rile me up."

Julie hip-checked Evie. "Well, it worked. You sure seemed hot and bothered by the sexy single dad next door."

"Not hot, just bothered." In the most annoying of ways. "If you had rats in your walls you'd be lighting houses on fire in retaliation. And why are we still talking about him?"

"You're the one who can't seem to drop it. Talking about his fruit."

Evie felt her shoulders slump. "They gave him six weeks to do what he should have done a year ago, which means his front yard will look like a dumping ground during my mom's birthday party."

Julie stopped what she was doing to meet Evie's gaze. "Oh honey, I am so sorry. I know how hard you've worked on that party."

"It was going to be a garden party. Everything I've planned is for a garden party. I can't fit that many people in my house. The Beautification Board barely fits."

"We can fix this," Julie said with excitement. "We can line the walkway with pretty white tents and twinkle lights hanging from them. Make garlands from Gerber daisies. Then rent some of those silly white curtains to hang between your fence and his, like Kristen Bell did at her wedding."

"I don't have the time for garlands or Kristen Bell's budget. I barely have time to study for my placement exam." Another thing she was doing in secret. She didn't want to get too excited in case something came up—like life. But of course Julie had ferreted it out of her.

"So you're going to do it?" Julie wrapped her arms around Evie from the back but Evie was too busy prepping herself for Julie's reaction when Evie admitted she was a coward.

"I think so," she said and panic wove its way up her chest,

strangling her lungs with an insurmountable pressure.

She had one week to send in her response, which she would. She just had to decide if it would be "starting school in the fall" or "defer until next year." She wasn't sure how long it was going to take her to turn her dad's shop around but finishing her business degree had always been important to her. It was just one of the many dreams she'd lost sight of when she'd become a single mom.

She could almost feel the pride she'd have when she hung that diploma on the wall. It would make her the first person in her family to graduate college. Her parents had sacrificed a lot to send Evie to school. That she'd dropped out two years in had been a huge disappointment—to them all. With a degree under her belt she could help her parents' shop and then, maybe, even open her own professional organizing company—be her own boss of her own business. One she dreamed of.

"No more thinking or you'll think yourself right into a no."

After going over the shop's books, Evie was more than halfway there. A *no* didn't have to be a door shut, it could just be a *to be continued*. Only she'd had sixteen years of *to be continued*. And wasn't it time she did something for herself?

Then she pictured her father at breakfast that morning. Too tired from his treatment to even make it to the table. He said he'd try to come into the shop around lunchtime, but Evie wasn't holding her breath. In fact, she'd rather have him home, resting.

Lenard was so upbeat and sunny he shined. He was the reason Grinder had been such a success for so many years. He created unwavering loyalty from the moment he opened his mouth. People loved Lenard and Lenard loved people.

"Hey!" Julie snapped her fingers in front of Evie's face. "I see what you're doing, and stop it."

"He couldn't even make it up the stairs last night without losing his breath. I feel like it's getting worse."

"He just started treatment a few months ago. Give it time to work. Plus, your dad is as stubborn as you. He isn't going to let a little thing like his kidneys hold him back."

"I just wish mine had been a match." Because then all the worry and stress would be nonexistent. Lenard would be healthy, Moira would be happy, and Camila wouldn't have to worry that she might lose her grandpa sooner than any kid should.

"They'll find him a match. He's still young and otherwise healthy."

All Evie could do was nod. She set the order on the counter, called out the owner's name, and then went right into making the next order, glad to have something to do other than cry.

"Now, back to Jonah," Julie said. "I heard he showed up looking like a sexy lumberjack with his bicep tattoo and shaggy beard."

"Sexy isn't the word I'd use."

Julie smiled knowingly. "What word would you use?"

Delectable. Delicious. Dangerous for your wellbeing. "A dick head."

"Are you sure this isn't just the residual effects of Mateo Exposure?"

"Mateo Exposure is no joke. It's a serious affliction with long-lasting symptoms."

"Clearly. I mean when was the last time you had an orgasm?" Julie asked. Evie went to open her mouth and Julie shushed her. "I mean a man-made orgasm."

She couldn't remember the last time she'd had orgasm-worthy sex. Mateo wasn't the most patient of lovers. That should've been red flag number one. Evie already had a hard time getting out of her head and into the moment. It didn't help when your partner asked, "Are you there yet?" two minutes in. Then there was the white stick that changed everything. Who knew that two little pink lines could cause the man who claimed he wanted to marry you to burn rubber out of your life?

It wasn't that she hadn't had sex over the years. Okay, she could count the number of lovers she'd had on one hand and still have fingers left over. But raising a kid solo didn't leave a lot of room for dating.

Julie slapped a hand to her forehead. "Oh my God. You've never had an orgasm."

"I've had an orgasm."

"One that didn't include batteries?"

Evie remained tight-lipped on the subject.

"How did I not know this?" Julie covered her mouth with her hands. "This is even worse than I thought."

"Can you keep it down? I don't want the entire shop knowing just how pathetic my sex life is."

"Pathetic by choice."

"Single by choice," she corrected. "There's a difference. And I don't have time for dating. I'm barely keeping my head above water."

"Then maybe it's time you allowed yourself to go under for a few minutes. What's the worst thing that could happen?"

"I could drown?" Lose her family's shop. Miss her dad's appointments. Take her eye off the ball when it comes to Camila. The list went on.

"Who knows? Maybe a hot, young lifeguard would be there to give you mouth-to-mouth."

"I don't want a lifeguard, especially a young one. That's more my mom's MO."

"Then what do you want?" Julie rested a hip on the counter and pulled her phone from her apron pocket and started scrolling through her inbox. "Hypothetically speaking, of course. If the perfect man were to walk into this shop, who would he be?"

Evie hadn't even had a moment's peace to think about what she wanted in a partner. She hadn't gone into her twenties thinking she'd wind up alone. In fact, late at night, when the house was quiet and the world was asleep, she let her mind wander, wondering what it would be like to have a life partner. Someone who took the time to understand her and accept her for who she was. Someone she could rely on and share the workload and joyous moments with—and the shitty ones.

Maybe it was because she'd had a long day, or that the worry over her dad's health felt like an albatross, but hypotheticals felt like a fun distraction. "Okay," she said, handing a complimentary bagel ball to the next customer in line, her "Grinder" tee dusted with flour. "If I were to accept a date from a man, he'd have to be kind, funny, reliable, know his way around a kitchen."

"And the bedroom?"

"For sure the bedroom. My monthly battery budget is insane. And it would be nice to put on some silk and lace for someone other than myself." She laughed. "He'd have to be gentle, but all man and funny."

"You already said funny."

"Because it's important. If he can't laugh at himself or the chaos of life, there's no way he'll fit into mine."

"Anything else? Brunette, blond? Bad boy or boy next door? Charming or swagger?"

"Aren't they the same thing?"

"No, charming comes from confidence. Swagger is closer to cocky but in a good way."

The man who came to mind had both charm and swagger and had this whole bad-boy-next-door vibe about him, in his own rumpled, lackadaisical ways. Evie gave herself a mental shake.

That man didn't even own a razor—there was no way he could give her what she needed. And at this point in her life, an orgasm was the only thing on the table.

"Neither. I want sweet and romantic, the kind of man who would meet a stranger in a coffee shop and bring a single red rose. Or talk about bouquets of freshly sharpened pencils."

Julie rolled her eyes. "You mean, like Tom Hanks in *You've Got Mail*."

"Joe Fox is a role model for single men everywhere. Successful, driven, loyal, good with kids—"

"A liar."

"That's just a trope of the rom-com genre. And it was more of a mistaken identity than a lie, another trope. Oh, did I mention funny—"

"Twice."

"Loyal and"—*since this was just a hypothetical, what was the harm in asking the dating gods to deliver*—"a man who can give a woman an orgasm. Like a blow my mind, take me to another galaxy orgasm. But I don't think one like that exists."

"Is that a challenge to the Universe?" Julie asked.

Now that she thought about it, a date with a nice guy wouldn't be so bad. Getting all dolled up for someone else would be fun. Not that there was time for fun, but this was all hypothetical.

"I guess it is."

Chapter Six

Evie

On Tuesday morning, Evie sat in the break room, staring at her parents across the table. It was like being called to the principal's office, only she was the principal and her parents were the irresponsible party.

"I can't believe you let it get this bad and never said a word," Evie said to them.

Her parents shared a pained look before Lenard spoke. "We didn't want to worry you."

"Yeah, well your plan backfired. I'm worried."

She'd spent last night going through every bill, statement, and order and she still couldn't believe how close the shop was to going under. Sure, when she'd quit her job to work for her parents' shop, she figured it would be just long enough to fill in until they could hire someone to take over as general manager. After seeing the books, there was barely enough money to cover the day-to-day expenses, let alone hire a qualified and trustworthy manager.

How had the shop gone from booming to nearly bankrupt in just a year? And how had she been so distracted with her own life that she didn't see this moment coming?

"Just manifest what you want," Moira said. Her mom was dressed in skintight capris, a leopard print blouse, and matching heels. Her lipstick was red, her hair upswept, and her skin could rival that of a woman twenty years her junior. People often mistook them for sisters, which Moira loved.

Evie squeezed her eyes shut, took three deep breaths, even did an ironic *oh-mmm.* Then she opened them and pointed to the spreadsheet that was so red it resembled Jackson Pollock's painting, *Mural on Indian Red Ground.* "Yeah, the invoices and overhead are still here. I hate to say this, but we're going to have to find a way to increase revenue and decrease spending."

"No," her dad said. "I know what you're thinking and we are not raising our prices."

"Or cutting employee hours," Moira added sternly.

Evie hated where her mind was going, but it was closer to letting go of a few employees. "We don't need six employees working on a Tuesday afternoon. Maybe at one time, but not anymore."

"We're a family here," Moira said. "And family sticks together, especially through the lean times."

"Mom, we aren't lean, there is no fat left on the bones. We're bleeding money."

She flipped the spreadsheet that she'd painstakingly created but neither parent even spared it a glance. It was like if they didn't acknowledge it then the problem didn't exist.

"Our employees depend on that money to feed their families," Lenard said, and even though he was dressed in a boldly patterned, fitted shirt with his trademark smile, Evie noticed the slight wrinkles around his mouth, the lightly jaundiced eyes, and the labored breathing he was trying to conceal. He'd worked the register for less than an hour before Evie demanded he sit down.

More worrisome than his obvious exhaustion was that he'd listened to her.

"If we don't make serious changes, and I mean now, we aren't going to be able to feed our own family."

Lenard clapped his hands. "Then we reach out to the community, have a good, old-fashioned Rainbow Raising. Maybe host Gay All Day Saturdays where coffee comes with a free scone."

"That's a great idea, Lenny," Moira said, pride and excitement lacing her voice. "Maybe we can do a few bake sales. Gloria had been tinkering with the idea of selling her empanadas to local shops before her husband passed. People love her empanadas. It would be good for sales and good for her to have a purpose again."

Evie sighed. "We'd have to have Rachael Ray and Gordon Ramsay cooking if we want to make a dent."

Moira ignored this. "The Smut Club is looking for a new place to host their weekly book club meetings."

"That's exactly what we don't need. A bunch of old ladies ordering a cup of tea and then taking up half the seats for three hours. We need new customers."

"This was the first queer-owned and -operated shop in the state. We made a supportive and inclusive place for the community, and I know they'll support us in our time of need."

Oh, how Evie wished it was that easy. She'd run the numbers twice and was no closer to finding a solution. Her parents had sacrificed a lot for Evie over the years, giving her a place to live when she became pregnant with Camila, stepping in as babysitters and second parents when needed, even paying for part of Camila's private school in the beginning—not to mention helping with the expenses that came with competitive cheerleading. So she was determined to repay that generosity by saving the coffee shop. Even if it meant going against their wishes.

"We need to add to our customer base. We're surrounded by corporate towers. There is no reason why the suits can't come here for their morning latte. We just need to make a few changes to attract them," Evie said. "It wouldn't take a lot. Some fresh paint, modern accents, maybe even take out some of the community tables and opt for some smaller, double occupancy tables."

"And turn this place into a pseudo boardroom?" Lenard said, horrified. "I've worked hard to make this place unique and homey."

"You have a blown-up centerfold from the June 1972 *Cosmo* magazine of Burt Reynolds in the buff hanging in the bathroom with a swiveling heart over his penis, so that when a customer lifts the heart an alarm sounds notifying the entire shop they're a pervert."

"It tells us they are curious and open. And this place is more than a memorial to Burt's penis, it's a place that encourages people to share their coffee with others, old faces and new. Sitting alone goes against everything this shop was founded on."

"It will still be that. Professionals come in, they buy coffee, and they go about their business without taking up tables for the regulars."

"Is the shop going to be okay?"

All three adults looked up at Camila, who was standing in the doorway to the office. She was in her barista uniform, wavy brown hair pulled into a high ponytail, her light-brown eyes dialed to concerned.

Dang it, how much had she heard?

"It's going to be fine, sweetie," Lenard said with a brave smile.

"Everything is just fine," Moira added. "Nothing for you to

worry about."

Camila looked at Evie, unconvinced, waiting for the truth. Evie didn't want to lie but she also didn't want to worry her daughter with adult business.

"What do you need?" Evie settled on.

Camila rolled her eyes. "Whatever. I should expect secrets from you guys."

"What does that mean?"

"Dad told me."

"About?" Evie asked, a ball fisting in the pit of her stomach that was in the exact shape of a Mateo-made problem.

"The wedding. And how *you* won't let me go. How you never let me do anything. God, you're so overprotective and controlling I can hear the helicopter blades whirling every time you enter the room."

What?

That ball ignited into a fireball of sheer rage. That *asshole* was pinning this whole thing on her? And he did it knowing Evie would rather take the fall than further ruin Camila's relationship with her dad. If Camila knew the truth, she'd hate her dad forever. If Evie took the blame, she'd be mad, but she'd get over it.

"That's not fair. Camila, I wanted to talk to you about it but..."

"But what? You forgot to mention Dad was getting married?" Camila said, the accusation in her tone bordering on disrespect. "You're just jealous because Dad is happy and moving on and you're still stuck here and your life is going nowhere. I'd never do this to my daughter."

"Enough," Lenard said. "Your mother tried to talk to your—"

"Coach," Evie cut in, giving her dad a death glare. "But she reminded me it's the same week as cheer camp and you can't miss that. It's mandatory."

"You just don't want me to go. Admit it!"

"I want you to go, I really do, sweetie. But you have camp that weekend."

"It's Dad's wedding," she whispered, and all that anger from a moment ago turned into heartbreaking anguish. "If things were reversed and you were the one getting married, I bet you'd see things differently."

It would never be an issue because Evie would never plan something as important as a wedding without a) talking to her daughter first, and b) making sure her daughter could come. Camila was the most important person in Evie's world, and she'd do everything in her power to keep her daughter from getting crushed. Even if it meant lying.

"I'm really sorry, sweetie," she said, making a mental note to reach out to Mateo—with a knee to the nuts—and ask him what the hell he was thinking putting the blame on her. Not only was Evie shouldering the blame for her daughter not being a part of the wedding, it was clear by the lack of tears he also hadn't told her the truth about the baby. "Your coach made it clear that camp is mandatory."

"Funny thing, I asked Coach and she said she would excuse me from camp so I could go. So you want to go with another lie?"

Evie's heart stopped. She'd never lied to Camila except for this.

"When I talked to your coach she said it would leave her in a lurch. You are their main flyer, the center of every pyramid."

"I'm also Dad's daughter and that's more important." And that was Camila's breaking point. Her eyes filled with tears and her breathing became slightly hitched.

"Camila." Evie reached for her, the urge to pull her daughter into her arms overwhelming. Though still upset, Camila accepted the comfort.

"Plus, you need an adult to fly and between the shop, Grandpa, and—" She almost said prepping for her entry exam. "It's just not feasible."

Camila sniffed and pulled away. "Heather would have probably even made me a bridesmaid."

Heather would have done no such thing, and Evie was afraid that deep down Camila knew that. The uncertainty in her daughter's body language, the way she bit the inside of her cheek to keep her lip from trembling, and how she kept her gaze downcast told the story of a girl who'd suffered a lifetime of disappointments and was just waiting for the next blow.

Evie went to take her daughter's hand, but Camila tucked it into her pocket defiantly. Evie's heart sank over what she was about to do, but anger was better than anguish. "You made a commitment to your team and we honor our commitments."

If the rest of the world abided by that same rule, Evie's life would be so less stressful.

"You always say family comes first, so where's your commitment, Mom? Punishing Dad?" Camila said with enough disappointment in her voice to slice Evie's chest.

She exchanged a look with her parents, who were as worried about how the news would affect Camila as Evie was. Evie put a hand on her daughter's shoulder. "There's something else I want to talk to you about."

Camila rolled her shoulder, causing Evie's hand to fall. "I'm done talking. Plus, some guy is asking for you."

"I'll get it," Moira said quickly and stood.

"They didn't ask for a manager, they asked for Mom by name. Which is creepy."

Evie's heart flip-flopped. Not that she thought some guy asking for her by name was creepy, but because the only people who asked for her by name were suppliers and vendors. Who were likely looking for their overdue money.

Evie watched her daughter storm out, then looked up at the ceiling to blink away the tears. She felt her mom's arms wrap around her, pulling her in for a warm and comforting hug.

Evie held on, burying her nose in her mom's hair and breathing in the familiar scent of Chanel No. 5 and simpler times.

"You're doing the right thing," Moira said softly.

Evie pulled back. "Then why does it feel like I'm lying to her?"

"Because you know that she can't stay mad forever, but the truth would haunt her for a lifetime."

With a jerky nod, Evie smoothed her hands down her leggings. Even the thought of a supplier pulling their business made her palms break out in panicked sweat.

She made her way down the hallway and felt like a dead man walking when she saw the man at the counter. He was dressed in a very official-looking suit, with a mustache and glasses and very official-looking energy.

"May I help you?"

"Evie?" he asked.

"That's me."

He looked her up and down and sighed a relieved breath. "You're even prettier than the video."

"Excuse me?"

"Oh, I'm Sam." He held out a bundle of pencils. Pink and red with freshly sharpened, pointy tips. "And these are for you."

"I don't understand."

He ran a hand down his face. "I knew I should have just opted for flowers, but my mom said a bouquet of sharpened pencils would be romantic. Prove that I'm a good listener, which I am by the way. Communication is the key to successful relationships. Wouldn't you say?"

If that were the case, then Sam must struggle with relationships because he was talking but not a word was making sense.

"I'm a little lost here."

"You're Evie, the You've Got Male girl, right? The one off ClickByte?" ClickByte was a social media app where people uploaded videos about anything and everything. Weird thing was, Evie didn't even have an account, so why was he bringing it up?

When Evie didn't answer, he pulled out his phone and navigated to the ClickByte app and a few swipes later there was Evie, in Technicolor, talking about her ideal man.

"Okay, if I were to accept a date from a man, he'd have to be kind, funny, reliable, know his way around a kitchen."

"And the bedroom?"

"For sure the bedroom. My monthly battery budget is insane. And it would be nice to put on some silk and lace for someone other than myself." She laughed. *"He'd have to be gentle but all man and funny."*

"You already said funny."

"Because it's important. If he can't laugh at himself or the chaos of life, there's no way he'll fit into mine."

Sam seemed neither funny nor the kind of man who could give her an orgasm. He looked as if he'd talk her right to sleep. No, he was not Evie's type—if she had a type. Which she did not. The closest "type" she had was F O X, her battery-operated boyfriend who was the undefeated champion of the World of Os.

"Where did you get this?"

Sam looked confused. "On ClickByte. I thought about messaging, but you know what they say about the early bird and all that. My favorite video is the one of you twerking in the kitchen to Britney Spears."

"There's more than one?" she croaked.

"Oh, a new one is posted every day."

Evie looked down the counter to Julie, who was smiling, and

Evie shot her a look that could make Bundy confess and beg for mercy. Julie's smile just widened.

"I am so sorry, Sam. But I'm not really dating right now."

Sam looked relieved. It wasn't as if Evie were looking for a date, but did he have to let her off the hook so easily? "Can I at least get a video with you to get our moms off my back?"

Evie gulped. "My mom set us up?"

"Kind of. She showed my mom the video, my mom got excited about grandkids, and well, here I am, holding a bouquet of pencils."

First, Julie was going to die, quickly, followed by her mother. "I'm sorry that you were roped into this."

Sam didn't answer. Without warning, he hit record. "So, I'm here with the You've Got Male girl, uh, Evie. I'm not her Joe Fox, but I know he's out there. For the record, guys, go with a single red rose, you might fare better than a bouquet of pencils."

"It wasn't the pencils—"

But Sam had already hit stop. Evie watched in horror at the number of hearts that immediately lit up the screen. "How many followers do you have?"

"Not me. You've Got Male. I tagged your account in the post. I bet this will have a hundred thousand views by the end of the day."

"A hundred thousand views?" She tried to swallow but horror was too far lodged in her throat.

"Good luck finding your Joe Fox."

• • •

"You posted a video of me?" Evie snapped at Julie, who didn't even bother to look apologetic. Nope. Her ride or die had sold her out and looked proud of herself.

"Multiple, actually. And girl, you are a hot commodity. Thousands of guys want to date the famous You've Got Male girl. Just check out your account."

"I don't have an account."

"You do now."

"You made me an account?"

"You weren't going to and what are friends for if not to be the best wing-girl on the planet?"

Evie crossed her arms. "A good wing-girl would ask permission first."

"Yeah, I'm more of a seek-forgiveness-later type."

"You told a strange man where I work."

"That was kind of a mistake. The Grinder logo was on your shirt."

Julie opened the video and pointed to the logo, but Evie was too focused on her frizzy hair and smudged mascara to notice. "Then there's this one." She swiped up and another video of Evie offering bagel balls popped up. She swiped again. "And this is my personal favorite."

Evie was sucking on a popsicle like she was a porn star. "It was hot in the kitchen and I needed a blood sugar boost."

"Well, your sucking technique is five stars because this is the most viewed video. Over a million views. The public loves it."

"Julie," she groaned. "I don't have time for this."

"You said you don't have time to go out and meet guys, so I brought the guys to you."

"Social media isn't the answer to everything."

"Maybe not, but it can get you laid."

Chapter Seven

Evie

Evie never considered death by shock a realistic scenario. That was until she pushed through the kitchen doors and re-entered the shop and saw the crowd of people. And it wasn't just your average crowd of coffee-goers, it was overflowing with men in suits and ties, holding roses.

She, however, was so not rose worthy. As she carried a tray of toasty bagel balls in one hand, with a dollop of frothed cream on her right boob, her face glistened like a glitter bomb from sticking her head in the coffee bean roaster.

It took everything Evie had not to bolt right back through those swinging double doors, down the hallway, and lock herself in the office—where her dad was known to keep a bottle of bourbon in the bottom drawer—and devour this fresh batch of balls. But that'd probably only give Julie more camera fodder.

The shop was busting at the seams with customers. Every chair was taken, every inch of standing room filled. Then there was the intimidating line, which went out the door and down the street—nearly every eyeball was zeroed in on her. And standing at the back of the room, holding hands and looking delighted with themselves, were her parents.

A hush settled over the crowd and the room stilled. Evie's stomach sank. Ignoring the whispers, she worked her way through the crowd and walked straight up to Julie, who was doing double duty on the espresso machine and steamer like it was an Olympic sport.

"What did you do?" Evie whispered harshly.

"Me?" Julie said and didn't bother to look apologetic in the slightest. "Why do you think I had anything to do with this?"

"Because there are men holding roses, people staring at me, and you reek of guilt."

"Fine. I think it's from the last video."

"What last video?" Nothing from Julie. Not even a peep. "*What* last video?"

"You're going to hate me," her friend said with a gigantic smile. "But I posted a video of you holding Waverly the other day. It was such a picture-perfect moment."

"Why would you do that?"

"Because there was so much demand from your fans that I had to give them what they were begging for." Julie made a swooping gesture to the crowd that had their phones aimed at Evie—likely recording. "Plus, your mom forced me to."

She glared at her parents. They waved back.

"Before you unfriend me, let me point out that your fans love coffee. In fact, this is the busiest day we've had since I started working here. A bunch of them voted for Grinder as their favorite coffee shop in Denver."

"I don't want fans. I don't want the male species coming in and complicating my already complicated day. And I don't want roses." But she did want to win Denver's Best Coffee House, so a little of the irritation faded at the possibility of being one step closer to her goal. "How many people voted?"

"We ran out of flyers. Plus, every hour I offer half-off drip to anyone who shows proof that they went online and voted for us."

Well, that was something.

"How many votes do you think we've accumulated?"

"Today? Hundreds."

"Hundreds?" And it was only lunch. If they kept up this kind of pace they might really stand a chance of winning. "You could have at least warned me about the ambush."

"And risk you bolting? No way. Not to mention that your mom would kill me if I spilled the beans. She's been vetting bachelors all morning."

"Vetting?" Evie spotted her mom, who was talking up a tall, dark, and handsome man. Her dad was squeezing the man's bicep, giving it a test drive. Evie wanted to remind them that she didn't do tall, dark, and halfway-out-the-door anymore. But what was the point? They were fully committed to the cause and Evie was starting to worry that they wouldn't stop until they married her off.

"No losers in this bunch," Julie said reassuringly. Evie didn't feel reassured. "Now, get out there and show them what a catch you are." With a resounding smack on the rump, she shoved Evie out from behind the counter and said, really loudly, "Bring on the bachelors."

Evie turned to flee and bumped into a blond Gen-Z-er who looked cheer-squad peppy and Instagram ready. "And here she is now," the coed said into her phone, which was on a selfie-stick and streaming live. A bright light beamed in Evie's face. When she blinked away the floating dots she noticed someone holding a ring-light on them.

"Evie of You've Got Male!" The woman pushed up next to Evie, shoving her phone in Evie's face until she was front and center on the woman's screen. Evie took in her appearance, and it was worse than she thought. "I'm Tasha Hart and my ClickByte handle is LoveByte, a profile dedicated to exploring love on social media platforms, and you, Evie, have been bitten by Cupid."

She'd like to bite Cupid right back. *Hard.*

"Once bitten, twice shy," Evie said with a forced smile, smoothing her stray hairs back into her ponytail. It didn't help.

"Well, your fifty thousand follows disagree."

She looked at Julie, who was looking back, so incredibly proud of herself.

"How are things going in the world of love and romance?" Tasha asked.

"Pretty slow. However, the coffee world moves at the speed of light, so if you'll excuse me."

Evie tried to move but Tasha blocked her path. Evie went left and right and left again, but she was trapped.

"Just go about what you normally do. This will make you more relatable," she whispered, then turned back to her phone. "We're coming to you live with Evie of You've Got Male. It's a balmy day in the heart of Denver and spectators have flocked to Grinder, one of the oldest coffee houses downtown, to see our bachelorette as she heats up the coffee scene while making one of her famous Everything I Brew I Brew for You mochaccinos."

"It's our daily special," Moira said to the crowd.

Evie's irritation was boiling as hot as the espresso machine. Unfortunately, there were too many witnesses to scald her loved ones with her famous mochas. So Evie went about her business, walking back around the counter and over to the machine, while Tasha gave blow-by-blow commentary on Evie's every move.

"What's an Everything I Brew I Brew for You mochaccino?" Evie whispered to Julie.

"It was your mom's idea." She pointed to the board and saw a new collection of romance-inspired drinks. Love is in the Latte. Cupid's Cappuccino. Fabio Frappuccino. Bodice Ripper Blended Brew. Chai on Love.

Evie rolled her eyes. She was reaching for the cocoa powder when the ring-light came into her periphery, nearly blinding her.

"Look at how she steams up that cream," Tasha said. "Those hands are capable and proficient, but with a gentle touch, fellas."

A round of hoots filled the air and she heard her mom above the crowd say, "She gets that gentle touch from me."

"Who's going to be the first one to give our bachelorette a rose?" Tasha said.

"Bachelorette?" Evie choked out and that's when she realized just how big this hoax had become. The men with roses seemed to have doubled and now they were standing in a line, flanking the counter. Each one looked more excited than the last. The only things missing were the limos and glamorous mansion.

Evie had walked into her worst nightmare.

"First up, we've got Steve the Stockbroker coming to us from Boulder." Tasha waved over a man in an expensive suit who looked like a *GQ* model with a dadbod. "Steve, tell us why you're here?"

"For this beautiful woman, of course," Steve the Stockbroker said to the camera.

Evie snorted. She was dressed in a frumpy uniform, her hair looked like a feather duster, and she didn't have a speck of makeup on.

"I've got a lot to offer any single mom," Steve said. He had the kind of voice Evie imagined the Most Mysterious Man in the World had. Which was another thing Evie didn't do—mysterious.

"All my friends tell me I'll make the best dad. I'm a partner at my firm, I cook like a five-star chef, I'm a great catch, and I've got a weekend home in Steamboat Springs."

Of course Steve the Stockbroker would have a house in Steamboat Springs. He also had a superhero complex. And an ego that he clearly needed to have stroked.

"Evie," Tasha said, "the only question is, will you accept Steve's rose?"

Evie looked at the rose, then at her mom, and narrowed her eyes.

Vetted, my ass.

Evie plastered a pleasant smile on her face and said, "Sorry Steve, but it will have to be a pass."

Unfazed, Steve looked deep into the camera. "If anyone out there is looking for a single, successful Sagittarius, just hit me up. My handle is @Steve-Broker. I prefer petite blondes who work out and have an adventurous side."

Evie was neither petite nor blond. And Stockbroker Steve was clearly looking for a social media boost. Her gym membership expired six years ago and the last time she'd given in to her adventurous side she wound up pregnant and alone.

Evie turned to escape back into the kitchen. She hadn't even made it a foot when Tasha snagged her arm.

"Don't give up yet," Tasha said. "You're one *no* closer to that big *yes*! Which brings us to Travis from TechStar, who came from Fort Collins. Travis, tell Evie a little about yourself."

Travis looked like a typical tech guy in his skinny jeans, untucked dress shirt with rolled-up sleeves, and hair with that perfect wave at the front like he'd just come from the hairdresser. He also had on a watch that likely cost more than Evie's life savings and probably spoke a hundred different languages.

"Hi, Evie." He clasped her hand between both of his and was

about to say something else when his watch *ping*ed. Maintaining hold of her hand, he flipped it over so he could see the face of his watch. "So nice to meet you," he said distractedly, then looked up at her like that was a normal greeting.

"You need to get that?" she said, trying hard to hide the hope in her voice. She failed. Not that Travis noticed. He was checking his notification.

"There. I'm all yours." But his phone chimed again, and again he glanced down.

"Does your watch vibrate? Because that could be fun," Tasha said and then winked suggestively at Evie.

"Why don't you tell us about yourself," Julie said, sliding up next to Evie.

"Five years ago, I created a motivational app that pairs personality traits to influencers and helps them target their audience. I've helped thousands of entrepreneurs reach their goals through visualization, strategic planning, and leveraging their natural strengths. Social media is my jam, which is why I was so excited by this idea of finding love over ClickByte."

"Well, I'm not really big on social—"

His phone *ping*ed again. This time in rapid succession.

Ping. Ping. Ping.

He held up a single finger and dictated into his phone, "Meeting in twenty. Period. Bring the Strafford proposal. Period." Without missing a beat, he looked into Evie's eyes. "I'm adventurous, I've been skydiving, climbed Everest, and I'm on the waitlist to go to space. I mean, YOLO."

"Do you know your phone doesn't work in space?" Evie mumbled and Julie hip-checked her.

"So if you're open to leaping without a net, will you accept this rose?"

Julie held up a hand. "That'll be a hard pass, Travis."

"Totes understand. Not a good personality pairing anyway."

"Evie, here comes your perfect *yes*," Tasha said. "I promise. Ernie is an engineer and a single dad from Englewood."

Tasha didn't have to mention his job description, Ernie looked 100 percent engineer. He also looked to be at least ten years Evie's senior. But his hands were shaking with nerves, and he seemed like a sweet man, so Evie softened her smile and said, "Hi Ernie. It's nice to meet you."

"Nice to meet you. As for me, I like long walks on the beach and dogs." His voice cracked so he cleared it. "I knew the moment you talked about the significance of a single red rose that I had to come. Did you know that a rose's perfect structure collects and purifies water and its shape inspired an engineering study for water purification? They're doing research on it at the University of Texas in Austin."

"That's fascinating, Ernie. But sadly, there are no beaches in Denver, and I'm allergic to dogs."

"Does that mean you're not accepting my rose?" he asked.

"Sorry, Ernie, but I'm going to have to say no. But I'd love to make you a Cupid's Cappuccino. On the house."

He smiled nervously. "That would be great."

"Coming right up." Then she looked directly into Tasha's phone. "And that concludes today's installment of You've Got Male."

Chapter Eight

Evie

"You're ruining my life with this whole ClickByte thing!"

In a testament to just how crazy her life had become, it wasn't Evie who was screaming the accusation, it was Camila.

She hadn't even turned the CLOSED sign around when her daughter stormed in.

"I'm sorry. *Your* life is being affected?"

"Yes!" Camila said, throwing her hands in the air as if Evie were the exasperating one. "Sabrina saw the video of you dancing and shared it with the cheer team. This is so embarrassing."

"How do you think this makes me feel?" Evie asked. "If you want to scream at someone, take this up with Grandma."

"Dad's even seen it." Camila's voice cracked a little and Evie's stomach bottomed out.

Mateo was the last person she wanted to know about the You've Got Male clusterfuck. It was bad enough that he was getting married and having a baby with a woman he was going to give everything he'd promised Evie and never delivered on. Mateo was such a narcissist that he would think Evie did this stunt to find someone because she was jealous that he'd moved on.

Even worse, she could tell by her daughter's expression that something had transpired between her and her father. And just like that, all the frustration from the day vanished and in its place came deep concern.

"What else is going on, Cami?"

Camila shrugged like it was no big deal, but she could tell by the way her daughter's body was curled in on itself that what went down was a huge deal. "I realized today that Dad won't be at camp, so he won't see me compete."

Which meant that her daughter would only have three people in the crowd on such an important day.

"Oh, baby." She pulled her daughter into her arms and instead of merely resigning herself to the embrace, Camila clung to her.

Evie breathed in the moment. Camila might be growing up, but she would always be Evie's baby and mothers protect their young. Only, it seemed that Evie had failed on that front, too. No matter how hard she pushed Mateo to be more involved, he just lacked the ability to put other people first. He never missed a child support payment, and was always contributing his half of everything, but when it came to emotional intelligence, that man should've been studied in a lab. Because the person who needed that cure was Camila.

"I should have known better," Camila whispered. "But I thought that, maybe, this time would be different."

Evie usually led with the truth, but there was only so much truth a person could take and Camila had gone several rounds with Truth and was about down for the count. "Me too, baby.

Me too."

Camila stepped back and wiped her tears. "Ryan said Dad's an asshole and that he'd bring all of his friends to the competition."

"He's a really good friend." And that was another reason why Jonah and Evie could never revisit that night.

Camila's phone *ping*ed with an incoming text. "That's Ryan. He said he'd pick me up from the shop so we can study together."

"That sounds fun. Just be home by dinner. Grandpa is making his lasagna."

"If things go late, I'll text. And lasagna is always better the next day."

"Dinner," Evie repeated.

And just like that, the teenage-tude was back with a dramatic roll of the eyes. Without another word, Camila marched out the café doors and hopped into Ryan's truck. But just when Evie thought that her daughter would drive off without a goodbye, Camila turned in her seat and waved Evie's way. Evie waved back and stood at the threshold until the truck disappeared down the street.

Dead on her feet, Evie turned the locks. Tossing her apron on the counter, she took in the shop and sighed. It looked like a hurricane blew through. Hurricane ClickByte had again left a path of destruction in her wake. Sales were up, but she didn't have the bandwidth to dole out any more rejections. She was barely holding things together as it was—saying no to bachelor after bachelor was taking its toll.

This all needed to end.

With renewed determination, she walked back toward the office to tell her mom just that. Only when she hit the threshold, she came to a full and complete stop.

There were four chairs arranged in a circle, three of them

taken by Julie, Moira, and Lenard. Evie had a sinking feeling the fourth was for her.

"What is this?" she asked. "Some kind of intervention?"

"We're calling it a sex-tervention," Julie said earnestly.

"I'm not having sex."

"Oh, we are well aware, dear," Moira said.

Needing a drink for this conversation, Evie walked straight past the confessional circle, to the desk, where she opened the bottom drawer and rummaged through. She pulled out the only bottle and held it up. "Seriously, Dad, all you have is Aperol? What happened to the bourbon?"

"I'm more into spritzers these days," Lenard said, as if that were reason enough to have an aperitif hidden in the desk.

Evie put it back. "Of course you are."

Julie kicked out the chair and it slid across the floor to bump into Evie's shin. "For the sake of vibrators everywhere, you need to pick one of these men. Just go on a date with a couple of them. See what transpires."

Evie plopped down. "You met the same guys I met, right? No, I'm done with this whole thing."

"I can always set you up with one of my men," Moira said. "In fact, I know the perfect guy. He's an architect."

"Let me guess," Evie said. "His name is Art."

"No, it's Dwane. He's twenty-seven, with biceps like he lifts tanks daily, and has a core of steel."

Evie found herself rolling her eyes just like Camila had moments ago. "Mom, I'm not dating a guy whose, uh, steely core you've considered."

"ClickByte isn't going to go away. In fact, your followers have doubled since Tasha Hart got involved," Julie said.

"I don't want followers," Evie said.

"Think of it as streamlining the dating pool. It will make

your dating life easier."

Evie snorted. "You seriously think this will make my life easier? Between Cami, the shop, dialysis and, well, other stuff"—*like going back to college*—"I don't have time for suitors interrupting my workflow and sucking up whatever bandwidth I have left after a long day."

They all shared a look and it was as if a whole conversation was going on between them, with Evie on the outside.

"Girl, you so need to get laid," Julie said.

"I think what they're trying to say is we just want you to find happiness," Lenard said quietly, resting his hand on Evie's knee in that supportive way he always did when her mom started applying the pressure and sharing her opinions. Her mom might be a busybody but her dad was her rock and protector. "You don't have to find it in a relationship. But I don't want you to live your life being afraid, sweetheart. I can't remember the last time I saw you happy."

Evie's heart sank. *When was the last time she'd been happy?* She couldn't remember, either. That her parents noticed made her heart ache. The last thing she wanted was to worry them and she could tell they were worried. Worried with the same fierceness that Evie was about Camila.

"I get that," she said to the group. "But this is getting out of hand."

Julie snorted. "Are you kidding, you have thousands of guys wanting to date you."

"Plus, look at the shop. It hasn't been this busy in years," Lenard said with a huge smile. "I wasn't sure about your idea of expanding our customer base, but I have to admit I see your reasoning. This week proved it."

"All it proved is that you guys have your nose too far into my business," Evie said. "Plus, this kind of traffic is temporary. As soon as I pick a guy people lose interest in this stunt and we'll have the same problem."

"Not if we make your dating life a novelty. Something people can follow. America loves a good love story, like Prince Harry and Meghan Markle," Moira said.

"I doubt a prince will come and whisk me off my feet."

"But a man courting you, a man found online couldn't be more perfect in today's day and age," Julie said.

"We don't know that."

"This is why you need to get laid, Miss Debbie Downer," Julie said.

"I counted this week's earnings and if we keep this up we won't have to lay anyone off," Lenard said with so much hope in his eyes Evie felt it all the way in her soul.

Julie's mouth fell open. "You were going to fire people? We're a family."

Moira crossed her arms. "See."

All that Evie could see was that she needed a beard—and ASAP. It was the only way to get her family and America off her back. Plus, she needed a break from all the crazy.

Chapter Nine

Jonah

Jonah wiped the sweat off his brow and took a long sip of iced tea. Maybe if that Beautification Board deadline wasn't counting down like the timer on a nuclear bomb, he could have justified staying inside today and playing hooky from adulting. Instead of his Sunday routine of staying in his pjs until noon, napping with Waverly after lunch, and watching football with Ryan, he was sweating it out under the blistering September sun—which wouldn't let up until fall came on the scene—trimming back the damn pomegranate tree.

His sudden motivation had nothing to do with the way Evie looked holding Waverly and everything to do with needing to make some headway in his life—and this was an actionable goal. It was also a reminder of just how badly life had chewed him up.

He didn't need to do the work himself. He could focus on the job search instead, and then once he got one, he could hire a company to come and make his yard look like Martha Stewart lived here...*no.* That kind of thinking had led to his problems, and to the garden that had been Amber's baby going to shit on his watch.

The flowerbeds were filled with weeds, the hedges and trees overgrown, and her roses were bare branches. Three of the many things he was going to fix. Maybe fixing the yard would jumpstart fixing his life. One thing at a time.

Jonah set a mason jar of iced tea on the fence, grabbed the trimming shears, and walked up to the pomegranate tree that launched the neighbor-war of all wars. And for the first time, instead of thinking about his wife, he found himself smiling over how ticked Evie had been with his basket of pomegranates. How those full lips had pursed, and those beautiful brown eyes narrowed in his direction. Man, she was as prickly as a porcupine. Jonah wasn't usually into prickly but on her he found it sexy as hell.

Reaching over his head and placing the cutters at the crossroads of a branch, he snipped, sending leaves and debris raining down on his face.

"What the actual fuck, Dad?" Ryan said and Jonah could hear his son's feet pounding across the slate pathway until he was right behind him.

Jonah looked at his son, who nearly topped Jonah's six-foot-one frame. "Language."

Ryan ignored the warning. "That's mine and Mom's tree."

There was a frantic and emotional nature to Ryan's voice that had Jonah taking a softer tone. "I'm just trimming it."

Ryan yanked the shears out of Jonah's hands. "No, you're killing it! We prune it in the spring," he said, and Jonah noticed the way his son once again used the present tense when referring to his mom. "Not a few months before winter. You'll damage the branches, and it will die." His son's voice cracked on the last word.

"I didn't know," he said apologetically. "But I have to trim it back or we'll get fined by the Beautification Board. And your mom wouldn't want some stranger in her garden."

Was there no way to push this off? No, he couldn't afford a landscaper. One he hired and definitely not one the board brought in.

He couldn't believe that this was all coming down to his kid's feelings versus a stupid—and out of his budget—fine. If it hadn't been for that meeting, the last five minutes wouldn't have happened, and Ryan wouldn't look close to tears.

"I don't care about the board. It's my tree. Don't ever touch it again." Ryan threw the shears on the ground and stomped down the pathway, heading for his car.

"Where are you going?" Jonah called out behind him.

"Anywhere but here."

"I know you're pissed, but until those grades are up, you're staying here and studying."

"Fine. Whatever." He burst through the front door and slammed it loud enough for the tree to tremble.

Jesus. What just happened? It felt like every step he took forward was the wrong step. And he desperately needed to find the right direction, only his compass was malfunctioning.

"I'm sorry. I didn't know the tree was so important," Evie said from behind him, and he dropped his head to his chest.

What had he just done? Ryan clearly needed space and instead of giving it to him, Jonah had sentenced him to an afternoon in the one place that didn't allow his son to breathe.

"Sometimes I feel like navigating Ryan's emotions is like walking through a minefield with a blindfold on."

He looked up and, Lord help him, Evie looked like a PTA president and the gorgeous girl next door had a love child. She was wearing a flowery sundress that flirted around a pair of legs long enough to lock around his waist. Then there were the tiny buttons that went from cleavage to thigh—buttons he wanted to undo with his teeth. Her shoulder-length hair was sleek and silky and made his fingers itch to slide through it.

A combination of animal attraction and irritation coursed through him. Animal attraction because, *damn,* just look at her. Irritation over the fact that his failings as a dad were no longer private. Evie must think he was parentally inept—*again.* Then there was her stubbornness in ignoring this surface-of-the-sun heat that arced between them.

If the way she was staring at his bare chest was any indication, she was remembering that night, too.

"My eyes are up here," he said, because she'd been eye-ogling the happy trail that led to the forest. His pecs bounced and she jumped back with a gasp. He laughed.

"Don't flatter yourself. You have leaves stuck to you." She reached out and plucked a leaf off his chest, careful not to touch him, then held up the leaf as proof. "See."

"Then why do you look like you want to stick a wad of ones down my shorts?"

"I do not!"

"Uh-huh."

"I'm here on official business," she said primly.

Unless "official" referred to her stance on him going to town with those buttons, he wasn't interested. "If you came with more HOA to-dos, leave it in the mailbox. I'm kind of stretched thin at the moment."

Evie looked at the driveway behind her, likely for an escape, but surprised him by stepping closer and extending a container of cookies that she had been holding behind her. "I come in peace."

He closed the distance. "Are those your mom's snicker-doodles?"

She smiled. "Two dozen."

"It will take more than some cookies to turn my day around." Which was a lie. Just being close to her made the pressure between his shoulders relax.

She set the cookies on the fence next to his tea. "How can I help?" Suspicion skated up his back. "Why do you look so startled?"

"Because you've never once offered to help," he said and her gaze quickly darted away. "So why don't you tell me what's going on?"

"I've had a week, too," she admitted. "Do you want to talk about yours first?"

"I think I need something stronger than iced tea for that kind of chat."

Jonah walked to the deck and grabbed two beers by the neck from a cooler. Spending time with her would be anything but a hardship, but when he twisted off the cap and extended one to Evie, she eyed it like it was Pandora's box.

"Is that such a good idea?"

"Probably not." He took a long pull and leaned against the railing.

"What am I doing?" she whispered to herself.

"Staring at my chest again," he informed her, since she didn't seem to know that her gorgeous eyes had darted south.

"Then maybe you should put on a shirt."

"Didn't know that a little sweat would turn you on."

She nervously tucked her hair behind her ear. "I'm not turned on."

"Did you know that you play with your hair when you're lying?"

"I'm not lying."

"Really? Then why do you look like I just asked you to play

strip Jenga?"

"That's a game?"

"It is now," he said and she laughed.

"Look, I just spent my morning with my dad at dialysis, the afternoon going over the shop's numbers for the third time, and I'm avoiding an important conversation with Camila. I can barely manage things as they are, so this probably isn't the right time for me to be making questionable decisions."

"Then let's make a good decision. You, me, those beers, and nothing more than two friends throwing back a few. I won't bite." She reached for the beer but he didn't let it go. "Unless you ask me to."

She yanked the beer from his hand and sat next to him. The step wasn't very wide so their thighs brushed when she sat. She tried to scooch away but there wasn't enough room so her attempts only caused their bodies to rub back and forth.

He tapped her bottle with his, then took a sip. "Now why are you buttering me up?"

"Am I that obvious?"

"You brought me cookies and they don't look laced."

She stared up at the sky as if seeking divine intervention. "I need a favor."

It must be a doozie because he knew she worked tirelessly to appear like she had it all under control. Accepting help, especially from him, went against her cool-as-a-cucumber facade.

"My family's driving me crazy," she said. "Like batshit crazy." Funny, that. Evie was driving him crazy every time the bottom of the short-enough-to-ride-above-her-knees skirt moved with the summer breeze, tickling his leg.

She took a long sip, nearly draining her bottle.

"You need another?"

"No. Yes." She laughed but the lines around her eyes didn't

crinkle. "My family and friends have become obsessed with my dating life."

Jonah was a little obsessed with her dating life, too. Like wanting to know if she had one. And if she did, was it serious? And why did that bother him so much?

"To the point that they have schemed behind my back to find me my soulmate using social media. I've gone viral, Jonah."

"That sounds like a you problem," he said.

"Men show up at my work with roses, asking me out on dates, professing their undying love, and trying to convince me that we're a perfect pair. I have to publicly turn down each one and it's not only embarrassing, I feel awful. I don't want to be the turn-down queen," she said. "There was practically a *Bachelorette* episode shot at the coffee house the other day, which was streamed live on ClickByte. Someone even left a poem comparing my body to a Ferrari on my front windshield. It's not just my family and friends now. It's as if all of America has an opinion on my dating life."

"You want to hear my opinion?" he asked softly, making sure to have zero judgment in his tone. He knew how many cooks she had in her kitchen. He'd been around her family and friends enough to know how much they ran over her wants and needs. Never in a malicious way, it came from a place of love, but he imagined the outcome was the same—Evie feeling like her life wasn't her own.

"Nope."

He bumped her shoulder with his. "That's a shame because I was rooting for Ernie."

"Are you shitting me?" She smacked his bicep. "You let me tell the whole humiliating story and you already knew?"

He chuckled. "Well, I didn't know about the poem. And a Ferrari, huh? I'd say you were more a Chevrolet SUV."

She glared at him. "You just downgraded me from a sports car to an SUV."

"A sleek and sophisticated SUV that is efficient and dependable and safe. I would trust it with my family."

Shock and tenderness filled her eyes, and when she spoke her voice was barely a whisper. "Even if I did make you almost kill Ryan's tree?"

He rested his hand on her leg and gave it a squeeze. He tried not to focus on the way her silky skin felt beneath his palm, or the way his thumb moved back and forth along the gentle slope of the knee. "Even then."

Evie's phone rang. She didn't move to answer it, just tilted her beer back and downed it in one gulp.

"I'll let you get that and"—he paused—"thanks."

This was his chance to get out of there, but instead Jonah found himself saying, "It could be your prince coming to save you."

"I'm not looking to be saved. Plus, I don't believe in princes. Unless they come bearing wine, then I might think about—"

Her phone rang again.

"You should probably get that," he said again but didn't move.

Evie looked down at the screen and groaned.

"Ernie?" he asked.

"No. It's the butcher from Marnie's Meats and More. My mom gave him my number after he saw my video."

"And you're avoiding him because you don't want to date a butcher?"

"I'm avoiding him because I don't want to—"

Her phone rang again.

"You can't just keep ignoring him and hoping he'll go away."

"You know what? You're absolutely right." She handed him

her phone. "Here."

"No can do. I'm not into butchers."

"Neither am I. Just answer and tell him I'm already taken," she begged. "Then we'll be even."

"Even?"

"From me picking up Waverly at the last minute the other day."

The phone rang, louder and more demanding than the last time. Evie rubbed her head as if the ringing was causing her acute pain.

The phone gave one final ring and went silent. Evie sagged against the steps with relief.

It immediately rang again.

"You don't have thirty seconds to help an old friend out?"

"Fine. I'll do it. But then we're even. Agreed?"

"Agreed." There was a raw vulnerability that nearly did him in.

He took the phone. "What do you want me to say?"

"Make something up. Be creative."

He hit speakerphone. "Evie's phone, who's this?"

The phone remained silent.

"Hello?" he prompted.

"Brad," a male's voice came through the phone. It was perturbed and pissy and, Jonah was pretty sure, presumptuous. "Is Evie there?"

Evie's big brown eyes gave a please-don't-rat-me-out plea. "Unfortunately, she's a little indisposed at the moment." Jonah flashed Evie a wicked smile, and wariness stopped her cold. "Hey baby, your bra is over there. No, hanging from the ceiling fan." Then back to Brad. "Women, am I right? Anyway, can I take a message?"

"Wrong number."

The line went dead.

Evie blinked at the phone and then him. "Ceiling fan? That's what you came up with?"

"You said I could be creative. Should we call Brad back and ask his opinion?"

She jerked the phone away. "Don't you dare. I mean, now he thinks we were…"

"Were what, sunshine?"

Evie blinked twice and then this amazing smile overtook her expression. "Oh my God! That was actually perfect!"

"I'm sorry? Did you just compliment me?"

"I'm as surprised as you are." She turned to face him. Her eyes went wide as saucers, her lips slightly parted as she drew in a breath. It was an a-ha expression if he'd ever seen one. His gut told him to run. "He thinks I'm taken."

"Wasn't that the point?"

"Yes. And it worked perfectly on Brad." She clapped with glee. "Now we just need to convince America that I'm off the market."

"We?" A sinking feeling started in the pit of his stomach and his warning bells sounded. "How do you intend to accomplish that?"

"By getting myself a fake boyfriend. And since you and I are at the bra-on-the-ceiling-fan point of our relationship now, and I trust you, I was thinking that you'd make the perfect—"

"You hate me."

"Hate is a strong word. But our dislike of each other makes it even better. It will ensure no lines are crossed!"

Dislike? That word was like a stake through his chest.

He jerked his hand away and stood. "Nope. Never going to happen."

"Just hear me out." She was standing now, too, and since

they were still on the steps, they were within kissing distance. He could feel her breath skate across his skin when she spoke. "By the time they announce the Best Coffee Shop in Denver, I'll have a better handle on the shop. The publicity alone will be enough to pull us out of the red."

"It's that bad?"

"We're a few months from going under and my parents are acting like we're short milk money. Please, Jonah, I just need a few weeks of the appearance of being off the market to get my family off my back."

"You make it sound so easy."

"It can be. All it would be is maybe some hand-holding, a couple of casual and public dates, and we upload a few videos. Maybe I play fairy godmother and give you a little makeover. Easy peasy."

"I'm not seeing an upside to this." Plus, it would take more than a little bippity-boppity-boo to turn his life into Prince Charming status. He was as far from being a prince as Evie was from letting rats destroy her grandmother's roses.

"How about I help you get your life in order? I'm a professional organizer, or I was, and you need some organization in your life."

Ouch. She wasn't wrong, though. He lifted a brow. "You really aren't helping your case."

"Please, Jonah. Between my dad's health, the shop, Camila, and now ClickByte, I'm desperate."

"So your solution is to lie to our families?"

She dropped her forehead to his chest. Her voice was threadbare. "I don't have time for a real relationship. I've put my goals on hold for so long, I don't want to do it again. I just want a break from it all."

He wanted to be that break for her. Wanted to be more than just her neighbor who occasionally shared a beer. What he wanted, he couldn't have. She'd made that crystal clear. Plus, there was Amber and her memory. And the kids. God, Ryan would kill him if he started dating his best friend's mom. And when these weeks were up, what would that mean for their relationship? She could finally be within kicking distance and knee him in the nuts.

Then there was the obvious.

"Do you think you and I spending time together like that is a good idea?" He cupped her hips and let his fingers slide low on the curve of her back. Then he leaned in and ran his nose along her cheek and nuzzled her ear. She shivered. "Do you think that we can be around each other, pretending that we're having sex, and not cross a line?"

Evie's breath hitched, but she pulled back to stare him down with those sultry eyes. "I can. Can you?"

Jonah grinned. "What if I said I couldn't?"

"Then I'd call you chicken," murmured Evie, running her hands up his arms gently.

Just then, Evie's back porch door banged open, and she jumped back as if she'd been scalded. The distance between them might as well have been a chasm, filled with all the reasons why Jonah couldn't let himself get that close to her.

"Sorry, sunshine. You're gonna have to figure this one out on your own."

Chapter Ten

Jonah

Whoever said that parenting got easier forgot the big "not" at the end of that statement. Jonah would take a sleepless night of feedings over one more day of potty training.

Waverly had awoken to a wet bed, Ryan still wasn't talking to him, and Jonah had accidentally smeared grape jelly on the sleeve of his suit. Then there was his schedule that had flipped him the resounding bird.

He was expected at Grinder in thirty minutes to meet his old boss about a possible job opportunity, Waverly had refused to wear anything but her mermaid costume, Ryan left the interior light on in his car so the engine wouldn't start, meaning Jonah had to beg Evie to handle carpool on her morning off, and he still couldn't stop thinking about her proposal. A proposal that was as ridiculous as the amount of time he'd spent weighing the pros and cons.

He'd trade in his left testicle for another adult to help him navigate the morning. Maybe both if that person also doubled as a toddler whisperer because Waverly wasn't just refusing to wear shoes—because what do mermaids need with shoes—she was also clinging to his leg like a defiant little koala. Then there was the preschool teacher who was blocking his entrance into the classroom.

"What do you mean she has to be completely potty trained?" Jonah asked. "Since when?"

"Since she took off her diaper and did a finger painting on the wall of the dress-up room," the teacher said.

"Her mom was an artist. It runs in the family."

"I'm really sorry," she said.

"When I got the potty-training policy notice, I thought I'd get more time than a single week." He looked at his watch and realized he was late. A month ago, he would've blown off the meeting, but something inside of him had changed. Maybe it was the momentum of the to-do lists. He definitely wasn't trying to prove he didn't need organization. But damn if it didn't feel good to try again. And he wanted to hold onto that feeling. "Look, I get it, you have rules, but I promise you we're working on it. Can you make an exception this one time?"

"If it were up to me, I would," she said with genuine apology—and a hint of blatant interest—in her eyes. "But it's completely out of my hands. I'm just a parent volunteer."

Jonah gripped the back of his neck. He didn't need to go in today. But he knew his old boss was always in the best mood on Monday morning, the earlier the better, relaxed from his long Sunday golfing. As the day wore on, Frank's mood would get worse. Getting him early increased the chances of him listening to the reasons why he should hire his top earner back, even if Jonah hadn't worked in two years. Every cell in Jonah's body was telling him that he needed to make this meeting. If he did, he could finally afford to hire someone who knew how to prune a pomegranate tree right. It was time he took the next step.

"Who do I need to talk to?"

"Unfortunately, Ms. Hathaway, and she was part of the splatter mural, so I don't think she'll be as easy to convince."

"Ms. Hathaway was the one who told me to use underwear instead of pullups, since it confuses them. So I used underwear."

"That explains why she wet her panties three days in a row."

"So I should go back to pullups?"

"You should potty train her. If you want…" She hesitated, and her cheeks turned pink. "I'd be willing to walk you through it. Maybe over coffee?" Her eyes lingered on his mouth. She was cute in a soccer-mom kind of way with pretty brown eyes, lush lips, and couldn't be more obvious than if she'd tattooed her number to his forehead, but all Jonah felt was the urgent need to shut things down.

Just like the other day, a woman who probably had a PhD in Potty Training had offered her help to clean up his world. Unlike the other day, he wasn't interested.

"Thanks, but I think I can get a handle on it."

She handed him a paper. "My number, in case you change your mind."

"Thanks, and have a good one," he said, walking away and wondering what the hell he was doing. He clearly needed help in the parenting department if he had any chance of impressing Ms. Hathaway, but the thought of a beautiful woman walking in his and Amber's house, knowing it was more than an offer for nannying, made his gut churn.

At least the thought of this woman. Which was a firm reminder of why Evie's fake dating scheme would never work.

• • •

"I swear she's a sweetheart and quiet. So quiet, she'll probably sit in the corner and read her book the whole time I'm in there," Jonah said to the receptionist.

Stacy, as the nametag proclaimed, eyeballed Waverly, who was staring up at her with the smile of an angel and gave two innocent blinks of those long lashes. Her mother's lashes. God, if Amber could see him now. Nearly broke, two years unemployed, his life a disaster, begging his old boss, Frank Rochester, for his job back while using their daughter as arm candy to get in good with the receptionist.

"He's really busy this morning, Jonah. Like really busy. He has zero fuc—" Stacy looked at Wavery, who was looking back with excited wide eyes, waiting for her to finish the dirty word. *Sorry,* she mouthed.

Jonah waved a dismissive hand.

"Her brother is seventeen. She's heard it all."

Stacy did not look impressed at his parenting skills. He did not give a fuck. Not today. Today Jonah had to get into Frank's office and convince him how instrumental Jonah could be to their success. How he could take them to the next level. Problem was, Frank hated kids, hated parents more. Thought they took the focus off work and misplaced it on other things like family and having a balanced life.

Jonah had to prove to him that he could do it all. Right after he proved it to himself.

Fake it till you make it, buddy.

"Seriously, today is not the day to go in there. The last guy came out crying."

"You know Frank, he loves me."

"Loved. Past tense. You left and he sent out a memo that you were dead to him."

"My wife had terminal cancer."

"The memo also said that was a you problem."

Jesus, was he really this desperate? He looked down at his daughter, thought of the bills stacking up, the bank balance, the impending fine, and felt dizzy. Unless he got a job ASAP, he'd have to break into Amber's life insurance settlement and that money was for the kids' college and wedding funds. Something that was not happening. So yes, he was that desperate.

"Five minutes with Frank. You watch Waverly and I pay you a hundred bucks. In return, I give you a free hour of my time to talk about your investment portfolio. And you know what an hour of my time is worth."

"If it's worth so much, why are you here?"

Because he hadn't heard back from a single company he'd reached out to. No one wanted to take a chance on a new hire with an unexplained resume gap, especially at the stage he'd been at. Other brokers probably thought he was crazy to quit his job months before a big promotion, or thought something must have gone really downhill. He didn't regret quitting. But trying to find a job after two years of being a stay-at-home parent was no joke. It made him really empathize with moms trying to get back into the workforce after sacrificing their careers to raise their kids.

"This is the best firm and I know if Frank gives me the chance I can prove myself and get back to handling eight-figure accounts again in six months."

"Two hours."

"Deal."

"But I'm not babysitting. She has to entertain herself."

"She is an angel, I swear." He was going to hell for that lie. Or maybe his baby could hold on for five minutes. And maybe the Beautification Board would give him an additional six weeks.

Jonah took Waverly by her chubby little hand and his heart burst with light and love so bright it nearly blinded him for a moment. Was he really going to do this? Was he really going to hire a nanny and let someone else raise his kid while he pulled eighty-hour weeks?

Just the thought of it brought on an acute case of heartburn. Or maybe it was heartbreak. Old-fashioned heartbreak. Either way, it knocked the wind out of him.

He went down on his haunches and looked Waverly in the eyes. "Daddy is going to walk through that door for just five minutes. Until that big hand is on the five, then I will be back. And because you've been such a good girl, I'll let you play Purrfect Pet Shop on my phone. And that's Stacy. She's going to be there if you need anything."

"You mean if there is an emergency."

Jonah shot Stacy a death glare. "If you need *anything* because you're three, and three-year-olds need adults sometimes to feel safe. And this is a safe place, right Stacy?"

Stacy rolled her eyes. "Whatever."

Jonah was rethinking this whole thing. "You know what? Never mind."

"I got her." Stacy stood up and walked around the desk and sat next to Waverly. "Go. Before I change my mind."

"You're a lifesaver."

"And you owe me *three* hours."

Jonah didn't have time to argue. He strolled straight into Frank's office, never slowing down as he pushed through the door.

Frank was as big as ever, his spare tire hanging over the pleats of his slacks. The buttons held on for dear life as he swung the golf club back and swung forward with intention, sending the ball sailing into the air on the simulator. Even though it was a perfect swing, the ball veered left.

Maybe slamming open the door hadn't been the smartest

decision because Frank flung the nine iron and let out a long string of words even Ryan and his friends hadn't learned yet.

"I told you no one was to fucking disturb me while I was fucking working." He spun around, expecting to see Stacy, and came to a dead stop when it was, in fact, not Stacy.

"Out!" he roared. "Get the fuck out of my fucking office. I told you to never fucking come back."

"Actually, you told me to get back to my fucking desk and get back to fucking work," Jonah quoted verbatim. "I'm ready to do that now, sir."

One could never tell how Frank was going to react, so when he burst out laughing and walked over to give Jonah a hug, Jonah felt his lungs exhale. There was a fifty-fifty chance of how this would turn out and it had spun in Jonah's favor.

He looked down at his loafers and breathed in the canistered air and oxford-white painted walls and wondered if it had. Or if this was like returning to hell. He didn't really like who he was now, but looking back he hated who he'd been then.

"How the hell have you been?" Frank gave Jonah a slap on the shoulder. "Still up to your elbows in dishwater and dirty diapers?"

"I have a nanny for that now."

"About time you saw the light. Never met a nanny who couldn't do a better job at raising kids than their parents. Just look at my five. All nanny raised. All turned out just fine."

One was an addict. One was on trial for insider trading. The youngest lived on his dad's yacht, and the other two worked for Frank. And his wife didn't work. She just didn't want to get elbow deep in dirty diapers. Or things like parenting and emotions.

"So about the job?" Jonah prodded, knowing he'd promised his daughter he'd be back in five minutes.

"I've been meaning to fire Henry. Father of new twins. You

can have his office."

"You can't fire him because he's a new dad."

"You want the job or not, son?"

Did he want it at the expense of someone else? Hell no. But did he want a big fat paycheck in his account? Desperately. And he knew that Rochester, Lemon, and Links was the only firm in town that would trust him with large accounts. And it wasn't like they would keep Henry even if he declined the job. But taking the job was wrong...right?

Shit. His moral compass was all over the place. Desperation could do that to a man. *There were other jobs,* he decided, *ones that didn't require taking some poor new dad's desk.* It would likely be closer to an entry-level job, working on smaller accounts until he could prove himself. But would it make enough to cover the mounting bills?

He was wading through the giant pool of Frank-sized shit—*how had he forgotten about this*—when he felt a little sweaty palm slide into his.

"What the hell is that?" Frank bellowed as if he'd just seen a seven-foot-tall cockroach.

"Da-da, I went poopoo," Waverly said.

Jonah looked Frank in the eyes. They were bulging, bloodshot with rage. There was even spittle in the corner of his mouth.

"I almost did, too, honey. Daddy almost did, too."

Chapter Eleven

Evie

The birds were chirping, the sun was out, her parents weren't at the shop, and not a single suitor was in sight. What a glorious day. The only storm cloud around was the conversation with Jonah from the other day.

None of it sat right. Not only had she inadvertently hurt Ryan, she'd asked Jonah to lie to his family. What kind of person asked that of a friend? A desperate one, that's who. She thought back to their near-miss sex-capade and knew that he had made the right decision by turning her down. But rejection still hurt.

However, she wasn't going to think about Jonah right now. She was going to think about her good day.

"Barbara," she said, setting an oversized mug on the counter. "Hazelnut latte for Barbara."

Evie went back to the register and asked the next customer, "What can I get you?"

"Fifteen minutes of babysitting."

Evie had to blink. She knew the voice but barely recognized the man in front of her.

Jonah?

He was wearing a charcoal suit with a deep blue button-up and his hair was actually styled. Well, as close as it could come to a style when he clearly needed a haircut. Then there was his beard, now more like a five o'clock shadow on his ruggedly masculine face that had her traitorous heart taking a nosedive into her stomach.

Double-checking that her mouth wasn't gaping open, she said, "Look around. I'm one of two baristas here."

His eyes widened as if just noticing that there were other people in the shop. "I know this is a big ask, but I'm desperate."

Well, she was embarrassed. She'd hoped to go at least a week before she had to see him—long enough for them both to forget her ridiculous proposition. She could still taste the whipped cream from being pied and there he was looking larger than life, and sexier than a desperate man had the right to look. But beneath the good looks was a frazzled father.

Waverly had her arms locked around his neck, there was a suspicious brown stain on the cuff of his shirt, and he had the look of a parent who was one temper tantrum away from going under.

"What happened to daycare?"

"They won't let her come back until she's potty trained so I hired a sitter for the day and she was a no-show."

"You're not helping your case here," she said, repeating his words from the other day.

"I deserve that," he said. "And we've been working on it. Look, I really need just fifteen kid-free minutes. I have a meeting with a potential employer and it's a big deal."

She catalogued his outfit. Now that she'd collected her

tongue up off the floor, she had a chance to really see what he was wearing. "And you're dressed like that?"

He looked down, clearly baffled. "What? I'm in a suit."

"That's like two sizes too big." He'd clearly lost the dadbod he'd had while married. Now he had the body of a runner, which made sense, since she saw him hit the pavement every morning after he dropped the kids off at school.

"It's all I had. Is it that bad?"

She walked around the counter and started undoing his tie. She whipped it off and went to work undoing the top two buttons of his shirt. Her fingers brushed his Adam's apple and there went that nosedive sensation again.

Her gaze flew to his and she found him staring at her lips. He didn't even bother to hide his interest. "Trying to get me out of my clothes, Evie?" Her name was said on a low rumble that sent her pulse racing.

She shook her head to clear it. "Shut up while I'm trying to be nice. Here." She took Waverly from his hands and plopped her on her hip. Oblivious to the heated tension in the air, Waverly started playing with Evie's hair. "Lose the coat."

"I've never undressed in public, but I think I like it."

"It isn't an undressing. It's an emergency fashion intervention."

It reminded her of the other intervention, which reminded her of her steamy dream last night that led to a meet-and-greet with her battery-operated boyfriend this morning that had her body going from warm to surface-of-the-sun blazing.

"He's supposed to arrive any minute. All I need is twenty minutes."

"You said fifteen." But Evie was already breathing in the sweet scent of baby powder and peanut butter, causing her hormones to go into a baby-induced frenzy.

"You said yes." He looked behind him to another man in a suit. Only this one, lord help her, had a red rose. "Or I could ask your mom and leave you to your suitors."

"Gee, what a choice the universe is giving me. I have to pick between two men who are trying to commandeer my morning. I already have a family of hijackers to contend with." And if she'd had time to spare it would have been spent studying for her entrance exam.

"I know what I'm asking, and I promise I'll make it up to you."

She sighed. She didn't want to be an asshole, it was only fifteen minutes. And she knew what it was like to be a struggling single parent desperate for a lifeline. Plus, time with Waverly wasn't a hardship. "You owe me."

"I'll bring over a tray of my famous spaghetti."

Her mouth began to water. "With homemade noodles?"

"Homemade from a box."

"Then I expect a big bottle of wine to go with it."

"Noted," he said and that was his cue to leave, only he stood there, staring at her. She was staring back and something new passed between them. Something dangerous and intriguing. He cleared his throat. "I should…"

"Yeah. You should."

But neither moved, and the moment grew until it was hard to breathe without taking in his yummy male scent. Or the way his eyes dilated and his nostrils flared.

"Cookie," Waverly said, reaching her pudgy fingers out toward the jar of cookies on the counter, effectively breaking the moment. She was as relieved for the distraction as she was disappointed. Which made no sense at all.

"I promise I'll make it fast," he said and turned around, heading for a man who was waving him over. Evie watched him walk away and couldn't drag her eyes off the way his ass filled out those slacks.

"Are you Evie?" the next customer in line asked. "Of You've Got Male?"

Evie looked at the rose and sighed. "I'm Evie of You've Got a Toddler with a Dirty Diaper. You want to help with that?"

Chapter Twelve

Jonah

Jonah approached the table, where Kyle, the director of finance for a midsized firm, was grinning as if he'd watched the fashion debacle unfold.

Kyle stood and welcomed Jonah with a handshake. "For a minute there I thought you were going to stand me up, but Jake said you were top of your class and admired your work so I decided you were worth the wait."

Jonah had met Jake freshman year at Cornell. They were randomly assigned to the same dorm. They immediately hit it off. So when Jonah decided to get serious about getting a job—one that didn't require getting someone else fired, brown-nosing it to climb the ladder, or sacrificing his family—he reached out to Jake. His firm wasn't hiring but he hooked Jonah up with Kyle.

"Just having a morning," Jonah explained. "Sorry about that."

Kyle waved it off. "No worries. My wife nitpicks my clothes

all the time."

"Oh, she's not—"

"Hell, she practically dresses me." Kyle froze, then swallowed hard. "Sorry man, I forgot. Jake told me about your wife. That's rough."

Jonah wondered what people saw when they looked at him. It was clear by the concern on Kyle's face that it was not the ballbuster broker he'd once been. *Because you aren't the ballbuster broker you once were.*

But he could be. All he needed was one person, *just one,* to take a chance on him.

"It was. But I'm ready for the next chapter."

"The kid yours?" He jerked his chin toward Waverly, who was perched effortlessly on Evie's hip, like two pieces to the same puzzle. Something uncomfortable tightened in his stomach.

"Just turned three."

"She's cute. I have two. Nine and thirteen. Let me tell you, the teen years will make you go bald. Some days all my daughter is missing is the plastic heels and a pole." Jonah thought of his own baby and shivered at the thought.

"I have a seventeen-year-old son, so I get it. Broody as hell."

"So this next chapter. What does it look like? Because, I'm going to be frank, we aren't really looking for anyone right now. But if the right kind of person comes along, we will always find the room, if you get what I'm saying."

"I am that person. I know on paper I have some gaps, and decisions that I would question if I were in your chair, but when my wife was diagnosed and I heard the word terminal? I knew I couldn't give one hundred percent of myself to my wife and job, so I quit."

"I heard you were mere months away from being named partner."

"I was. Which speaks to my ability and work ethic. It also speaks to the way I work with clients. My past employer won't give me a glowing recommendation—"

"Frank is the devil incarnate. I can assure you we run our company differently."

"Good to know, because while my daughter is in preschool and I'll be hiring after-school help, things come up that are out of my control. Like today. And I don't have a partner to rely on."

The second that last sentence came out of his mouth he wanted to reel it back in. Because the slowly built confidence in Kyle's eyes fizzled.

"I get that family comes first, but I need someone I can rely on, and sometimes that means making a hard call or working through dinner or over the holidays."

"I hear you and agree with you."

Kyle relaxed. "Why don't you email me your resume and a list of client references, and I will take a look at it and get back to you. You were at the top of your game and impressive as hell."

Jonah didn't like the past tense Kyle used on that last line, but he knew his former clients would sing his praises.

Jonah reached into his bag and pulled out a crisp white paper. "Already have it." He slid his resume and referral list across the coffee shop table and Kyle gave it a quick glance.

"Prepared. I like that."

They shook hands, and when Kyle left the shop Jonah walked over to the counter where Evie was effortlessly amusing Waverly while serving her customers like a pro. A lifetime from now, when he thought back to this moment, he would remember the way Evie looked holding his daughter. She had Waverly on her hip in a little apron and Grinder tee, helping with the whipped cream. And what a breathtaking picture that made.

Something shifted inside him.

She must have felt his energy because she looked up at that precise moment and their gazes snagged and stuck. After a heavy moment, she turned to her employee and asked, "Julie, can you handle things for a minute?"

Julie looked from Evie to Jonah and back to Evie and gave a dramatic brow waggle. "Take all the minutes you need."

Evie rolled her eyes, then grabbed another cookie for Waverly and walked around the counter.

"You don't have to stop for me," he said, even though that was exactly what he wanted—to sit down with her and tell her what had just transpired.

"This seems like more of a sit-down conversation. Not one casually thrown over a counter." They walked to a table in the back and sat. He expected her to hand over Waverly, but instead she bounced his daughter on her knee. "I want to hear everything."

That comment hit him in the chest. He hadn't had this kind of excitement since he almost made partner.

"I think it went well. Better than well. Maybe closer to great."

Her face lit with genuine excitement. "Oh my God, Jonah! That's amazing."

"He didn't seem to care that I'd quit a prestigious job to be a stay-at-home dad. He agreed to really look at my resume and call my former clients before deciding."

He stopped and Evie smacked the table. "You can't leave me hanging with two-line items. Tell me everything!"

A little surprised that she wanted to hear all about it, and uncertain about the rusty way his chest expanded, Jonah went into every detail about the meeting, getting more excited by the moment, until he got to the part when he brought up Amber and being a widower.

"I should have left it alone. I know it makes people

uncomfortable. And it was like he went from looking at me as a viable candidate to a broken and inept has-been."

"I'm sure it went in one ear and out the other. I mean, what kind of man would use that against someone?" Evie said. "Plus, I see it as a strength. For you to go through that and come out the other side with your family still intact? That takes courage, determination, and power."

Her positivity shined through her and was so contagious he couldn't help but smile.

He ran a hand down his face in disbelief. "It's terrifying. Now that this is a real possibility, I have to get my shit together for the actual interview."

Because there was going to be an actual interview. He was going to manifest the shit out of that.

"You can do this, Jonah."

He had to. But he also couldn't do this alone. That was a fact. He needed help. More than that, he needed a professional organizer. "Remember that offer you made the other day?"

She lifted an amused brow. "You mean the one you shot down?"

"Maybe I was a little hasty."

"No, you were right. It is a ridiculous idea."

"Give me three reasons why this can't work."

"Easy. We hate each other." She ticked up a finger. Then another. "Our lifestyles clash. And your life is a disaster. You should have a walking hazard sign around your neck."

"Your life isn't all rainbows and sunshine."

She crossed her arms stubbornly. "Then why do you call me sunshine?"

"Because while you pull this June Cleaver act with everyone else, with me you are all fire and brimstone."

"You just proved my point. And if you want another reason,

here." She handed him an estimate from a landscaping company for his yard if he missed his timeline.

He glanced at it, then crumpled it up. "This is bullshit and you know it."

"I agree. And FYI, I vetoed it, but the rest of the board saw the progress you've made and voted to hire Karlson's son's company if you fail to comply."

He ran a hand down his face and looked at the ceiling. "Shit. Shit. Shit! I can't afford this." He looked at Evie. "I can't afford this. Not without breaking into the kids' college fund, which is a nonstarter."

"You still have a month."

"Hazard sign. Remember?"

Evie remembered how hard it had been in the beginning to be in it alone. But she'd never really been alone, she'd had her parents. Jonah had himself. "I'm not saying yes, but what are you offering?"

He looked dumbfounded. "Seriously?"

"I'll hear you out."

"If you help me get my life in order, I will help you convince the world you're off the market."

She snorted in disbelief. "It's going to take more than a few weeks. Plus, I was delusional. We could never convince people we're together."

"Kyle thought we were a couple at first."

"He did?" Was that a blush on her cheeks?

"He did. And you know what? When he thought you were my wife—"

"Wife?" she choked.

"He didn't remember I was a widower. And he treated me differently. Like I was complete and a man who could do the impossible. Because in my past life I *could* do the impossible."

Except for when it came to saving his wife.

Evie rested her hand over his. As if she knew what he was thinking, she said, "Don't go there. You were Superman all the way through."

Resting his elbows on the tabletop, he leaned forward until he could see the flecks of gold in her eyes and rested his hand over hers, letting the warmth sink in. *Getting too close, Jonah.* "Who's chicken now, Evie?"

She scoffed. "If this is going to work, we'd need to lay some ground rules," she said, her tone all business, no bullshit. Her attention flickered to their hands, but she didn't move. "First rule, touching is permitted only in public and only for show."

"What kind of touching are we talking?" He waggled a naughty brow, needing to lighten the mood and get back on track convincing Evie that her plan was brilliant.

"I'm being serious."

"So am I. If this is to work, then we need to set some concrete lines so we are on the same page. So clearly hand-holding is okay." He flipped his hand over and laced their fingers, testing it. She stiffened but eventually relaxed. "How about cuddles, hip holding, and ass grabbing. All tastefully done of course."

She yanked her hand back as if bitten by a viper. "How can ass grabbing be tasteful?"

"I am the king of tasteful, trust me."

She seemed to consider this. "Only if the moment calls for it."

She blushed. Interesting. The idea of his hands on her ass got her hot and bothered. It made him wonder what else got her motor running.

"Is this moment calling for it?"

"No. Neither is it calling to seal it with a kiss. A handshake will do fine." Evie stuck out her hand and Jonah took it, then placed a gentle kiss to each knuckle before releasing her hand. She rolled her eyes. "Remember, this is just fake."

It had to be. Dating in public while having a strict no-sex pact, and then breaking said pact behind closed doors, had the potential to blow up in their faces. When they reached the end of their agreement and things ended, someone could get hurt.

"Any more rules, sunshine?"

"One. And it's the most important one. No one falls for the other. We both agree that this is a transactional relationship."

"Am I Richard Gere or Julia Roberts in this scenario?" he wanted to know.

The set of her chin suggested irritation. "This is serious."

"I am being serious. I've always wanted to walk into a store and say 'Big mistake. Huge.' Then do a mic drop."

"As long as you're wearing a wig and dress, I'm all for it. But this is a tit for tat. Even-steven situation. Nothing more. Got it?"

"Got it. But in case I forget to tell you later. I had a really good time."

Chapter Thirteen

Evie

"Drop the diaper and back away," Evie said.

Evie hadn't even finished her morning mocha and her day had literally turned to shit. She'd gotten up early to go over some of the shop's vendor invoices when Camila had called her from next door, saying it was an emergency, and turned Evie's mess of a morning into a crime scene.

The stench alone blew her back a step, nearly taking her out at the knees. The visual—*oh God*, the visual. The giant finger-painted, poop-smeared wall was like the metaphorical landscape of her life.

Wielding tongs and a beach towel, she crossed the threshold of her neighbor's nursery. She was stuck in a standoff with a diaper-lobbing toddler, who—in the three-minute argument between Evie and the coffeepot that was overflowing—had pulled a diaper-Houdini, then smeared herself with the entire contents of the dirty diaper. From the tips of her wheat-blond mohawk to the bottoms of her chubby little feet, Waverly left a mess in her wake wider than the Colorado River.

Jonah better be the best damn beard of all time.

"I say we go at her like she's a greased pig," Lenard's eternally humored voice said from beside Evie. He was standing shoulder to shoulder with Evie, like a fellow soldier preparing for battle.

"Or we can bribe her with a cookie and when she's distracted wrap her up like a burrito, then take her outside and hose her off," her mother said. Today she was wearing her hair in wavy curls, a polka-dotted sundress—*Pretty Woman* style—with stilettoes on her feet. She was also standing beside Evie. Then there was Camila, who was behind Evie, using her body as a shield.

"She's not a dog," Evie said.

"Sink or shower?" Moira said to Lenard.

"I'm not sure Jonah wants to wash his vegetables in a sink doubling as a makeshift changing table," Evie said, noting that he was suspiciously MIA.

"Hose it is," her parents said in unison. Even though they'd been divorced for over a decade, they were inseparable. Which was a testament to her mother's generous spirit.

"Jonah," Evie called out, her voice one octave shy of manic. "My parents are about to power wash your kid."

Only silence answered back.

"Where is he?"

"Um, he said if there was any problem to call you and you'd help out. There was a problem so I called you," Camila said. "I told Mr. Stark that I'd watch Waverly until he got back."

"And he's where?"

"Having coffee with someone."

"Of course he is."

What had she agreed to? That was a question she'd been asking herself all week. Yes, it had been her idea, but she'd clearly been out of her mind when she'd come up with it. Desperation could make people do crazy things.

Like staging a fake relationship to trick America. Was she willing to lie to her family to get them off her back? Sadly, yes. While Evie hadn't posted anything on ClickByte, someone had videoed her and Jonah holding hands, and she could already see a reduction in suitors. Better still, other fans of the account were continuing to pour through the doors, but Evie was starting to wonder if she'd ever have privacy again.

For heaven's sake, she had taken to wearing a ballcap low on her forehead, an oversize sweatshirt, and hunching over to make herself as inconspicuous as possible just to get groceries without incident. But this. This!

This was not a part of their pact.

She whipped out her phone and angrily whipped off a text.

Evie: My parents are about to corner and hogtie your kid like cattle.

She waited five seconds and when no dots appeared she pocketed her phone and shot Camila her mom-glare.

Camila grimaced. "He offered me a hundred bucks to get her ready for school."

"It doesn't look like she's ready," Lenard said, amused.

"I swear she was dressed. I looked away for one minute and when I came back she was like this," Camila said.

"You looked away or stepped away to talk to a boy?" Not willing to break eye contact with the two-foot-tall terrorist who was holding the room hostage with threats of instigating a poop war, Evie didn't meet Camila's gaze. She didn't need to. The guilty silence was answer enough.

"Well, it's time to earn that money."

"I can't. I have a game today and if I get my uniform dirty, Coach will freak. Plus, she's covered in..." Camila made a gagging sound. She'd not only inherited her dad's features and ability to deflect, she'd also inherited his sensitive gag-reflex.

"Evelyn darling, you hold the towel out wide," Lenard instructed, taking Evie's hands and spreading them all the way out to her sides. "Moira, you dangle the cookie and coo softly."

"And what will you do?" Evie asked.

Lenard shrugged as if the answer was obvious. "Look fabulous." He clapped his hands once. "Now, on with the show."

Evie was about to tell him that the show needed more direction when Waverly's little eyes slowly blinked and she took a step forward.

Everyone around Evie held their breath and took a giant step back. Waverly stopped, confused. She took another little toddle and they took another step bringing them up against the hallway wall.

As if reading the energy of the room, Waverly's little lips formed a perfect little circle and her forehead scrunched. Her lids blinked rapidly and her hands fisted. *Oh boy*. Evie knew that look. That was the look of a kid who was two minutes from a meltdown.

Waverly plopped down on the floor, her bum leaving a fresh print on the hardwood, and lifted her little arms in the air. "Uppie. Uppie, Ve-Ve. Uppie."

"Awww. She wants a hug," her parents cooed, but Evie noticed they didn't move forward to intercept the chocolate-covered cutie.

"Uppie," Waverly said again, this time with a little more force, and what was Evie to do? She was already late for work, had agreed to a carpool switch-aroo, and clearly she was the only adult in the room brave enough to face poop.

"Come here, sweetie." Holding her breath, Evie bent at the waist and wrapped the towel around Waverly's roly-poly body and lifted her into her arms. Waverly rested her smeared cheek on Evie's crisp, white shirt and let out a yawn. "How does a nice warm bath sound?"

· · ·

Waverly was clean and dressed for school by the time Jonah had finally answered her text with an ever-so-helpful nugget of wisdom.

Jonah: Running late. On the way. Sometimes a hogtie is necessary. Take pics.

Evie: Helpful as always.

Jonah: Why aren't you at work?

Evie: Our daughters conspired against me.

Jonah: So it's a regular Monday?

Evie: This isn't what I signed up for.

Jonah: When life gives you poop, reach for the hose.

Evie didn't bother to respond. She put her phone away and cracked open the door to Jonah's bedroom. It looked exactly how it had when Amber had been alive. Cork-colored walls, crisp white linens with bright yellow accents that matched her sunny personality. Only instead of the pristine presentation, it looked as if a dry cleaners had exploded, followed by a category-five hurricane.

The bed was unmade, and there were piles and piles of unfolded laundry. Some were on the floor, some hung up, and some just a crinkled mess spilling out of the hamper. She couldn't tell if they were dirty or wear-ready. Or at least that's what she told herself when she picked up one of the few folded shirts and gave it a big whiff.

A strange unfurling happened in her stomach. Warm and tingly and pheromone-induced.

Holding her breath so as not to be transported into a dreamy cologne commercial with a half-naked Adonis emerging from the water, she slid the shirt over her head. It dwarfed her, landing mid-thigh. She shuffled through another basket and found a pair of sweats. Ten sizes too big but it would have to do.

She was mid-pull when the hairs on the back of her neck went on alert.

"If you wanted to get into my pants that badly you just needed to ask," a familiar voice said from behind and damn, if she hadn't just stepped even further into it.

Chapter Fourteen

Jonah

With a squeak, she yanked the sweats up and over her dancing-frog-patterned-thong-clad ass and spun to face him. "How nice of you to join the party."

"Didn't know I was invited," Jonah said, thoroughly amused.

"You were supposed to be the host. I was supposed to swing by and pick up your kiddo for daycare. Lunch packed, ready to go was what you told me."

"I was having coffee with Mrs. Gomez about Raoul's life insurance policy and, well, I showed up for coffee and she had a huge spread. I think I'm the first guest she's had over since becoming a widow."

And Jonah knew how that felt. He'd spent nearly six months avoiding people. It was the only way he knew how to navigate through the grief without pulling the people around him into that pain.

"Last week was the first time she's shown up to a board

meeting since the funeral. She said she only came because you'd stopped by her house earlier and she wanted to help you out. But really *you* were helping her out."

"So you no longer think I set out to ruin your meeting?"

"It was more of a hijacking."

He looked at Waverly, who was sitting on the floor, dressed in ruffles and bows, quietly flipping through a picture book, like she wasn't a toddler going through her terrible twos. Then he looked at Evie. She looked as if she'd gone through a carwash. The bottom half of her hair was wet, she wasn't wearing even a stitch of makeup. Then his body registered what she was wearing—one of his shirts—which was sexier than he expected. The usually primped PTA mom looked like she'd rolled out of his bed.

It looked perfect on her.

"Kind of like what you did to my morning," she added.

"I didn't mean to."

"I know, but you did. I barely have enough time for my own family, I can't completely take on someone else's. Not without sacrificing my own. I said I'd help, not be a stand-in."

"I know and it won't happen again." She didn't look convinced. "Let me take you to dinner to make it up to you," he said. She hesitated. "Nothing behind it. Just a thank-you for going above and beyond." That was Evie to a T. She put her heart into everything, even if it was at a cost to her. She already had a small country depending on her to keep things afloat. He didn't want to be one more hole in her boat. "Bet we can stem that tide of suitors even further."

She seemed to consider his offer. Her eyes softened, her shoulders seemed to sink. That's when he knew she was going to say yes. And then what? They'd find themselves alone and all the circling they'd been doing would reach its breaking point. And they'd end up in bed and—

He looked at his marital bed and his lungs refused to take in oxygen, his throat refused to open, and his head refused to let him go there. For God's sake, he still slept sideways in his bed, with his head on one side and his feet hanging off the other.

When Amber passed, waking up without her was too much. The empty space in his bed was a metaphor for what was going on in his chest. So he'd decided to sleep on her side of the mattress. It didn't help. He tried the middle, sleeping side to side, buying a new mattress. Nothing worked.

He could have slept on the couch but he didn't want to worry Ryan more than he already was. So Jonah slept sideways—it was the only thing that had worked. And even though he'd become accustomed to his wife's absence, he still couldn't manage to make the switch. Which made him wonder if he could sleep with another woman in this room.

He looked up and found Evie studying him intently, understanding and hurt in her gaze. "That's why we have ground rules, Jonah."

Chapter Fifteen

Evie

Evie pulled a bottle of pinot from the fridge and popped the cork. Pouring the wine nearly to the rim of the glass, she took a big swig and plopped down on one of the barstools at the island.

God, today had been a long day. She'd been on her feet for ten hours straight with her head under the frother and her hands in the coffee roaster. Today, her dad had dialysis and Julie was shooting a wedding, so Evie manned the ship solo. Camila stopped by after practice and worked the counter for a couple of hours, which Evie was grateful for. Her daughter had been in a good mood, chatting about school and her friends and some boy she'd met. It was as if Hawaii-gate never happened.

Twice, Evie started to tell her about the pregnancy and both times she'd lost her courage. It was the first day Camila had been happy and open, like her usual sunbeam of a daughter, and Evie wanted to hold on to that for just a little while longer. Plus, the more Evie thought about it, the more convinced she became that this should be Mateo's story to tell. Of course, provided he didn't find a way to blame this one on her, too.

Evie was tired of being the fall guy. It was time Mateo stepped up to the plate, and she was going to tell him that. Tomorrow. Tonight she had a date with a bottle of wine and a bubble bath. If she could get Camila out of their shared bathroom long enough.

"Any new suitors today?" Moira asked, breezing into the kitchen with so much grace it was as if she were floating on air. She was dressed to the nines, her hair effortlessly perfect, and her makeup smoky. All she needed was a martini in hand to double for Faye Dunaway—her early years.

"Four," Evie said. "All carrying roses. But you knew that because you and Julie have been impersonating me online and responding to men's messages. Not to mention sneaking videos of me doing embarrassing things, like bending over to get the bagel balls out of the oven."

Moira poured herself a glass of wine and slid onto the other barstool. "There are a few women in there, too. Don't be so singular in your quest for love."

"Not looking for love. Or a date, for that matter."

"And you aren't keeping up with the sheer volume of potential partners You've Got Male has attracted." Moira took a delicate sip from her glass. "It would be rude not to respond and as your mother it's my responsibility to make sure you aren't rude."

"As my mother it's your responsibility to listen to your child when she tells you how she feels."

Evie was interrupted by a knock at the door.

"Would you mind getting that?" her mom asked, taking a leisurely sip of wine. "It's probably Marty. Or is it Mark?"

Evie rolled her eyes. "You don't even know who you're going out with?"

"All I remember is that he's a Gemini, which should balance

a little of my Aries fire. Plus, Gemini is represented by twins, and I've always wanted to date twins."

Not wanting to hear her mom's theory about the sexual prowess of a Gemini, she set her glass down and made her way to the door. She opened it and her greeting died on her tongue.

Had her mom taken the whole twin thing too far? Because standing on the porch were two men. Well "men" was a bit of an overstatement. One was maybe twenty tops, the other early twenties. Both were dressed nearly identical. Skinny pants, different color graphic tees, with tan boots and a hoodie.

"Can I help you?" she asked.

"Is Camila home?" the younger one asked. That's when she noticed the bouquet of flowers he was holding.

"Nope. Not happening," Evie said. There was absolutely no way this guy was age appropriate.

"Seriously?"

"I'm her mom, and I am always serious when it comes to twenty-year-olds dating my sixteen-year-old."

"I'm only nineteen."

"Yeah, it's still a no." But the kid didn't budge. She eyed the other man. "And you?"

"I'm here for Moira. Are you her mom, too?"

Evie slammed the door in their faces.

"Where are your manners?" Moira *tsk*ed, then opened the door. "Good evening, gentlemen. And which one of you is Mark?" The one who looked older stepped forward.

"Milo." He held out his hand.

"Of course," she said breezily, elegantly shaking it. "Moira and Milo. We're going to have a fun time, aren't we?"

Lenard walked up behind the two of them and kissed Moira on the cheek. "Have fun, sweetie. But not too much fun."

"Who's that?" Milo asked.

"Oh, my ex-husband. We're a very progressive family."

He smiled. "Right on."

"This is your date?" Evie asked. "And you had him pick you up here?"

"I'm a gentleman, ma'am," Milo said to Evie. "I take my Cougar Catch matches seriously."

"You find dates on an app named Cougar Catch, but you call me ma'am?"

Milo shifted nervously from side to side. "You seem like a ma'am kind of woman."

Before Evie could respond, Camila appeared from behind her grandfather. She was in a dress much like Moira's, only it was shorter and tighter. "Hey, Dexter."

Evie's hand flattened to her chest. "Dexter? Like the serial killer?"

Dexter's brows caved in with confusion. "Who?"

"Never mind. This"—she waved between the two mismatched teens—"isn't happening."

"Oh, it's happening," Camila challenged. "You said I needed an adult to go to the wedding. Here's my adult." Camila went up on her toes and kissed the guy. Dexter seemed surprised but not disappointed as if that was a green light for other things.

"Exactly, he's an adult. You're a minor, and in the state of Colorado, I am in charge of you until you're eighteen."

"My body, my choice."

Evie opened her mouth but nothing came out. What could one say to that? Plus, she was so shook by Camila's comments and blatant disrespect that she didn't know how to proceed. Wasn't she just happy and sunshine-y three hours ago? There was no way Evie was that moody at her age...right?

Moira's hand rested on Evie's shoulder. "Why don't you let her go?"

"Because he has to be pushing twenty-five."

Lenard looked him up and down. "I put him at twenty."

"He said he's nineteen," Camila said. "And we can hear you."

"Nineteen is too old," Evie said.

"Ryan is almost nineteen and you don't freak out when I'm with him," Camila said.

"Because he's our friend."

"Well, Dexter is Ryan's friend. So one degree of separation."

"And one degree from getting his ass kicked if he even decides to take things past hand-holding." The serious-as-shit voice came from the shadow behind the porch.

Then Jonah appeared, holding a grocery bag, and his gaze was dialed to locked and loaded.

"Hey, Mr. Stark," Dexter said with a large gulp. "What are you doing here?"

"I should ask you the same. Does Ryan know you're taking out Camila?"

"Uh, yes sir. He was there when Camila asked me out."

All five sets of eyes flew to Camila, who was toeing the porch plank with a pair of thigh-high boots that looked suspiciously like Moira's.

Evie was about to send Camila to her room like she was six and throwing a tantrum when Moira said, "Milo, how about we make this a double date?"

"Seriously?" Camila blinked as if she'd never imagined that she'd get a yes out of this situation. Meaning, she was purposefully setting Evie up to be the bad guy.

"As long as your mom's okay with it," Moira said and Evie felt torn. She didn't want to reward this behavior, but if Camila was going to go on a date with a guy who was a little too old, what was safer than with Ryan's friend—who was clearly already scared shitless of Jonah—and a sixty-five-year-old chaperone?

"I can't believe I'm saying this, but be home by ten."

Camila jumped into Evie's arms and gave her a kiss on the cheek. "Thanks Mom. We'll be home by eleven."

"Ten or no deal."

Camila rolled her eyes, but she was grinning from ear to ear. "Fine. Ten."

"That gives us four hours to paint the town red," Moira said, and Evie wondered just what she'd agreed to.

Chapter Sixteen

Evie

"You need me to put the fear of God into him?" Jonah asked with a tone of protectiveness that had Evie's heart taking a nosedive to her stomach. Here was someone who wasn't even blood related doing something Camila's own father had never done for her.

"Yes," she said as the brake lights of Milo's car disappeared into the night. She sighed. "Am I being too protective?"

Jonah walked up the steps to her porch, not stopping until his big body filled the frame of her doorway. He was dressed in flip-flops, cargo shorts with a million and one pockets, and a simple black T-shirt that clung to his biceps and a jaw-dropping chest she tried her best to ignore. Nothing even close to the kind of dress clothes her suitors at the shop had worn, yet he managed to light her south-of-the-border furnace. Then there was the full grocery bag he held in his arm, the neck of a wine bottle and a baguette sticking out the top.

"Do you feel like you're being protective?" he asked.

She snorted. "What kind of therapy crap is that?"

He smiled and, *oh boy,* was she in trouble. "Crap my therapist says."

For the first time that day, Evie actually laughed and, just like that, all the pent-up stress was replaced by something lighter. She pointed to the bag. "What's that?"

"A thank-you for potty-gate."

"I already said you didn't have to do that."

"I wanted to," he said. "You saved my ass with Way. Again. And I haven't thanked you for having my back with the board, even though I did sic rats on your grandmother's roses. Our families have been friends for over a decade, we've been neighbors for over a decade, and I don't want fruit trees and ClickByte to come between our friendship. "

"Well, this isn't public, so not part of the deal. And friends is all it can be."

He seemed to think that over and nodded. "Deal. Then how about you invite me in for a friendly dinner. Ryan is on babysitting duty, and I have a bottle of red and a bowl of my famous spaghetti."

"Famous, huh?"

"Well, it's famous for being the only thing I can really cook without burning it."

"Jar or homemade sauce?"

"A little of both?"

She considered the ramifications of inviting him in, then remembered what they'd just agreed to—friends. And he was right, there was a lot of history between them, and it would be a travesty to see it all go to waste.

"I already have a salad in the fridge."

"Talk about a perfect pairing." There was that smile again that set her furnace ablaze. Which was a problem because south-of-the-border blazes didn't fit into this new "just for show" pact.

"A drama-free dinner sounds nice," she said and backed up so he could enter.

"Are you saying the neighbor-war is over?"

"I wouldn't say over." She led him to the kitchen. "But we can put the feud on standstill for one night."

"Then I better make the night count."

He swept past her into the kitchen, the scent of testosterone and yummy male lingering in his wake. It had been a long time since she'd had a man over for dinner. Long as in, the last man she had at her dinner table—and she wasn't talking about Paul with the receding hairline who worked mall security, Stan the steam cleaner salesman, or any of the other strangers her mom randomly invited to dinner as Evie's plus-one—had been Mateo.

Oh, Jonah had eaten at her table in the past, but there was always family around. Tonight, it was just them. The girls were on a date and her dad had retired to bed, leaving just Evie and the mysterious single dad next door. Because that's what he was to her—a mystery. She knew him as a husband, a dad, even as a neighbor, but she'd never known him as only her friend.

She looked at the table and then at Jonah and suddenly it all felt so intimate. Too intimate. The kind of intimate that could derail her carefully laid plans.

"Why don't you grab the wine opener and take a seat at the counter."

He gave her a knowing grin. "You afraid I'm going to whip some candles and flowers out of the bag?"

She swallowed. "Are there candles in the bag?"

"Do you want there to be candles and roses?"

"Candles would be a strict violation of the rules. That's just like you to break the rules week one."

"Cool your panties, sunshine. No flowers."

"Good. Store roses have never done it for me," she said and

brushed past him to grab the salad out of the fridge.

"What does do it for you? Asking for a friend."

Thank God her head was stuck in the fridge because she did not want him to see her blush.

Ignoring his question, she asked, "Have you heard back from Kyle?"

"Radio silence. Which might be an answer."

She spun around. "Don't do that! Don't undervalue yourself. And don't think the worst. "

"Working on it. And how about you? You sign up for the placement exam yet?"

"You remember that?"

"I do." There was something in his eyes that might be called *care*, but Evie didn't want to see it. She didn't know how long it had been since someone had thought of her needs. Grabbing the dressing, she busied her hands with that instead.

"Working on it. I still have some time. I am still weighing the pros and cons of doing it now rather than postponing a year when the shop is in a better space."

"In a year there will be another excuse and then you look up one day and three years have flown by and you're thirty pounds heavier, your garden is overgrown, and you're sporting sweats with a hole in the crotch."

"That's a visual I didn't need. But point taken."

"Sign up for the exam before you pro and con yourself out of it being your choice. If there was one takeaway from Amber, it is to value when you can make a choice and not have one made for you."

Evie opened her mouth to say something soothing, but knew he was done with that topic. "So, how did the meeting go with Mrs. Gomez?"

The expression of appreciation he sent her way did funny

things to her. And for a moment she forgot why he annoyed her so much. "Strange."

"Strange how?" She found a container of crumbled blue cheese, tongs from the drawer, and gave the salad a quick stir.

"I went in to just give her advice on how to handle the claims and find a broker. She said she'd already met with bigger firms, and it didn't feel right. She wanted to work with someone who understood what it's like to lose someone you love."

Evie went to bring the salad to the island and stopped short. Jonah had set their places with plates, dinnerware, and wineglasses. The steaming pasta was in a beautiful white bowl, which he'd brought from home, and he was uncorking the wine.

"I *can* set a table. I'm not completely inept."

"I didn't say that."

His eyes sparkled with challenge. "Maybe not aloud, but you thought it."

She neither confirmed nor denied his statement. Instead, she set the salad down and slid onto the barstool next to him. "Do you mind if I have my pinot grigio instead of the cab?"

"White wine with this sauce? That's criminal. In fact, I don't know if I could trust someone who drinks white with a clearly red-wine dish. Do you put ice in it, too?"

"No. And pinot is a neutral wine."

"Unless you're choosing white because I brought red."

She snorted. "No. I really prefer white. Now, back to Mrs. Gomez. Did she hire you?"

"I said I'd think about it."

"What's to think about?"

"I don't have a job, Evie. I don't have a firm backing me. I can't confidently say that I'd be the best guy to handle her money. I told her about the interview and we are going to revisit it when I'm employed."

"Sounds like you are going to pro and con yourself out of a great way to dip your toes in the water." She reached out and touched his hand. Sparks ignited but she didn't move away. "You can only hide from the world for so long. Trust me, eventually you have to get back out there."

"I will. I just want to do it right. I'm still interviewing and sending out resumes while I wait. It's kind of like screaming into the Ether, but maybe I'll get a few hits." He took a sip of wine and swallowed. "How long did it take you after Mateo split?" he asked.

She waited until he finished filling her glass, then took a long sip. She hated talking about this. She was sure Jonah had received the lowdown from Amber at some point, but somehow the idea of telling him directly felt somewhat comforting.

He must have mistaken her silence for hesitation because he waved off the question. "You don't have to tell me if it brings up bad feelings."

"Not bad. Mad. At first, I was hurt. Then I was embarrassed. Nowadays, I fluctuate between exasperated and pissed."

He chuckled. "How long were you together?"

"A little over a year. I found out I was pregnant six months into dating. He immediately proposed, then one night he drew me a bath and said he was going to go get some ice cream. He never came back. I called every hospital thinking he'd been in an accident, but then I got a notice that our bank account had been cleaned out. I was seven months pregnant."

Jonah's expression was priceless. "I've always had this gut reaction to punch your ex. Now I know why," he said, and that protectiveness was back. Only, this time it was directed at her. And she wasn't sure how *that* made her feel. "I can't believe you even let him in your life after that."

"I do it for Camila's sake," she admitted. "I hoped that just because he was a bad partner wouldn't mean he couldn't be a good dad. He's failed on both fronts."

"Amber told me he was a deadbeat, but I never knew how bad it was. It must have been hard to go through that all alone. How old were you?"

"Nineteen. But I had my family, who've been this amazing support system. Mateo might not be all that involved but Camila receives three times the love." Not wanting to ruin the meal with any more Mateo talk, she asked, "Where do your parents live?"

"My dad died in Afghanistan. And my mom lives in Boulder. She's been great, but she's a lot older than your parents, so being a weekend grandma is about all she can handle. And I wouldn't want her to take on more. She worked three jobs to keep the roof over our heads. She deserves to spend every moment of her retirement being retired." He rubbed a hand down his face. "Does single parenting get any easier?"

"It did after I came to the conclusion that, while I wanted to be perfect at everything, the perfect mom, the perfect employee, the perfect daughter, I was going to screw up on every front. As a single parent, perfection isn't an option."

"You seem like you're holding it together pretty well."

"It's all a facade. You saw my room the other night. It was filled with clutter, bags of goodwill stuff, weeks and weeks of unopened mail and bills. I hide it in there before every board meeting so people think I have my shit together."

"Sunshine, I couldn't see anything past those Gnope panties."

"Friends don't comment on other friends' panties."

The air crackled. "Then why have you been staring at my lips?"

She jerked her head away. "You have a little sauce on the corner of your mouth."

"Liar."

He was so spot on she was surprised her pants didn't burst into flames.

Chapter Seventeen

Evie

"Nothing about that is okay," Camila said loud enough for everyone in line at the market to hear, while holding her phone in Moira's face. Evie ducked her head and pushed the cart forward to distance herself from the conversation and hopefully go unscathed.

Moira rested her hand on Camila's and lowered them. "Don't worry, honey, he's all yours."

"Gross," Camila said with enough teen angst to fuel a heat-seeking missile. "I am not going out with a guy you matched with."

Evie came to a stop and whipped her head around to look at her daughter. "Hold up. You two are matching with the same guy now?" Camila picked up a candy bar and pretended to study the ingredients. "How old is he?"

Silence. Even though her daughter's back was to her, Evie knew she was rolling her eyes.

"Camila?" she pressed.

"Twenty-one."

This whole thing was getting out of hand. "You let a twenty-one-year-old slide into your DMs?"

"Mom, no one says that anymore."

"Well, no one in this house is going out with a twenty-one-year-old. He is age inappropriate for both of you." She glared at her mom. "New rule, no younger than me for you. And no one older than Ryan for you," she said to Camila.

"You always were such a party pooper," Moira said.

Evie dumped one—make that three—chocolate bars into her cart and wondered if she had enough time to run and grab another bottle of wine. Scratch that: Tequila. "I had to be, with two free spirits as parents."

"Your spirit could be free, too, if you'd just get laid," Moira said and Mrs. Lichfield, who was walking past the checkout line, shot them a scathing look and Evie felt her face heat. She gave the woman an apologetic smile. It didn't help. "Which is why I invited Susan's son to dinner on Friday. You remember Susan from my yoga class. Her son is divorced, handsome, and an entrepreneur."

He was also balding, with a beer gut, and put sugar and cinnamon in Turkish coffee. Evie didn't trust someone who doctored up a nine-dollar, exquisite cup of paradise. That would be like adding ice cubes to a high-end pinot grigio. As for him being an entrepreneur?

"He owns his own *hot dog stand*," Evie said, but Moira just waved a dismissive hand. Oh my God. This dinner was going to happen, no matter what Evie said. The only thing that would get her out of another awkward blind date was—

"Plus, I'm dating someone."

Moira blinked. Twice. Then dramatically flattened her hand

to her chest. "I knew You've Got Male would work if you'd just let it." She pulled Evie into one of those swinging-back-and-forth kind of hugs. "And you're working it. I am so, so proud."

Evie looked at the cashier, who was shamelessly eavesdropping. She lowered her voice. "Actually, it's Jonah."

Camila promptly dropped the candy bar, her bored attitude morphing into horror. "You're dating Ryan's dad?"

Evie lifted her hand to tuck her hair behind her ear, then immediately dropped it. "Why do you sound so surprised?"

"You *hate* each other," Camila said.

"Love and hate are closely related," Moira said. "And it makes for some great sex."

"Gross," Camila repeated at the same time Evie choked out, "No one said love. We've only had one date."

Wow, look at the lies falling off her lips. Granted, they did have dinner and wine and if level heads hadn't prevailed, they might have even shared a kiss. Something that wouldn't happen again, since that was against their ground rules.

Moira clasped her hands. "It was the night we had that double date. Wasn't it? I knew something happened."

"How did you know?" Evie asked casually, as if talking about a date with Jonah was the most natural thing in the world.

"Lenard said he cooked you dinner."

"Who said it wasn't just a neighborly thank-you for helping out with Waverly?"

"Because I saw the nice wineglasses in the sink."

"Wineglass selection says a lot," the cashier said. "Does this mean You've Got Male is off the market?"

"Yes," Evie said loud enough for everyone in line to hear. "I am." She handed over her credit card and started packing her own groceries. "Before you start streaming this, I want everyone to know that we're just seeing where this can go."

"Oh honey," an older woman with a crop of curly gray hair said from behind—who had her camera aimed at Evie. "There's already a poll going on over how fast you're going to have sex. I put a hundred on a week tops."

It was Evie's turn to be horrified. Strangers thought that was okay to tell someone in the checkout line?!

"Can we stop talking about this?" Camila asked.

Moira put her arm around Camila's shoulder. "You should be happy for your mother."

"Why? Because she's dating my best friend's dad? Talk about awkward. I can't believe you didn't ask me how I felt about it first."

"You didn't ask me how I felt about you dating a nineteen-year-old first. You just invited him over."

"I know him from school. Plus, this is different."

"How?"

"Because it's Ryan's dad and now..." Camila looked at the camera aimed at them and threw her hands in the air. "Never mind. I'll be in the car."

"Honey," Evie began but Camila was already storming off.

Evie let out a sigh and went back to bagging her groceries. This was not how she'd wanted to tell her family. Especially Camila. Evie never imagined it would be easy, but she'd hoped it would be a little blip, not a blow-up in a public place. She'd handled this all wrong. But it was too late to change direction now. She was committed to the farce, and it would all be over in just a few weeks. Then life could get back to normal.

"Don't mind her," Moira said. "She's just upset because she's hormonally unstable. It will pass."

Evie wasn't so sure about that. She knew that her daughter had a massive crush on Ryan but was too shy to tell him. It was obvious to anyone who saw them that there were feelings. It was part of the reason Evie wasn't as worried about Camila's sudden boy-crazy phase. She knew the string of dates was her passive-aggressive way to make Ryan jealous.

Would Camila ever tell Ryan her true feelings now that their parents had "dated"? How badly had Evie's selfish need for privacy and space impacted her daughter's life? And their mother-daughter relationship?

"So, tell me about you and Jonah," Moira asked, and Evie was hyperaware that everyone around them had gone silent as if waiting for her answer.

"There isn't much to tell. There's me. There's Jonah. There was a single date. End of story."

"If that's what you think, you're more out of practice than I thought." Moira pushed the cart out of line and crashed into someone. "I am so sorry," she began and looked up. Her apologetic expression went furious when she realized it was Mr. Karlson. "You!"

Evie couldn't help but bite back a grin. Moira was as friendly as a Labrador, but whenever she was around Mr. Karlson she grew fangs. Maybe there was something to her talk about love and hate being two sides of the same emotion.

"Good evening, Moira," Mr. Karlson said smoothly. He was wearing slacks, a blue polo, and looked every bit the silver fox. "It's nice to see you, too."

Moira pushed her cart forward and ran into his again on purpose. "Out of my way, Karlson."

He smiled. "Why, when this is so fun?"

"When I think of you, fun is the last word I'd use."

"Clearly you haven't been thinking about me in the right way because I'm a lot of fun." Karlson winked and Evie swore her mom sucked in a breath.

"Then you should join my mom on Saturday for her new

book club," Evie said, and Moira kicked her in the shin.

"It's a members-only club," Moira pointed out.

"Then I guess I'll just have to join." He looked down at the cart and said, "If you'll allow me to help, I can pack your groceries in your truck."

"I don't need some guy to pack my groceries."

Karlson lifted a brow at the innuendo and Moira got flustered. "I'm not some guy. I'm a man. When you realize that, you know where I live."

And for the first time in her life, Evie saw her mom go speechless.

Chapter Eighteen

Evie

It had been three days since Evie had heard from Jonah. They'd agreed to move forward with this pretend relationship arrangement, but neither had made the next move. It was as if they'd been in a holding pattern, waiting for the other to step up. Even though Evie knew she was the one who'd asked for the arrangement, a part of her still wanted him to be the one to make the first move. *What? It was a woman's prerogative.*

Just when she was about ready to give in last night, he'd called and asked her out. Not *out* like on a date out, but *out* like going to the mall to buy some new suits. He mentioned something about grabbing a bite to eat after, but she claimed that she had to close the shop—then immediately called Julie to let her know she'd be coming in on her day off to close the shop.

"Play it cool, Evie," she whispered to herself. But cool had never been her strong suit. Case in point, she was standing on Jonah's porch ten minutes early because the second she'd hung up the phone last night her internal countdown clock activated.

The plan was to meet at eleven, but she'd been ready at ten thirty, and instead of playing another round of Relationship Twenty Questions with her mom or risk Moira interrogating Jonah when he showed up, Evie decided to walk next door. She thought that being proactive and seeing him on her terms would fill her with confidence, but as she lifted her hand to knock on the door her heart beat abnormally.

"Oh for God's sake, you're just picking out clothes together, not engaging in a secret affair," she mumbled under her breath. But the words *secret* and *affair* had chaos exploding through her chest.

Chin up, she gave the door a quick rap with her knuckles and waited.

And waited. Until she began to regret her early arrival. Not to mention her sundress, which had taken her twenty minutes to pick out, or her hair and makeup that she had spent the better part of an hour styling.

All for a ClickByte video, she reminded herself, but her brain called bullshit on the statement. This was a bad idea. An incredibly stupid, epically ludicrous, baddest bad idea ever. Which was why she turned to make a stealth escape. Only the door swung open.

Evie froze mid-step.

"Hey, Mrs. G," Ryan said, and Evie closed her eyes, silently berating herself for her lack of patience.

The idea of a faux date had her stomach in knots. Running into Ryan while she was dressed like a PTA mom on the prowl had her questioning her sanity. But it was too late to abort now.

Plastering a casual smile on her face, she turned. "Hey there, Ryan."

The teen was dressed in a pair of athletic shorts, a shirt with the high school football team's logo, and a ballcap. He had car keys in his hand and a gym bag slung over his shoulder with an expression that said she'd obliterated the "good" right out of his morning.

His eyes darted around, discomfort tightened his frame, and a suffocating awkwardness settled around them both.

Until this moment, there'd never been an awkward moment between them. Evie had read him stories under sheet-forts and sewn him a Batman cape for Halloween. She'd driven him to and from school thousands of times and he'd spent as much time at Evie's house as his own over the years. But it seemed within the span of a few seconds a gap the size of the Grand Canyon had opened up between them.

She wasn't sure if Jonah had told Ryan about their "relationship" or if he'd learned about it from Camila, or worse—from ClickByte—but it was painfully clear that he knew. And the change in status quo unsettled him.

Evie suddenly regretted talking to Moira about her dinner with Jonah. Especially in such a public setting. She'd never imagined that it would be filmed, but she should have counted on Camila telling Ryan everything. She only hoped that Jonah had the conversation with his son before the bomb was dropped.

"You okay?" Evie asked and Ryan shrugged, his gaze locked on his cleated feet. Evie took a small step forward and gentled her voice. "It's fine if you say no."

Ryan met her gaze, and there was so much betrayal and misery in them she considered just telling him the truth, blaming it all on desperation and insanity, but he spoke before she could.

"Then, no," he said. "I'm not."

"Is there anything I can do to make this any better?"

"Not unless you want to break up with my dad. Because this is super awkward."

"It doesn't have to be," she said quietly, because whether it was her or some other woman, Jonah was eventually going to start dating. Perhaps it would have been better, though, if that woman wasn't one of Ryan's mom's friends.

"But it is. Between you guys, my grades, Coach threatening to bench me, and my dad maybe starting a new job, my whole life is one big question mark."

Evie didn't know how she felt about being a part of that question mark for Ryan. The poor kid had enough uncertainty in his life as it was.

Just like Camila.

What had she done? It seemed so simple. A few public dates, maybe a kiss or two, a handful of ClickByte videos. She'd never considered just how deeply it might affect her relationship with Ryan or Jonah's relationship with Camila.

"No matter what's going on between your dad and I, we will always be here for you."

His gaze landed on someone behind Evie and a tingling sensation tickled her neck. Evie turned around and her mouth went dry.

Jonah was standing at the bottom of the steps in a blue T-shirt that was in a losing battle with his biceps. Then there was his face—clean-shaven and handsome as hell. Even though he had on dark sunglasses she knew his eyes would be intense.

Concerned for his son.

"Your girlfriend is here," Ryan said, then blew back into the house. "Later."

She waited until he'd started up the car before she said, "I should have waited for you at home. I'm afraid I've just made everything worse," she admitted. "I'm really sorry. Maybe we should forget the whole thing."

Jonah removed his sunglasses and there was that look—the

same one from the night of the meeting. Uncertainty. "Do you want to?"

"Well, maybe we should," she snapped, unsure why she was suddenly so angry. "With the way that just fell so easily from your tongue, like this hasn't just thrown our lives into upheaval— our families' lives! My concern was a sincere one, because of my fear of hurting our kids, and you give me some flippant question back."

"It wasn't flippant." His words were loaded with ridicule. "That was me being pissed that my kid found out through the grapevine. Not even from Camila, but Dexter told him after practice in front of his teammates. And I guess Camila is avoiding him at school. This whole thing has blown up."

"I am so sorry."

"Sorry doesn't fix jack shit." She heard bitterness spill over into his voice and her heart shrank.

Guilt mixed with some of her anger. Her voice barely above a whisper, she said, "Then we call it off. I tell everyone it was my idea, which it was. And that I dragged you into it."

When he spoke, his voice was soft and clear. "I would never let you take the fall. Plus I came to you. I got you tied up in this mess."

"We both knew what we were getting into."

"Honestly, this is embarrassing, but the person I'm really angry at is myself. I just heard back from Kyle." She could almost see the fresh battle scars on his ego. "I didn't get the job. He said they just couldn't take a chance on a guy who hasn't been in the business for the past two years."

Before Evie knew what she was doing, she just stepped down into his arms and wrapped him in a hug. To her surprise, he hugged her back, resting his jaw on the top of her head. They stood like that for a good moment or two.

It was when the embrace started to sizzle that she backed away and cleared her throat. "So what do you want to do? What is the best step forward for you?"

"I need your help, Evie. If I'm going to get Way potty trained, look like the candidate of the year, and fix up this yard, I need you."

Suddenly his yard and her nagging seemed so petty. She had no idea what he had been struggling with, and while she still wanted it completed before her mom's party, it didn't mean she couldn't be neighborly and help him accomplish it.

"I don't want to back out of the deal."

He looked down at her. "Neither do I."

She was shocked at the wave of relief that washed over her at his comment. She could attribute it to the ClickByte fiasco, or the humiliation that would follow getting dumped days after she'd told all of America they were dating. But neither of those reasons could explain away the hum that vibrated through her body over the way he was looking at her. Like he wanted to know what she had on under her dress.

"I really should have checked with you about how and when we told the kids."

"And deny the public at large an opportunity to bet on our sex life?" he said with a mega-watt smile. "Did you know that the majority of America thinks I can get into your pants in just two dates?"

"Good thing this is all pretend," she said, even though the tension between them was real as hell. By the smirk on his face, he knew it, too.

Only it wasn't chemistry that had her worried, it was connection. Specifically, the connection that was forming between them. A connection that was clearly having an adverse effect on the kids.

She crossed her arms over her chest and looked him up and down. "So I guess you ditched the lumberjack look?"

"You didn't mind the lumberjack look the other day." He ran a hand down his jaw. "But if you like the lumberjack, he's only three days away."

"I think your new clients will prefer clean-shaven. Everyone knows that lumberjacks spend their days playing with their wood."

"Everyone knows that wood needs regular maintenance. It's a lonely job but someone's got to do it," he said with a grin and the image alone had her tongue turning to dust. "I'm taking applications."

"Maybe you should post on ClickByte."

Chapter Nineteen

Jonah

"My eyes are up here, sunshine."

"I was looking at the belt." Evie sounded offended, but Jonah couldn't help but notice that she tucked a strand of hair behind her ear while setting the record straight.

She was sitting in a blue velvet, high-backed chair right outside of the dressing room at an upscale men's clothing store. Her long legs were crossed, her posture prim and poised, but she couldn't hide the heat in her eyes when he came out from behind the curtain.

Seemed sunshine had a thing for a man in a suit. Or maybe it was the way a man stood when he wore one. Jonah felt as if he were a superhero who'd just tied on his cape—invincible.

It had been a long time since he'd felt in control, but right then he felt as if he could take it all on and come out on top.

"So?" He held up his hands and did a little spin and noticed she was working really hard to keep her gaze on his.

"I think they're a little snug around the, uh..." She waved a hand south.

He looked down and then up at her innocently. "The uh, what?"

She waved a hand toward his crotch. "You know."

He strode toward her until they were toe-to-toe, looking down into her eyes. Then he rested his hands on the chairback and leaned over until her full lips were inches from his. "Yeah, but I want to hear you say it."

She let out one of those shotgun laughs, like a joyful burst that erupted from the belly. It made him want to make her laugh all over again.

"I bet you do," she said, then pushed against his chest, shoving him back. "But instead, I'm going to grab you a larger size."

Jonah watched her walk away, her hips swaying like only a woman could pull off, and she was a woman all right. Something his dick didn't have a hard time remembering. Which was why the crotch was a little snug. The pants weren't the problem. It was the woman.

He closed the curtain and sat down on the changing room bench, doing multiples of three in his head to get the image of her in that dress out of his mind. When he'd pulled up outside his house and saw her standing on his stoop, his mouth had dried up.

She was one hell of a beautiful woman. And she didn't even know it. Which was another part of the growing attraction.

"Jonah?" Evie said from the other side of the curtain. "I brought you a bigger size and a few more things to try on."

He parted the curtain and met Evie's gaze. With a wink, he said, "One with more leg room?"

She smiled as if they shared a secret joke. The idea intrigued him. It felt fun and intimate all at the same time. Sexy, too. "If that's what you call it." She thrust forward a pair of leopard print pants.

He laughed. "I think you have me confused with Magic Mike but thanks for the compliment."

"No one could have a true Cinderella moment without pleather leopard print," Evie teased.

"Then I guess that makes you my fairy godmother," he said.

She smiled like the Cheshire Cat. "Then I guess you have to do whatever I say."

"As long as you don't make me walk around in glass slippers."

Chapter Twenty

Evie

They hadn't even ordered their food and already Evie wanted to ask for the check. Or maybe a raincheck that was to be cashed in never.

There she was, sitting in a booth and looking over the wine list, wondering what the hell she was doing. After their shopping trip concluded, Jonah offered to take her to dinner. At first, she declined, but then he'd pointed out that they still needed to make a video, and what was more date-like than sharing a bottle of wine by candlelight?

She'd begrudgingly agreed, but only for the sake of Operation Off the Market, so she'd gotten her mom to close up shop. She wasn't sure what she'd expected, but it wasn't a secluded, tiny table for two where their knees were playing bumper cars.

Playing footsie with Disaster Jonah was one thing. Doing it while he looked like a *GQ* model in his new suit and tie? *Sweet baby Jesus* was she in trouble. He hadn't just managed to make her forget about her problems; he'd made her laugh. He'd also made her feel things that weren't part of their fake relationship. Things that were responsible for the dopey smile she knew she was sporting.

She'd smiled so much over the past few hours her cheeks hurt. And that was nothing compared to how her hormones had decided to come out of hibernation and hum in the most inappropriate places. And at the most inappropriate times—like now while she was staring at his tie and imagining how it could double as a blindfold.

"Maybe we should go to the food court instead," she said.

"Why?" he asked. "Afraid you won't be able to keep your hands to yourself?"

She laced her fingers and placed her hands in her lap. "My hands are fine just where they are."

"If you decide they need a change of scenery, I have some suggestions." When she didn't laugh, he tucked a strand of hair behind her ear, callused fingertips sending shivers down her spine. "I'm just trying to lighten the mood. You've been on edge since we sat down."

"I'm not on edge. I guess I'm just nervous."

"So am I," he said quietly. "Maybe we should talk about it."

Worst idea ever. Because talking about it would expose the reason behind that dopey smile. It wasn't just about *GQ* Jonah, it was about the caring, tender, emotionally attuned Jonah that she was starting to know.

Evie didn't ask what-ifs when it came to men, but there was something about this new side of Jonah that ignited a lightning storm of what-ifs—most of them centering around that drunken kiss all those months back.

A kiss that was a mistake, but nonetheless had sparked a curiosity that continued to grow. A curiosity she had to squash.

Because while they needed to make people think this was real, she needed to remind herself that this was about as real as rainbow-farting unicorns. Reason being, his life was still a mess. When she'd been a professional organizer she'd worked with a lot of grieving people. People who'd recently lost a loved one and couldn't face the emotions that came with letting go. Evie would work with them, guide them and support them while they sifted through some of the most treasured times of their lives, times that had ended, so that they could unpack the grief and open a new chapter.

The widows and widowers were the hardest. Sifting through wedding pictures, their spouse's clothes that still smelled like them, the everyday items that symbolized the end. Something as benign as a toothbrush could unlock deep emotions because it was a reminder that their loved one was never coming back. It was Evie's job, and honor, to be the person who held their hand through the roughest patch of their lives.

So then, why hadn't she helped Jonah when Amber had passed?

Before she could respond, the waiter arrived with a bottle of wine and held it out for Evie's inspection.

"This is my favorite," she said. "How did you know?"

"It's my job as your boyfriend to know what you enjoy."

She tried to think of the last time a man had taken the time to catalog what her likes and dislikes were. She couldn't. She also tried to remember the last time she'd had this much fun with a man and came up blank again.

And when he looked at her like that, like she was the most precious thing on the planet, it was easy to see how fast she could fall into Jonah's life, which would mean she'd have to put her own on hold. It would further complicate her relationship with Camila—who was barely talking to her. And it would add a whole other family to her already long list of dependents. So it was a good thing this wasn't real.

The waiter opened the bottle and handed the cork to Evie. She sniffed it, then nodded. After the waiter left, saying he'd be back to take their order, Jonah picked up his glass and held it out to her. "To an incredible first date."

"Fake date," she reminded him.

"Sunshine, to everyone in this restaurant we are a couple enjoying each other's company."

He watched her over the rim of his glass, his expression intense and assessing to the point that she squirmed in her seat. The more time she spent with him, the higher the potential for things to go sideways. Even the slightest axis tilt would send the balls she was juggling crashing to the ground. And what a disastrous crash it would be, because those balls were made of blown glass, where the slightest tap would shatter them all.

"What else would people expect?" she asked, because it had been a long time since she'd gone to dinner with a man. And this man didn't fit into the normal categories. He wasn't a stranger, but their relationship had always been defined by their kids. Yet this was an intimate party of two, and she didn't know how she was supposed to feel about that. Or if she should feel anything at all.

"A lot of eye contact." His gaze locked on hers, humor and something warmer flickering in their depths. "Check. Hand-holding." He took her hand, even threaded their fingers together, and she ignored how perfectly they fit. And she especially ignored the flutter of butterflies that took flight in her stomach. "Check. Deep conversation."

"How deep?" she whispered.

"Why don't we start with the easy stuff and work up to the hard stuff."

She wasn't sure what he considered easy because she was having a hard time focusing while his thumb was skating over the back of her wrist. Evie said the only thing she could think of.

"How is potty training coming?"

He laughed. "Terrible. Any tips?"

"Let me break it down for you in three easy steps. Number one, when she uses the potty give her a treat. Two, when she uses the potty give her a treat. And finally, when she uses the potty give her a treat. You're going to treat it like it's Halloween."

"And hype her up on sugar?"

"It's not really about the treat, it's more about the attention. Women are pretty easy. They just want your attention."

"Are we talking hypothetical attention or specifically my attention, sunshine?"

She didn't answer, instead redirecting the conversation back to the kids. "I'm getting even more worried about how this is affecting our kids."

"How did Ryan seem?" he asked.

"Like he was angry but trying not to show it."

Jonah snorted. "So normal? He did mention that he and Camila had been talking about it a bit more. Camila also told him that your dad's shop is in trouble."

Evie didn't like to talk about family business with outsiders, but she felt like she'd been alone in this battle and could use a sounding board.

"More like one bad month from going under."

"How is that possible? Grinder is an institution in this town."

"Between Starbucks and other cafés popping up around town and my dad not cutting spending as earnings went down, it's a mess."

"It was packed the other day."

"That has more to do with ClickByte than the shop. And

I'm afraid once this is all over and people lose interest that the shop will go under. That's why I'm hoping to win this Denver's Best contest while we have the buzz from the socials. The free advertising alone could really turn things around. We just have to stay open long enough."

"Do you like working there?" His voice sounded sincere— not an ounce of judgment.

"You mean at the place I worked at as a teenager when I came home pregnant and single? Yeah, it's a real party."

"That bad?" The waitress passed by and he brought her hand to his mouth and kissed her knuckles.

For show, she told herself.

"It's not that I hate it. I love helping my family. But I miss being my own person. When I had a career, I had something that was all mine."

He stared at her for a long moment and something passed between them. A deep understanding that only two people who had sacrificed their needs for their loved ones could understand.

"I totally get that. I feel like I lost my identity the moment Amber was diagnosed. And it wasn't just quitting my job, it was like saying goodbye to a part of myself. An important part."

"Being a single parent doesn't leave a lot of room for dreams."

"What's your dream, Evie?" he asked and…had he moved closer? Or had she? Either way, their thighs brushed and his free hand rested on her knee. Her bare knee. The contact was electric.

"I want to finish my degree," she admitted. "I just don't know how that could work. With the shop, my dad's health, I just don't think the timing is right. Again." This was the third time she'd struck out.

"So you haven't accepted?"

She shook her head. "I have to take this placement exam first. But it's on one of our busiest days of the week and my mom will be taking my dad to dialysis."

"I don't know anything about making coffee, but I know how to manage people. Let me help."

An unwanted warmth that went way beyond attraction worked its way through her chest. "You don't have to do that. It isn't part of our agreement."

"It's something I'd do for any friend."

The word friend struck her wrong. Maybe it was the ambiance or the wine or the way his fingers were gliding over her knee, but it felt like something more complicated than friends.

"I have to think about it." She was so used to being in control, it was the only way her life worked. She'd rather miss the exam than be let down by a man again.

"I think it's best that we stick to the agreement," she said.

"You help so many people. Why are you so afraid to ask for help? Or even accept it when it's being offered?"

"Because in the past, asking for help meant disappointment when it came to the male species."

"I'd never let you down, Evie."

She swallowed thickly. "You don't know that."

"I do. And I think deep down you do, too."

Over the past decade she'd seen Jonah at his best and worst, his highest and absolute lowest. Terrifyingly, she'd found herself being drawn to both. Because if she felt this way over him when his life was a three-ring circus, how would she feel when he was the ringleader?

That was a situationship she didn't want to find herself in.

"Help goes both ways and I don't have any room for more strings. I might trip."

"Accepting help doesn't make you indebted. At least not with me. Plus, didn't you just get me the number for a gardener who came highly recommended? And a part-time daddy's helper?"

"That reminds me." She opened her purse and pulled out a folded piece of paper. "I also found you a cleaning lady. She works for one of the regulars at the shop."

"First, I will have you know that my kitchen counter was clean enough to eat off this morning. Second, that is exactly what I'm talking about."

"Me finding you a sitter or housekeeper is part of our arrangement, part of me helping you get your life in order." A fact she needed to remember.

That didn't mean that her heart didn't melt when he ran his thumb over the inside of her wrist and said lowly, "You're doing more than helping me put my life in order. You're putting it right."

"I am?"

"Yeah," he said, and she found herself getting lost in those ocean-blue eyes. "Evie?"

"Yeah," she whispered back.

He cupped her cheek and angled her head until her lips were a breath from his. "You ready?"

She was nowhere near ready to kiss Jonah, yet she didn't pull away and he slowly lowered his head. In fact, she met him half way and then—

Then his mouth was on hers, gentle and probing, more of a caress. Nothing to warrant the way her heart was pounding or her blood was surging through her body. By the way her nipples were popping their corks, she'd think they were playing that game of strip Jenga.

He shifted, pulling her lower lip between his. Intentional. Practiced. Perfect. As if he'd been thinking about this moment for months. And if she were being honest with herself, so had she.

They'd both been circling each other since that night a few months back, desperate to see if it really was as incredible as they remembered. Newsflash: it was even better. It was, hands down, the best kiss she'd ever experienced—and yet their mouths were barely moving.

There was a whole lot of movement happening beneath the table, though, as she parted her legs so he could slide one of his between and lock them into place like a missing puzzle piece.

Jonah slowly pulled away and she leaned farther into it, trying to fill the growing space between their lips. She slowly opened her eyes, expecting him to look as dazed as she felt. But he was smiling.

"Do you think they caught that?"

She shook her head to make sure she heard him right. "What?"

"The kiss. The couple behind us was filming." He ran the pad of his thumb down her cheekbone. "Why, sunshine, were you kissing me just for the sake of kissing?"

"No." She batted his hand away, her stomach sinking. "We have an agreement. And that was all according to plan."

Chapter Twenty-One

Jonah

Jonah waited until his mom had picked up Waverly for a girls' day and walked into the family room to talk things out with his son.

Evie was right the other night to be worried about how their arrangement was affecting the kids. Which was why Jonah had given it a lot of thought and decided he'd provide Ryan with a platform to express his feelings on how things progressed from here.

Man, the other night.

This fake relationship was turning into a problem. Namely, that Jonah was no longer a fake-it-till-you-make-it kind of guy. He'd lost that ability when Amber turned down the medical trial and he knew he was going to lose her. Pretending not to feel his feelings seemed like he was robbing them of the time they did have left.

So faking it with Evie suddenly had lost some of its appeal.

He hadn't kissed her because someone was filming them. Hell, once they'd sat down he couldn't focus on anything but her. He barely remembered what he ate, he was too engrossed in their conversation, hanging on every word she gifted him. He heard her breathy little moans, felt the kiss, and that made all kinds of feelings rise to the surface that he was not ready to deal with.

He should have told Ryan about him and Evie the moment they made the agreement. Finding out his dad was dating would be hard enough. Finding out through the grapevine must have sucked.

It was no wonder the kid was pissed. One minute Jonah was right there with him in the trenches, the next he was rebooting his career and diving headfirst into the dating pool. Or so it seemed. If Jonah had told him directly, Ryan could have gotten pissed or sad or all the emotions that came with seeing the people around you, the people who were supposed to be sharing the same grief, healing and moving forward.

It wasn't moving on. Jonah would never move on because that implied leaving Amber behind. But he was ready to move forward. Even if it meant engaging in a fake relationship.

It was time he pulled his head out of his ass and helped his son move forward, too.

Ryan was sitting in the middle of the couch, scooched down low, a baseball cap turned backward, and his bare feet propped up. There was a dirty plate, a bowl half-filled with chips that had long since gone stale, and two empty soda cans littering the coffee table. So much for having a counter you could eat off.

Two days was all it took for the house to look like a teenage-sized tornado had blown through it. He ran a tired hand down his face, then entered the room.

Jonah knew that Ryan was aware of his presence, but the

kid didn't even acknowledge him, just kept playing his video game.

"Mind if I join in?" Jonah asked.

The response was a bored shrug, but Jonah would take what he could get, so he picked up the spare controller and sat on the couch. To his surprise, Ryan restarted the game in two-player mode.

All it took was five minutes for Jonah and Ryan to fall back into their Saturday pattern they'd had when Ryan had been younger, playing video games, razzing and joking with each other. Jonah even got a few laughs out of Ryan. It felt good. Normal.

"So I'm guessing you want to talk," Ryan broached, eyes glued to the screen.

Jonah chuckled. "Am I that obvious?"

"You just don't play video games anymore."

That brought Jonah up short. He had hundreds of memories of them sitting on this couch, killing zombies or enemy combatants. "Sure, I do."

"When was the last time we hung out? Besides family dinner?"

Jonah opened his mouth to say just last week, when he realized that he couldn't think of the last time it had been just him and Ryan, hanging out and doing guy stuff without Waverly or interruptions.

"You're right and I'm sorry. I've let other distractions suck up my time and that's on me."

"Whatever. I get it."

"But you shouldn't have to." Jonah wanted to pause the game but knew that the best way to keep Ryan talking was to play it casual—two guys shooting the shit. "How do you feel about me dating?"

Ryan's fingers paused ever so slightly on the controller. "You have to start sometime. I guess now is the time," he said. "Are you going to start inviting her to family dinner and stuff?"

Ryan was ten steps ahead of the reality of the situation. By avoiding the conversation, he'd left Ryan to wonder what family life was going to look like.

"Family dinner is family dinner. And this family is you, me, and Way, and I don't see that changing anytime soon."

Ryan's shoulders visibly relaxed, a clear indicator that he'd been stressing over this. Maybe even hesitating every time he came home not knowing if his family would look different than it had when he'd left for school. Just like when Amber had died. The kid had gone to bed with a mom and awoke to a fractured home.

"How do you feel about it being Evie?"

"I guess if you had to date someone, I'm glad it's her."

Jonah released a breath he'd been holding since Ryan's run-in with Evie the other day. "If you're not, you can tell me."

Ryan paused the game to look at Jonah and he could see the honesty in his expression. "She'd never try to take Mom's spot. Plus, I think Mom would like that you two were together."

Jonah swallowed thickly. He liked that his son approved of Evie. Until that moment he didn't know how important it really was.

"You do?" Jonah asked. "Why?"

"She was nice to Mom when Mom was sick and took care of me and Way when Mom died. Mom loved Evie, so I guess it's okay if you love her, too."

Relief and panic waged war in his gut. Relief that Ryan thought Amber would be okay with things—encourage it even. Panic because love wasn't, and never would be, a part of the equation. Sure, he'd kissed Evie because he'd wanted to. And yes, he was attracted to her like a bee to pollen, but their arrangement was there to keep anything more than lust and like to form.

Something he needed to remember.

"I'm not looking for love, kiddo. Evie and I are just seeing where this thing can lead. We enjoy each other's company, have a lot in common, and have only been on one date—unless you count the dinner I made her."

Was this where he told his kid the truth? And how would the truth affect Ryan? He'd just told Jonah he liked Evie and thought Amber would approve, and it was all a lie.

"Maybe you should talk to your therapist about this," Ryan said. "Because it's kind of weirding me out. Plus, I've got practice and have to get ready."

Ryan flicked off the television and stood, but before he could leave Jonah grabbed him for a hug. To his surprise and delight, Ryan hugged him back.

"I've missed this," Jonah said gruffly.

"Me too," Ryan said, then pulled back and walked up the stairs.

Jonah made a note to schedule an appointment with his therapist, then swiped off a text because there was someone else he wanted to talk to first. He knew Evie was at work, saw her speed out of the driveway at six that morning. No doubt she was slammed with customer orders, employee gripes, family drama, and possible suitors with roses and promises of Prince Charming ways.

It was the last one that got him typing.

Jonah: How would you like to show off your landscaping prowess?

He reread the text. Delete. Delete. Delete.

Jonah: You want to smell the roses?

"That's what you're going to send?" Ryan asked, startling Jonah. He looked over his shoulder to find his son transfixed on his phone.

"How long have you been standing there?"

"Long enough to know that you're way out of your league with Evie."

Didn't he know it.

"Then what do you think I should write?" he asked, wondering if he was desperate enough to take dating advice from a teenager. The answer was a pathetic yes.

Ryan grabbed the phone. "How long have you been dating?"

"Two weeks."

Ryan shot him a look. "You've been dating for two weeks and gone on one date? It's worse than I thought," he said. "Where do you want to take her?"

He wanted to take her somewhere that she could relax, that didn't put too much pressure on the date. Somewhere that was like a coffee date but without the coffee. And he knew just the place. "The garden store."

Ryan lifted a brow. "Seriously? You're going to take her to look at manure?"

"I'm going to take her to look at the roses." She'd been wooed for weeks by pricks bringing her a single store-bought rose. Jonah was going to give her a whole garden shop full of garden-quality roses. Plus, he saw how often she and her mother spent in the yard, knew that she loved gardening, and knew she'd appreciate an afternoon to smell the roses.

Ryan handed over the phone. "Here."

Jonah's gaze flew to the screen at the already sent, no permission asked, text to Evie.

Jonah: We've been dating two weeks and have only been on one date.

"That's it? No question? No asking her out?" Jonah asked.

"It's to the point without cornering her to accept. Women like to have options. And you want her to go out with you because she wants to, right?"

His brain reminded him that the dating was for show. But the rest of him said he wanted her to say yes because she wanted to spend the afternoon with him.

"You're right. How long do I wait for a response before I just call her?"

Ryan snorted. "Call her? Dad, that's so last century. You wait. How long she takes to respond will tell you a lot of things."

"Like?"

"Well, if she answers back in under a minute, think of yourself as the icing. The best part of the cake. They're into you," Ryan said. "Fifteen minutes they are still interested but they're working their way through the cake to make sure they want the frosting."

He couldn't believe he was asking, but... "What about longer?"

"Then oven is on, the cake on the center rack, so they know you're there, they're just a little sidetracked with other things."

God, his life had come down to cake metaphors. What was wrong with him? He was about to put his phone away when it lit up.

Ping.

Ryan looked at the phone he was still holding. "Not bad. Forty-five seconds. This is good."

"What does it say?" Jonah asked.

"She said, 'Ideas?'"

Jonah threw his hands in the air. "What the hell does that mean?"

"That she's open but putting the ball in your court to plan it. So what do you have planned?"

"Tell her I'll pick her up at four," he said, and Ryan started typing. "Wait, be sure to ask if that works for her. I don't want her to feel cornered."

Ryan rolled his eyes. "She's already signed up for the frosting, now she's looking for confirmation that you know how to frost a cake."

"Even so, make sure she knows this is on her time."

"Your life," Ryan said and hit send. He handed Jonah back his phone but held onto it. "You're not going to wear cologne, are you?"

"I was thinking about it. Why?"

"It reminds me of Mom. And if it reminds me, it will remind you. I just don't think Mom would want to be a third wheel. Now go on, Dad. It's up to you to make it a great second date."

• • •

Once Evie agreed to the date, the morning took on a sloth-like attitude, moving so slow Jonah was going to lose his mind. To keep his excitement and nerves under control he decided to send out some resumes, then clean up around the house. It started with the kitchen and family room, and ended with him working in the yard, pulling weeds and prepping it for its makeover.

He hadn't a clue as to what the final product would look like, but he figured ripping up the dead to make room for the living was a good start. Even though there was a cool fall breeze, summer was still hanging on, leaving Jonah ripe for the picking.

He hopped into the shower, skipped the cologne, and raced out of the house. By the time he hit the car he was sweating again—this time with nerves.

They were taking it date by date, and since this was only date two, he wanted to play it cool so he was picking her up at work rather than the old-fashioned knock at the front door. Plus, she'd just finished her shift. So he'd be picking her up in front of her employees, so there was no going back. Maybe that was why he was so nervous.

He knew what a risk they both were taking with their families, their professional lives, their other relationships. If things went sideways, it could negatively impact their lives, which was the opposite of why they'd agreed to this arrangement in the first place.

So when Jonah got a text from her that she'd meet him at the garden store he knew what that meant. She wasn't ready to deal with the onslaught of questions that would arise if he'd picked her up at Grinder. It should have given him relief, but for some reason a wave of disappointment washed over him.

Then he looked at what she was wearing, and those nerves were back. He was so out of his league.

She had on a pair of ass-hugging black jeans, knee-high suede black boots, and a light-pink fitted tee. He'd never seen her wear anything like this and he liked it. It was like the girl next door and a biker collided, leaving behind one sexy-as-hell woman.

She was standing by the entrance to the garden and home center surrounded by a bright mosaic of flowers, her hands in her back pockets, rocking back and forth. By the way she fidgeted with her hair he could tell she was as nervous as he was.

"You look incredible," he said as he approached her.

For the first time since he arrived, she met his gaze. "I do?"

He chuckled. "Yeah, sunshine. You do."

She looked down at her clothes and laughed. "Don't let Julie hear you say that or I have to pay her fifty bucks," she explained. "She actually dressed me. In her clothes. She said I couldn't go on a date in my work uniform."

"You would have looked equally as stunning," he said and

meant it. The woman was as sexy all dolled up as she was in sweats sans the makeup and working in her yard.

"Thank you," she said, and he was pretty certain she was blushing. "I wasn't sure what to wear, since you didn't let me know where we were going until five minutes ago."

"I thought we'd keep it casual and fun, so I picked Everything But the Kitchen Sink."

"When I saw your text, I was surprised."

There were those nerves again, stemming from uncertainty. "Unless you'd rather go somewhere else."

"Are you kidding?" Her smile was so radiant she glowed. "I love this place. I can't even think of the last time I came here with time to peruse."

"I figured we could check out some plants for my yard and maybe I can get you a rose bush for your garden."

Her lashes fluttered. "You want to buy me a plant?"

"I figure all the other guys brought you roses, so I wanted to get you something, too. But something that will last."

She nibbled at the lower lip he wanted to kiss. "You don't have to buy me anything."

"It's something I'd do for my girlfriend and since we've been dating two weeks, I figure it's time to start wooing you."

"Hang on." Without another word she raced to her car.

What had just happened? Had the plant been too big a gesture? Right as his brain was spinning with all the possible scenarios of that moment—like if she was going to come back or bail—she was back at his side.

"I have a present for you. It isn't anything big, and I've been sitting on it because I didn't know how to give it to you, but the moment seems right." She handed over a poster-sized, rolled-up tube of paper.

"Are you gifting me your Nick Carter poster?" he teased.

She snorted. "You wish." Her smile was shy. "If you hate it, it won't hurt my feelings."

Whatever it was he knew he wouldn't hate it. Hell, even if it were a Carter poster he'd hang it above his bed. But it wasn't a poster—it was blueprints.

"What is this?" he asked quietly.

"I had some ideas that I think would make your yard look nice. I'm nowhere near a professional landscaper, but I was just sitting at the kitchen table and this idea popped into my head. It will look like you spent top dollar but no one will know you're on a tight budget."

It wasn't just an idea. It was a full-on master plan for both his front and back yards. It was gorgeous—and affordable. He hated that she had figured out his financial woes, but in a way, it felt nice to have someone to talk to about it. "This must have taken you hours." Hours he knew she didn't have to spare.

She shrugged it off, but he knew that this was more than just blueprints. He wasn't sure what it meant, but it confused the hell out of him.

"You didn't have to do this," he said.

"I wanted to. I was so hard on you about your yard. Think of this as an olive branch."

Oh, it was more than an olive branch, but he'd dissect that later. "Is this because you want me to kick my butt into high gear?"

"Yes and no. I did this because I wanted to. But I also have some skin in the game."

"I knew there's more to the story than concrete-staining pomegranates and rats in the roses."

She looked away, guilt etched in every beautiful feature on her face.

"Spill. What's going on? Why is this so important to you?"

She sighed as if hesitating, then lowered her voice as if she was about to impart secrets of national security. "You have to promise not to say a word to anyone. Only one other person on the planet knows what I'm about to tell you."

He took her hand. "You can trust me."

At the word *trust* she flinched ever so slightly, and it made him wonder just what kind of assholes she'd been spending time with.

She looked over her shoulder, as if expecting to find an influencer with their phone poised to record her every word. "My mom is turning sixty in a few weeks and I'm throwing her a surprise party."

"She'll love that." He didn't know a lot about Moira, but he knew that she loved to be the center of attention.

"She can smell secrets from a mile away. When I was a kid, Christmas was a joke. She'd just pick up a box and smile, as if she already knew what was inside. And she did!"

"And you want to really surprise her?"

"Yes. She surprises everyone. And you know what they say about how people do for others what they wish someone would do for them?"

He didn't think that she realized how much insight she'd just given him into her mind. Evie was the queen of accountability, always being there for her loved ones and helping carry the load. Did that mean she wished someone would do that for her?

"I want to do that for her. I want it to be a garden party at the house with all her friends and family. And I want it to be perfect."

Now he understood why she'd been so upset the night of the board meeting. "And my yard would be an eyesore that would bring your party down—and not to mention the rats."

She sank her teeth into her lower lip. "Yes."

"Why weren't you just straight up with me?"

"I already told you. The more people who know, the greater the chance that my mom finds out and the surprise element is ruined."

That was part of the story, but his gut said she wasn't telling him the whole truth.

"You didn't think I'd care," he guessed, and the look on her face said he'd hit the nail on the head. Guilt washed over him. Had he really pushed things so far that she thought he'd purposefully sabotage her party?

"I don't think you're an asshole, Jonah," she said and, thank God, it seemed she meant it. "I just didn't know if you were ready and I felt guilty that I needed you to be ready. Then Karlson kept calling and I took the easy way out and blamed it on the Beautification Board."

"So when that backfired and they gave me six weeks I blew your plan?"

Her silence was all the answer he needed and, man, he felt like a jerk. He was starting to realize just how many people derailed her plans on a daily basis. Little things like sleeping in. Big things like going to college and quitting a job she clearly loved. He didn't want to be one more person who made her life complicated.

"I will have the yard done by the time the party is here."

Her eyes lit with unexpected surprise. "Really?"

He cupped her cheek. "Really, sunshine."

She visibly swallowed and he could see the pulse at the base of her neck pick up. "You don't have to do my proposed plan. I meant what I said. If you hate it, no harm, no foul."

"I love it."

It was the perfect solution to his problem. And he was

starting to think he'd found another perfect solution. Too bad it wasn't real.

"Now how about we go pick out a rose bush."

"My mom loves roses. I'm more of a peony kind of girl."

"I have no clue what a peony is, but I'm treating you to the biggest one they have."

Chapter Twenty-Two

Evie

Everything had changed and Evie was terrified she'd fail the college placement test.

"Two plus two equals you're screwed." She groaned and stood, stretching her arms over her head. Using her pencil, she twisted her hair up off her neck and secured it in a bun and walked across the kitchen. She poured herself a cold glass of lemonade and took a long sip, pausing to look out the window at the yard next door.

Holy hotness, her heart stopped. Right there in her chest.

It was possible she was losing her mind.

The afternoon sun was high, creating clear blue skies, green grass, and temperatures hot enough to melt the rest of the clothes right off a man's body. Something she hoped would happen because there was Jonah, all heat-slicked biceps and glistening abs on display that even a cold glass of lemonade couldn't quench.

With one last thump to the chest, her heart went on standby, and Evie knew that she wasn't over that kiss.

No matter how many times she told herself to get back to studying, she couldn't help but stare. One look out the window and her mouth went dry—the exact opposite of what was going on in her panties.

What. A. Sight.

Across the fence and directly in front of her was the location of Jonah's new flower garden. And standing in the middle, in a pair of low-slung shorts and no shirt, his skin slick with the day's rising temperatures, was the troublemaking man next door and that I-run-marathons-for-fun body of his. The one that had every single mom in the neighborhood straining for a better view.

Women like me, she thought and watched as, in one fluid motion, Jonah bent over—all the way over—so he could pull a tree from its plastic pot. She wasn't sure what this obsession was about. Didn't care. All she knew was that the best ass in the state was practically begging her to look her fill.

And look she did—until the ice in her glass had all but melted. He kept digging so she kept staring, amazed at just how well he filled out a pair of shorts.

You are in so much trouble. How was she going to keep up the ruse and not jump his bones? Oh, that's right, because hooking up with your fake boyfriend, who happened to be your neighbor, was a dangerous move. Even thinking about him like this was dangerous. They'd struck this ridiculous deal for a reason—that reason being she didn't have the time, nor desire, to date.

"This is all for show," she reminded herself, rising even higher up on her toes when he lifted the large tree and settled it in the pre-dug hole, causing his calves to flex. The sheer amount of exposed muscle was enough to make her hyperventilate. "And so was that kiss."

But in the moment she had thought it was real, and she had

kissed him back. What did that say about her frame of mind? That she was a crazy woman. Who had better things to do—such as study for her placement exam so she could sign up for classes.

No exam. No college.

Not to mention, she had to pick Camila up from cheer practice in an hour. And her parents would be here when she got home. Which meant she needed to take advantage of the rare private time she had left. Only Jonah took that moment to glance behind him—and directly into her kitchen window.

Even though the sun was shadowing most of his face, she could still feel those intense blue eyes as they zeroed in on her. Ass of the gods still to her, he straightened and, *Lord help her,* gave a shake of his bootie.

Evie could have panicked and ducked down, but what was the point? It would only add to his smugness. So she dialed her expression to bored and pretended as if she were refilling her glass with water. He wasn't buying it. In fact, he abandoned his flower bed and walked closer to the fence line, his gaze never wavering from hers.

Her palms began to sweat, and her heart kicked back into gear, going from zero to stroke-out in two seconds flat. He leaned over his workbench and when he came back up he was holding a notebook. Scribbled in all caps was a message.

ARE YOU CHECKING ME OUT, SUNSHINE?

She made a big deal of laughing, then walked to the table to grab her own notebook. Shaking her head, she responded—with a big, fat lie.

JUST ADMIRING YOUR FLOWER BED.

He lifted a brow and, flipping the page, wrote her another

message and held it over his head like it was a boombox and they were reenacting *Say Anything*.

SO WAS I. AND I HAVE TO SAY, SUNSHINE, YOUR FLOWERS ARE LOOKING EXTRA PERKY THIS MORNING.

Evie looked down at her shirt, which was more fitted than she usually wore, and praised the bra fairies for inventing the pushup. She quickly answered back.

I REALLY WAS JUST LOOKING AT YOUR NEW LANDSCAPING.

He threw his head back and laughed and she found herself laughing back. Not ironically, but an honest to God from-the-gut laugh. And it felt good—freeing. A lightness settled around her and she realized that she enjoyed his company. Even when there was a fence and window between them, he could still make her laugh. And that had to mean something.

He held up his notepad.

THERE WE GO AGAIN WITH YOUR INTEREST IN MY LANDSCAPING. MY TREE IS IMPRESSIVELY BIG. DON'T YOU THINK?

She gave an unimpressed shrug, but inside she wanted this game to continue. She responded…

IT LOOKS LIKE A SAPLING FROM HERE.

He studiously went to work on his reply.

THEN YOU NEED A BETTER LOOK.

Evie didn't feel like a college-dropout, stressed-out, frazzled single mom. She felt sexy and empowered. She felt like someone she'd almost forgotten existed.

Maybe it was the playfulness in his eyes or maybe it was because she enjoyed flirting with him, but instead of going back to work she scribbled a reply.

Our agreement didn't include landscape show-and-tell.

It also didn't include you objectifying me while I'm tending to my garden, he shot back.

You objectify me every time I wear blue.

I notice that you wear blue a lot lately. In fact, you're in blue now.

So she was. Funny, that. Out of all the T-shirts she owned, she happened to pick the tightest, bluest one of the bunch. Not that she'd let him know that.

I own a lot of blue.

Lucky me. And for the record I objectify you every time I see you.

Evie was never one who liked overt sexual attention from men, but from Jonah she couldn't seem to get enough. So his next comment sent her head spinning.

In fact I'd like to objectify you now.

His dark, hooded eyes said he wanted to do more than that and she found herself asking if she wanted to be objectified. Her nipples had no objection at all. But her brain? That was objecting like the opposing team at the O.J. Simpson trial. While her lady business was sustaining and entering damp panties and a thudding heart into evidence.

But could she cross that line with Jonah and still keep reality within sight? Because while this was all pretend, the butterflies tickling her stomach were real as hell.

Listening to the sane part of her, she wrote her reply.

SORRY. I'M BUSY STUDYING.

If he were discouraged, he didn't show it. In fact, his smile grew to cover his whole face as he held up his notepad.

I KNOW THIS GUY WHO IS A WIZ WITH NUMBERS. I BET HE'D BE WILLING TO HELP YOU FIND OUT WHERE X AND Y CROSS.

YOU NEED TO KEEP YOUR Y AWAY FROM MY X.

Evie waited with bated breath for his response, but before he could finish writing his phone rang and he pulled it out of his pocket to answer. Taking that as a sign from the Universe to get back to work, she walked to the table and went back to studying. Only she couldn't concentrate on the math problem in front of her. Her X was so busy wondering just how impressive his Y would be, she didn't notice that someone was at her back door until there was a knock.

She nearly fell off her chair.

It was Jonah. Still shirtless, notepad in hand, his arms stretched over his head as if holding up the doorway. Shoulders were on display, flat stomach taut and rippling with sinew.

She considered ducking under the table but he'd already seen her. And by the smile on his face he'd read her mind. He plastered his notepad to the back-door window.

MAY I BOTHER YOU FOR A GLASS OF LEMONADE?

Only if I can pour it all over your body.

AS LONG AS YOU STAY ON THE PORCH, she wrote back.

AFRAID THAT YOU'LL TEAR OFF MY CLOTHES IF YOU GET ME ALONE?

She made a big deal of rolling her eyes, then went to grab a glass, sure to sway her hips like someone was watching. And the heat on her backside burned hot enough to let her know he was watching.

Glass in hand, she strutted to the door, opened it. "Never even crossed my mind."

He smiled. "Liar."

She thrust the drink at him. "Here's your lemonade."

He didn't reach for it. He just said, "It's not for me. It's for you. You looked a little parched."

He was flirting with her, and she liked this open, playful side. In fact, stressed-out-single-dad Jonah was nowhere to be seen. In his place was an assured, animated, arousingly sexy man with enough swagger that had her lips daring her to invite him in.

He curled his finger through her belt loop and yanked her across the threshold. The liquid sloshed over the rim of the glass.

"What happened to keeping your distance?" she said haughtily.

"You said I couldn't come in. That doesn't mean that you can't come outside." He leaned in and pressed his lips against the shell of her ear. "Do you want to come, sunshine?"

"No." *Yes. Desperately.* Her X was already thrumming with desire. She squeezed her thighs together, but the pressure only made things worse. Her breath came out in short bursts as his nose nuzzled the sensitive spot behind her ear.

He slowly pulled back, just enough so that she could see just how dark blue his stormy eyes were, smell the fresh sweat and cut grass on his skin, feel his breath brush her lips. "You sure about that?"

"Yes. I think you should go before we cross a line we can't uncross."

The corners of his lips hitched. "Will do. As soon as you let go of me."

"You're the one who's holding—" She looked at her hand, which was wrapped around his bicep holding on for dear life. She told herself to let go, that she needed to let go, because eventually letting go was the plan, but instead she tugged him closer.

"So are you checking yes or no?"

"Are you asking if I like you?" she said to his lips.

"Oh, I already know you like me. I'm asking if you want me to devour you."

Chapter Twenty-Three

Evie

Evie was afraid to answer that question. Just like she was afraid of what would happen if she did. Because the flirty energy between them had shifted to something intensely powerful and heady. Something that wasn't going to go away until it was properly extinguished.

Maybe that was the answer to her hormone-driven problem. Sex.

Mindless, unadulterated, no-emotions-allowed sex. Or as he'd called it: devouring. She'd had sex, made love, and had her fair share of orgasms—sadly all self-given. But she'd never been a freak-in-the-sheets kind of woman. Between being a young mom, living in her childhood bedroom, and the utter lack of privacy, there hadn't been the opportunity.

But now? Her parents were gone, Camila was at practice, which just left her and her fake boyfriend—who had made her a very real offer. One she couldn't believe she was considering.

"Just sex?" she asked.

His eyes sparkled with amusement. "If that's what you want to call it."

"I like what you called it better," she said, because it didn't leave room for feelings or misunderstandings. It was blunt, raw, animalistic in nature.

"Is that a yes?" he asked, his voice as rough as tossed gravel.

"That's a yes to just this once," she said.

He cupped her hips and walked her backward until her butt bumped into the table. Taking the glass from her hand and setting it down, he let his gaze rake her body, catching on her breasts, her hips, the hem of her shorts. "Baby, if you come it's going to be more than once."

Her legs nearly buckled beneath her and, had she not been wedged between him and the table, she would have toppled over. "That's a big statement."

"We already established, I'm a big guy." He pressed her against him so hard that her good parts were aligned with his good parts, and she felt just how big he was. "With a big problem."

She slid her hand down his bare chest, loving how the muscles twitched beneath her touch, not stopping until she met the outline of his very large erection. It was heavy and pushed against the front of his shorts. "I can see."

She cupped him and he let out a groan that betrayed every ounce of pent-up sexual frustration. She cupped him harder and his eyes dazed, then his hand covered hers, stilling it.

"Maybe I overstated my prowess," he said with a chuckle. "It's just been a long time and I don't want to shoot my shot before I even get you out of these shorts, which, by the way, are going to star in my dreams tonight."

Her heart skittered to a stop. "Wait. You haven't since, um…"

He shook his head. "I mean, I know that we didn't, but I assumed that you'd..."

"There's been no one but you," he said, and it somehow struck a romantic chord within her. It also struck a tripwire in her internal warning center because romance had no business when it came to just sex.

And that's what this was. Just sex.

"There's been no one for me for a while," she admitted. "A long while."

"Then we'll take it slow together," he said and then his mouth gently pressed against hers. It wasn't quite a kiss so much as a greeting—an achingly gentle greeting that had her toes curling into the floor.

The second meeting of the lips was more of a promise of what was to come—and she had a feeling it was going to be her.

"What if I want to take it fast?" she asked, because slow didn't work for her. Her heart couldn't withstand slow.

"If fast is what the lady wants, then fast is what she'll get."

Before she could say another word, his mouth came crashing down on hers. One hand gripped her hair while the other journeyed down her body until it found her denim-clad ass.

"Can I take these off?" he breathed into her mouth, his hands already sliding under the hem and massaging the curve of her bare bottom. "I want to see just how perfect you are."

"I've had a baby, Jonah. I'm far from perfect."

"I'll be the judge of that." He looked at her like she was the most beautiful thing on the planet. "So, is that a yes?"

Evie swallowed hard and nodded.

"I need to hear you say it." His lips were on the gentle slope of her neck, his hands gripping and sculpting the sensitive skin where her upper thigh met her backside. "I need to hear you say that you want this as badly as I do."

"I want this." And to prove it, she unbuttoned her shorts and with a little shimmy, slid them off her hips, letting them fall to the floor—leaving her in nothing but a thong.

He took in her lace and that million-watt smile paid her a visit. "Blue? For me, sunshine?" When she didn't answer, he ran the pads of his thumbs down the back of the thin strap of sapphire-blue fabric that went into the valley between her cheeks. "Yeah, they're for me. Did you think about me when you got dressed?"

The honest truth? Yes. She'd seen him earlier that morning mowing his lawn, his white T-shirt clinging to his chest with the day's heat, his biceps showing off. She'd carried the image into the shower, while she'd participated in a little self-care, and then again when she'd pulled out the blue lace. Not that she knew he'd come over, but maybe she'd been secretly fantasizing.

"I think about you a lot," she admitted, surprising them both. "Ever since that summer night."

"The way I handled everything has been on replay for months. I've regretted my decision ever since. Which is why I'm going to make it up to you."

"You don't have to make it up to me. Just make me feel good."

He moved like lightning, his mouth taking hers in a hard, hungry kiss that had her head spinning. He devoured and dined, dipping his tongue into her mouth and sliding it against hers. She sifted her fingers through his hair to hold him to her and that rippling chest of his started to heave.

He nipped her lower lip, hard enough to sting, then pressed wet kisses down her neck, to the hollow of her throat and lower until he was hovering over her breasts. He brushed his lips over her nipple, then pulled her into his mouth through the material and a groan erupted from the back of her throat. He moved to the other side and back again, until her breathing was as erratic as her frustration. She didn't want to be teased, she wanted to be touched.

Skin to skin. His mouth on her with nothing between them.

She lifted her arms in invitation and he RSVPed to that party at laser speed. Her shirt was up and over her head, and before she knew it he was lifting her onto the table, stepping into the vee of her thighs and parting her legs.

His gaze ran down her, lingering and savoring, not coming back to hers until he'd made a few pitstops along the way.

"Christ, I knew you were beautiful, but you're even more stunning than I remember."

She felt herself actually blush, like she was eighteen again and discovering that her crush was crushing back.

"You've gotten even better," she said, dancing her fingers down his pecs to his abs, playing with the line of hair that disappeared beneath his shorts. She popped the button and toyed with the zipper. "It must be all that yard work," she teased.

"Or maybe I had someone I wanted to impress."

Her heart fluttered to a stop. Had she heard him correctly? Was she part of the reason behind his transformation? And if so, what did that mean for their arrangement?

"Stop overthinking it," he said. "You're an impressive woman, so I wanted to impress you."

Not wanting to read too much into that, she ran her fingers over his bulge and felt it swell beneath her hand. "Color me impressed."

"Sunshine, the impressing has just begun."

Evie groaned as he impressed his way down her neck to her shoulder. Using his teeth, he tugged her bra strap down her arm, then kissed his way across to the other side and with a gentle tug her bra fell low enough that her nipples were freed. Beneath his warm breath, they tightened into buds.

He took his time worshipping them and, leaving her bra in disarray, he kissed his way down her stomach, swirling his tongue around her belly button. His hands did some worshipping, too, making it clear he was an ass man. Gripping two handfuls, he straightened up and lifted her, right on to the edge of the table.

Without missing a beat, he wrapped a foot around the leg of the chair and drew it to him and then took a seat, his mouth unceasing. He ran his hands up her thighs, yanking them farther apart so that she was on full display. With any other man she'd be self-conscious, but with Jonah she felt beautiful. Desired.

Perfect.

It had been a long time since she felt perfect at anything. But in this moment, in the here and now, she gave in to the perfection. Reveled in it.

She spread her legs as wide as they'd go. "Go on. Impress me."

"You'd better hold on to something."

No teasing, no games. Jonah ran his tongue right up the center of her lace thong and Evie's head fell back on a moan. He licked again, then yanked the lace to the side, exposing her.

"Hold this, baby," he said, taking one of her hands and placing it on lace so that she could pull it to the side. "Just like that."

He settled in, like he was there for the long haul, then began to feast, baring his tongue against her most sensitive part. He set a pace that had her back arching and her core tightening. The perfect combination of flicks, licks, and scrapes that drove her crazy.

There was that word again.

She squeezed her thighs against his head to increase the friction and had to brace herself with her hands as she rode his mouth. But it still wasn't enough.

"Faster," she said.

Not only did he go faster, he added a finger to the mix. Then another. She felt the heat rising in her core, through her chest, and out to her fingertips. Her breath came in short bursts, her hips bucking, and she felt the steam rise higher and higher like a pressure cooker until she exploded. Hard and fast, her orgasm tore through her, her core coiling and spasming to the point of pain, until that pain turned into pleasure.

He rode it out with her until the very last tremor. And when her eyes began to refocus, he winked—and started rebuttoning his shorts.

"I thought we were—"

"I don't have a condom," he said, his jaw tight with sexual frustration. "I didn't come over here thinking that—"

"I don't have any, either," she admitted. "But that doesn't mean I can't help you with this." She cupped him with her hand and squeezed.

"You don't have to."

She stood and shoved him back in the chair. "I want to. I want to make you feel as good as you made me feel."

He hesitated, his body wound so tight she knew that one touch and he'd crack. So she ran her fingers up over the ridge and traced back down the length. "Let me make you feel good, Jonah."

She tugged at his shorts and with a rough chuckle, he lifted up enough that she slid them down his legs, along with his boxer-briefs. She was more than impressed—she was gobsmacked. He was massive.

He wrapped his fist around his girth, as if trying to ease the pressure, then gave a smooth pump. Her mouth watered.

"Let me," she said, replacing his hand with hers, then dropped to her knees. And just like he did, there was no teasing and no games—she took him in her mouth, swallowing him whole in one motion.

"Jesus Christ." He groaned roughly and that was all the encouragement she needed.

Evie gripped the base harder and moved her hand up along the shaft as her mouth descended. Impossibly, he grew even larger.

Using the flat of her tongue she skimmed the head and then traced the vein before taking him again. His fingers fisted in her hair and gently tightened as he pumped into her mouth. He wasn't aggressive, being careful to let her set the pace, even though she could tell he wanted to push all the way in. So she stretched her mouth as wide as it would go and took as much of him as she could.

She felt powerful, alive, like all her cylinders were firing at once.

His hands cupped her jaw and he began to pull out. "I'm about to come very quickly if you keep that up."

"I know," was all she said, then looking up at him through her lashes, took him again.

As if realizing what was about to happen, he said, "Christ, sunshine," and she felt him tighten inside her mouth.

She squeezed her lips as firmly as she could around him and rode out the pumps he was thrusting her way.

She found a rhythm that was somewhere between sex-crazed and sex-kitten—a rhythm that seemed to be his undoing. Because the next time she flattened her tongue and drew him in, his hands fisted at his sides as if he were too amped to touch her.

"Evelyn." Her name tore from his throat and his head fell back as he tightened and then exploded in her mouth. She took everything he had to give until his orgasm ended and his body was limp.

She released him and looked up to find him looking back with an expression on his face that made her belly flip. An expression that she didn't want to read into.

"Evelyn," he said again, this time a gentle whisper as he cupped her face and brought her to her feet, placing the tenderest of kisses on her lips. Then he pulled her onto his lap so that she was straddling him.

"Perfect," he said against her lips and kissed her again. She wasn't certain how long they sat there like that, her on his lap, his hands gently stroking down her spine, kissing like they were teenagers. But she was certain that it was as close to perfect as it could be.

And that could *not* be allowed to continue.

Chapter Twenty-Four

Jonah

"That's three for three," Jonah said, feeling a little full of himself.

"It was the treats, wasn't it?" Evie asked. She was sitting in the break room at Grinder with her laptop opened, a stack of spreadsheets covering the table.

"I feel like Willy Wonka has moved into my house."

"I went big-girl potty," Waverly said, proudly running to Evie and putting her hands in the air.

Evie lifted her onto her lap and snuggled her into her arms. The picture it made caused something in his chest to pinch painfully.

"You must be so proud of yourself. I know I am." Evie pressed a kiss to Waverly's fine hair, which was secured into two uneven pigtails. But the hair was up and out of her face, her bows were matching, and she'd actually used a big-person toilet.

He'd take the win.

"I wants cookie," Waverly demanded, all innocent and

mischievously.

"By the chocolate lipliner, my guess is you already ate your cookie," Evie said. Her eyes met Jonah's over his daughter's head and—*bam*—it was like a sledgehammer to the chest. Every detail of the other day came rushing back. And not just the naked part. It was the way she had felt in his arms and how her lips had melded against his as they'd kissed for the better part of an hour. They'd kissed until his legs went numb and his lips were swollen from her playful little nips. They'd kissed until they'd heard a car pull into the drive and then they'd laughed as he'd struggled to get back into his shorts with a raging hard-on and sneak out the back door.

He'd actually had to hop the fence like some horny teen boy who'd snuck into his girlfriend's bedroom late at night. Only she wasn't his girlfriend, not his real one, and he needed to remember that. Especially in these moments when the feelings were connected to his kids—who she was great with, by the way.

"She had two," Jonah said, and Evie laughed.

"Sucker."

"You said make it rain chocolate. I'm making it rain and getting results. She hasn't been sent home from school once this week," Jonah said.

"You haven't?" Evie directed the question to Waverly, then pulled her into a hug. "What a big girl you're becoming."

Waverly puffed her chest out a little, but then her body sank into Evie's as if taking in every ounce of female connection. He couldn't take his eyes off them, nor keep his thoughts from going to a dangerous place.

He'd seen Evie hold Waverly hundreds of times over the past two years, but this time was different. He was different. Jonah didn't know how, didn't like it, but it was the truth.

"If it's okay, you and I can go have a little tea party, Way,"

Lenard said from the door, only he wasn't looking at Waverly; his gaze was trained on Jonah. Laser sharp and filled with warning.

Jonah wasn't sure what his expression had said, but it was enough to throw Lenard into waiting-on-the-porch-with-a-shotgun mode. Jonah knew that both their families had bought the story hook, line, and sinker. Not Lenard. He'd been suspicious from the word beau.

"That would be great," Jonah said. "That will give Evie and me some uninterrupted time. To go over the books," he added quickly.

"Uh-huh," Lenard said, then held out his hand to Waverly, who took it with a gleeful squeal. Jonah watched the two of them walk out the door, but not before Lenard shot him another look.

Hurt her and I will break your face.

It was a ridiculous threat coming from a five-foot-nine, buck-fifty of a man who wore silky Tommy Bahama shirts. But Jonah's stomach hollowed out anyway. He wanted to say that Lenard was directing the threat to the wrong person, because if anyone was bound to get hurt it was not going to be Evie.

Oh no, Evie had been MIA since that day in her kitchen. The only way he could pin her down today was that they were going over the shop's accounting. He wasn't ashamed to use his number-prowess to get some alone time with her, only she'd picked a time when she knew Waverly wouldn't be in school. Well, it looked like she was losing her travel-sized shield and would have to deal with him one-on-one—and he intended to use this moment to his advantage.

"Thanks, Lenard," Jonah said.

"Uh-huh," Lenard said again as he disappeared around the corner holding Waverly's pudgy little hand.

The door closed. Silence fell.

"I've been going over what you put together. I can't believe you did all this work. It must have taken you hours," she said, not meeting his gaze.

"It's no big deal." He got up and walked around the desk, taking the seat next to her.

"It is. It can really help, maybe even get the shop into the black."

He knew what game she was playing. She wanted to make this about the arrangement. About a favor for a favor.

"I mean, sourcing the coffee beans from a different vendor is an interesting idea." She finally met his gaze, and he saw the genuine concern there. Realized how much pressure she was putting on herself to make everything work smoothly. Maybe she hadn't been avoiding him. Maybe she was just that overwhelmed.

If she needed to make this about work, then he'd give her the space she needed.

"But Dad's been buying from the same guy for thirty years."

"He's charging you twenty percent more than going direct." He rustled through the papers to find the invoice from their coffee supplier. "You could get it at Costco for less."

"Costco isn't authentic Italian beans."

"No, but this guy is." He located the spreadsheet of vendors he'd already vetted and pointed to the next line. "And this company supplies cups, lids, and containers for a fraction of the cost if you order in bigger quantities."

"This is great. It really is, and I appreciate all the time you put into this, but it's not going to move the needle enough to make enough of a difference."

Her fingers were in her lap, knotted in her apron. He reached over and rested his hand over hers in a supportive gesture and the air crackled between them. For the first time since they'd been left alone she met his gaze and, *whoa baby,* crackle didn't even begin to describe the electricity sizzling between them.

"You got this," he said with velvet confidence. "Just trust your gut."

"My gut isn't all that reliable. Just look at my life," she whispered, and not for the first time, he wanted to punch her ex in the face. It wasn't that he'd just left her to figure it out on her own, it was the constant minefield of problems that she was forced to wade through to make sure Camila wasn't hurt in the process of him "figuring out" his life.

"You are a smart businesswoman. It's how you managed to run a professional organizer business in such a competitive market. You know what to do, it's just hard to see the answers when you're treading water." He flipped her laptop around and clicked until he found the new business model he'd come up with. "You already identified the biggest solution and that's expanding your customer base."

"I've identified it, but I can't figure out how to make it happen. My mom thinks Get Grinding gratitude cards and bake sales are the answer."

"That could be a part of it."

"Seriously?"

"Not those exactly, but with a twist. What if you expanded what you offered food-wise? Like a larger selection of muffins, scones, and breakfast sandwiches? You can do gratitude cards, where for every ten coffees a customer gets a free breakfast sandwich. It encourages them to come to Grinder and gets them to try one of your new items."

"I can barely afford what I'm buying now. Why would I want to increase my costs and give things away?"

"I know this seems counterintuitive, but the only way to reach a new level is to level up. Find new customers by asking local businesses to hand out your Grinder gratitude cards, maybe even do a cross promotion with a few," he said. "I doubled my portfolio by offering a gratitude present to clients who referred friends and family. I reached out to life insurance companies and offered a finder's fee for every customer they sent my way. That's how I ended up with so many retired clients who needed help investing their spouse's life insurance policy. They were some of my favorite and most loyal clients."

"I didn't know that's what you specialized in," she said with a softness to her voice that got to him.

"After my dad died my mom received a life insurance payout. She didn't know what to do with it, didn't understand how she could make it work for her and live off the interest, and ended up burning through the money in a few years. She struggled a lot after that."

He didn't say the rest. After his dad died, he pretended to be the man of the house, a scared and confused ten-year-old who put on a show for the world that he could carry the burden of suicide. That he could be the strong one his mother could lean on. In doing so, he denied himself the opportunity to grieve—to unpack the anger and resentment and sorrow in a healthy way.

So when Amber unenrolled from the test study, he'd allowed himself to feel all the emotions so he could deal with them and not cling to them like the side of a cliff. But in letting go he'd somehow managed to fall so far that he began to wallow in it. Maybe it all ran together and became one entire shitstorm of grief that he'd drowned in.

Evie must have sensed some of the thoughts in his head. She turned her hand over and laced their fingers. "I am so sorry."

Jonah shook his head. "It's okay. It was a long time ago." He cleared his throat. "Anyway, like I was saying. I might wear a suit now, but as a kid I was lucky to get a new pair of shoes every year. I started my own business fixing old computers out of my garage and selling them for a profit when I was sixteen. I sold it to a larger computer repair shop when I turned eighteen and used the money to put myself through college."

"Sounds like you were really driven," she said quietly.

"Don't sound so shocked."

"I'm impressed."

"I know it doesn't seem like it, considering I let my life get to category-five status and my yard being the storm wreckage that everyone can see."

"Do you feel like the storm has passed?" she asked, but he knew they weren't talking about his life. She was asking about his heart. Was asking him where he stood—where they stood.

He tugged her until she scooted onto his lap. Sitting sideways, her legs dangled between his. He wrapped one hand around her waist, the other cupping her cheek and turning it so that she was looking at him. "Honestly, I feel like I'm in the middle of another kind of storm." One he could easily be swept up in. "But I think you already know that."

The way she swallowed hard told him that she did. It also told him that maybe he wasn't the only one getting swept away.

"This is just for show," she said.

"What we did the other day wasn't for show. It was about us."

"It was runaway hormones taking over the decision-making cortex of the brain."

"Maybe the first fifteen minutes, but the rest of it? You can't tell me that was just hormones."

Her face said that it wasn't, and that gave him a flicker of hope. "Which is why it can't happen again," she said.

Her statement should have extinguished any remaining hope on contact, but the fact that she was staring at his lips did the opposite. She might not want to want him, but she wanted him all right.

"How about this?" he asked, kissing the side of her jaw.

"Can this happen again?" He moved his lips to the other side, skimming her cheek as he went. "Or this? I know, how about this?"

He feathered a kiss right beneath her ear and he felt a shiver take over her body. He took her lobe between his teeth and bit down.

"Jonah," she whispered, "anyone could walk in."

"You're right." He gave her a chaste peck on the lips.

"Can you turn a little to the left so I can get a better angle?" someone asked from the doorway.

With a squeak, Evie leaped off his lap like her pants were on fire. Fitting, since her face was the color of a fire hydrant. Julie, however, looked exceptionally pleased with herself.

Phone aimed at them, she was videoing the entire encounter. It made Jonah wonder just how much she'd heard. Evie must have had the same fear, because she said, "How long have you been standing there?"

"Long enough to see that hot little neck kiss," Julie said to Evie.

"You better not post that," Evie said.

Julie smiled like it was Christmas morning, then punched her cell's screen. "Whoops. Too late."

Chapter Twenty-Five

Evie

"Are we going to lose the shop?" Camila asked. They were wiping down the tables and running through their closing routine.

Evie considered for a flash sugarcoating the whole situation, but then decided she had enough secrets. "I don't want you worrying about that."

"Mom, it's a family business. I'm part of this family, and I want to help but I can't if I don't know what's going on."

While Evie didn't want to burden her daughter with the weight of the shop, Camila also had a point. By the time Evie had reached middle school she worked in her parents' shop every day after school, and by high school she had her own key and was an assistant manager, closing three nights a week.

"It's bad, but I think with some serious changes we can save it."

"Why don't you use your ClickByte following to hype the shop?"

"Because social media doesn't solve everything." In fact, it caused more complications. Look at her. One video and now she had a fake boyfriend whose O-face she knew intimately.

"Lila's mom owns a pet rescue, and they have a huge following. She posts about cats and dogs and new fosters. She went from a few adoptions a month to over a hundred this summer. It works."

"Of course it works. Everyone wants to see cat videos. A coffee video would be boring."

"That's such a millennial thing to say." Camila picked a mug up from behind the counter and made a latte with beautiful coffee-foam art of a heart on top. She walked to a table, paired it with a bouquet of flowers and a romance novel Evie had been reading, then filmed it. She put some coffeehouse music behind it and posted. "See. Five seconds."

Evie looked at the reel and was beyond impressed. It looked professional, inviting, and more appealing than the ads her dad had taken out. "That would take me five hours."

Camila pocketed her phone. "Never mind. It was just a thought."

"It was a good thought, sweetie. I'm just so overwhelmed right now."

Camila looked behind Evie and rolled her eyes. "Right. I forgot you're dating your dead friend's husband."

"Camila," she scolded, but there was no heat behind it because Camila was right. All the safety guidelines that they'd put in place had flown out the window in one lust-filled moment and it had been weighing heavily on her heart. Not that she regretted it, but it sure did complicate things—things like her feelings.

"Sorry," Camila said without an ounce of "sorry" in her voice. "It's just that now things are super weird between me and Ryan."

"Do you want to talk about it?" When Camila didn't immediately shrug her off, Evie sat down at one of the tables and patted the seat next to her.

Camila lifted a slim shoulder and let it fall but took a seat anyway. Evie's heart bloomed with hope. It had been a while since Camila had confided in her and she missed the closeness—that unique bond between mother and daughter.

Evie squashed her impulse to ask more questions, knowing that if she pressed too hard Camila would clam right up. So she waited patiently while Camila clearly weighed the pros and cons of admitting she might not have the answers to everything.

"I went over to hang out," Camila began. "Ryan told me the guys were coming over and explained it was a team hangout. He's never minded before."

Evie bit back a smile. "Was Dexter one of these guys?"

Camila traced the rim of the coffee mug, her gaze riveted to the tabletop. "Probably."

"Maybe it wasn't so much sharing his friends with you. Maybe he didn't want to share you with his friends."

Camila's eyes slowly lifted to Evie's. "Why would he do that?"

Camila liked to play a big game when it came to dating, but it warmed Evie's heart that her daughter was still a naïve sixteen-year-old when it came to boys. "Because he's jealous of you dating his friends."

Camila rolled her eyes. "He's not jealous. He's the one who gave Dexter my number to begin with."

"Did you want him to give Dexter your number?"

"Dexter's a nice guy and he's fun to hang out with, but I think he likes me more than I like him."

That was music to Evie's ears. She'd tried to be cool with Camila dating a college guy, but she was afraid that dating a guy who was older and had more life experience would force Camila to grow up faster. She should be hanging out with friends her own age, people who were at the same phase in life, people with whom she had things in common.

"Have you told Ryan that?"

"No. Whenever I bring up Dexter, he changes the subject."

"You and Ryan have never kept things from each other. I think you should tell Ryan the truth. Maybe he'll be honest about why he's being weird."

"Maybe," she said noncommittally. "About the ClickByte posts, I can totally make them if you don't have time. All we need is an influencer or two to give us a shout-out and people will start coming here. I know that the kids at my school would start coming here if it was hyped up."

Evie knew that ClickByte alone couldn't save the shop. Although to a stranger looking on, it would appear by the sheer number of customers that the shop was doing phenomenal. And she had to admit, Grinder was gaining a steady stream of customers every day. Granted, a good handful of them came to see the place Tasha Hart filmed her famous LoveByte video. That short interview had over two million views, and Evie's account had grown to nearly a hundred thousand followers. But those lookie-loos bought coffees.

What if Camila was right and social media was an important piece of the solution, and not the problem she'd labeled it? She would reach people who'd never heard of the shop. Plus, it gave Camila a way to contribute.

"That's a great idea," Evie said and stood, pulling her daughter into her arms for a hug. While Camila merely tolerated the hug, she also didn't pull away.

• • •

"Cupid's Cappuccino for Alex," Evie called out and a woman, who looked to be Evie's age, approached the counter.

"Thank you," Alex said, but she didn't move—just looked at Evie with shy hesitation.

"Can I get you anything else?"

Alex looked over her shoulder at a booth in the corner that was overflowing with a party of ten, then back at Evie. Her face was flushed. "This is so embarrassing and you're going to think I'm crazy. But we were wondering if you'd come over to the table and say hi."

"We?"

Alex pointed to the booth, and the women all waved eagerly at Evie. "The You've Got Male-Mamas. I know it's a silly name, but we thought it was fitting since you're the inspiration behind our dating group."

"What dating group?"

"Well, we're all single moms who are ready for love. We saw your video and decided that since it worked for you, maybe it can work for us, too. So we formed a support group of sorts, where we help each other post Looking for Love videos, vet men, and we even use each other as wing-girls, coming here and sitting in the corner to make dating a safe experience."

"You meet here?"

"We all do. This has become one of Denver's hottest coffee-date spots."

Evie was floored. These women were actually using ClickByte to find their person. "Is it working?"

"Yes! Three of us are dating great guys, including me. Although I didn't post a video, I messaged one of the guys from your video and he responded back. We've gone on three dates, and he is the nicest man."

"Who?" Evie prayed to Elvis, Sinatra, and Buddha himself

that it wasn't Travis. Alex seemed like a sweet woman who deserved an attentive and present partner. Single moms are so used to putting themselves last, they deserve someone who knows how to put them first.

"Ernie," she said and her expression turned dreamy. "He's not my usual type, but he seems to be the perfect fit. He's sweet and kind and the most emotionally intelligent man I've ever met. It's still early days but things are looking very hopeful. And I love dogs, too."

"That's"—*unbelievable, unexpected, encouraging*—"amazing."

"It really is. Not only have we all met some great guys, we've formed this incredible group of women. We decided to start meeting here every Monday on our breaks. We bring our lunch, order some coffee, and talk about kids, guys, and sex. God, sex. You have no idea how long it's been. Between my three kids, I barely have time to brush my teeth, let alone sex."

Oh, Evie knew. It didn't used to bother her, but after the other morning it was all she thought about. She'd fantasized what would have happened if one of them had a condom, if they'd had the house to themselves for more than an hour, if…if…if!

Oh, so many *if*s it kept her awake at night, and her trusty F O X giving her pleasure in the shower every morning.

"But because of you, all the You've Got Male-Mamas made a pact to put dating and love as a priority," Alex said. "Some of us even shot our Man Wanted videos right here in the shop. See."

Alex took out her phone, pulled up the app, and played a video of one of the women behind them standing in front of the Grinder sign rattling off her list of boxes a man needed to check.

"They all did that?"

Alex nodded. "We aren't the only group, either. Last week, we ran into the You've Got Male-lorettes, a group of older Gen Z-ers who are doing the same thing. We also post updates every week and people are following us to see how our dating journey is progressing."

This was exactly what Camila was talking about. One person posted and the trend caught on. All they needed was the right spark and news of Grinder could spread like wildfire through the Denver area.

"We all figured that the Cupid Vibes are strong here. I mean, Grinder is practically a wishing well for love. It's said that if you wish on a penny and put it in the Lucky in Love tip jar Cupid will strike."

Well, that explained all the penny tips.

"None of us are at your level—"

Evie swallowed hard. "What do you mean 'my level'?"

"That video of you and Prince Jonah was pretty spicy. Not that I have to tell you. It has over a million views."

"A million?"

"Even my coworkers are talking about it. You're like the Kardashian of ClickByte."

"I don't know about that," Evie said to Alex.

Twenty minutes, ten romance stories, and a Cupid's Cappuccino later, Evie had not only made a new set of friends, she'd also picked the brains of ten new regulars on ways they thought Grinder could improve. Jonah and her mom had been right. All the ladies said that they'd eat lunch here if there were a selection of healthy food options. They also said they'd make it their morning coffee stop if there were a selection of definitely-not-healthy bakery items.

Which was why Evie was going to go straight into the back office and investigate the list of vendors Jonah had compiled once she was done here. Jonah's life might be a mess, but he'd helped declutter hers. Even sweeter, the man had somehow made a spreadsheet appear romantic.

"I have an idea! You should join some of us and go to Shoot Your Shot for Tequila Tuesday."

Shoot Your Shot was an upscale wine bar and local catch-and-release establishment for professionals in the downtown area. It was the Tinder of watering holes.

"Isn't that a weird place for a first date?" she asked.

"Laura has a first date with a single dad who illustrates children's books for a living—isn't that the cutest?—but she's a little shy when it comes to asserting herself. So she wanted an environment that encouraged a little risky behavior," Alex went on. "We're going to support her. Oh, we'll be standing on the other side of the bar, of course." Alex smiled conspiratorially, then lowered her voice. "We don't want them to know our level of crazy right off the bat. We have to reel them in first."

"Of course we do," Evie laughed.

Although for Evie, her man knew every one of her eccentricities—including the fact that she'd hung him out to dry with the Beautification Board. He knew her professional life, at present, was currently a dead end. Her home life was one Goodwill bag from the Clampetts. And her personal life required a beard. And he still looked at her like she was dessert.

"The girls and I would just get a kick out of you coming."

"We'll be there," Julie said, slinging an arm around Evie's shoulder. "Right, You've Got Male girl?"

This was normally the kind of invitation Evie could get out of by using one of her million excuses—all were valid—but something inside her was telling her to shoot her shot at being that fun, extroverted, and bold woman she'd been before. She'd spent the past sixteen years finding reasons to say no, maybe it was time to start saying a few yeses.

"What time are you meeting?"

Chapter Twenty-Six

Evie

Chaos. Zombie apocalypse chaos had erupted inside Grinder. And of course, it had to happen right on the day of Camila's overnight cheer camp.

A summer flu was spreading through her staff like the plague, leaving her down two employees. Julie wasn't scheduled to come in until four. Her mom and dad were at dialysis, Evie was scheduled to carpool some of the cheerleaders to camp, and she got a flat tire on the way to work. She'd managed to get the spare on, but she didn't want to chance driving on it to Boulder and back—not with a group of teens in her car. It was too dangerous.

Evie had already called three other parents to see if they could cover for her, but they either already had a carload of cheerleaders or they couldn't get off work. Since she wouldn't expect her parents to drop their lives to come to the rescue, she was SOL. So she'd called a service to come and change her tire. The earliest they could make it was three, which meant she'd be pushing it, since the girls were set to depart Evie's house at four thirty.

There was just no way she could do it all today.

It was times like this that she wished she had a partner—someone to help carry the weight. Someone to call when she got a flat, or to hold her hand when things got rough, or sit by her side and cheer with her when her daughter hit major milestones. She didn't need to be taken care of, but sometimes it would be nice not to have to take care of everyone all on her own.

It would be nice not to feel alone.

Her parents had given her all the support and love that they had to give—which was enough for five families. But as they'd aged it was as if the roles were slowly reversing and it was now Evie's time to give back. Only some days, she felt like she didn't have enough to give.

That she was coming up short and everyone was paying the price.

To add to the chaos, Tasha Hart from LoveByte had shown up earlier to interview some of the You've Got Male-Mamas about their journey of love in what Tasha was calling a social media social experiment. Even Ernie made an appearance, bringing his adorable twins along.

They were little, like travel-size little, and Evie gave a sigh of relief that she'd dodged that bullet. She'd raised her daughter, was looking forward to the next phase of life, and couldn't imagine starting over. Not that she was opposed to dating someone in the future—the far, far future—who was a parent. She just always imagined that they'd be in the same chapter when it came to parenting.

Another thing Tasha brought with her was her following. Hundreds of people filed through the shop, buying coffee and cookies and even Grinder's specialty roasted coffee beans—in fact, they'd sold out of their monthly stock in one day, and she had to order more.

What a problem to have, Moira had said gleefully. And her mom was right. There was a silver lining in all of this. New customers were discovering Grinder, raving about their signature drinks, and promising to come back again. So when Tasha had asked Evie to give them an update on her and Jonah's relationship, she'd obliged.

Which was how she found herself sitting at a table with a fresh coat of lip gloss, staring into the camera as Tasha held it in selfie mode. Tasha sat next to her, a crowd of onlookers circling them as the live interview started.

"LoveByte Nation wants to know how it feels to be the inspiring factor for many singles taking to social media for this social experiment," Tasha began.

"I don't know if I'd call it an experiment," Evie answered.

"Remember to look into the camera," Tasha whispered, and Evie tucked her hair behind her ear and smiled into the phone. Tasha slid back into her talk-show-host voice. "Then what would you call it?"

Fake. A fraud. A giant faux relationship that we're selling to the public at large. "Fun. I'd call it fun."

That answer wasn't fake. That was the I-swear-to-tell-the-whole-truth-and-nothing-but-the-truth honest answer. And if she were going for honest, it was also thrilling and exciting and all the other adjectives that came with sharing a secret with her sexy neighbor. Yes, it was stressful, too, wondering if and when they'd be found out. It was also scary to think that they'd blurred the lines last week in her kitchen. But right now, with the shop full of paying customers, she was starting to think that the reward outweighed the risk.

"Don't be shy now. We all saw that kiss. It was very honeymoon phase if you ask me." Tasha looked into the camera.

"What do you think, LoveByte Nation? Was that a honeymoon-phase kiss, or what?"

A giant cluster of hearts floated up the screen like a bouquet of balloons taking to the sky and hoots and hollers came from the customers in the shop.

"And where is your sexy plus-one?" Every eyeball looked around the store, as if expecting him—just like Ernie—to have come.

In her gut she knew he would have. So then why hadn't she asked him? It would have been the perfect time to give credibility to their ruse of a relationship.

Because you are intimately acquainted with his O-face. That's why.

Evie hadn't seen him since the honeymoon-phase kiss. Oh, sure, they'd waved to each other through the window, and even exchanged a few notepad conversations, texts about carpool—Evie had even babysat Waverly for a few hours, where they had two successful potty times—but she and Jonah hadn't talked about *it*. And she wanted to keep it that way.

Talking about it would lead to thinking about it, which would lead to dreaming about it, and possibly doing *it* again.

"He's—"

"Running a little late," a voice broke through the crowd and she froze. Which was the exact opposite of what her heart was doing in her chest—pounding like a jackhammer.

Jonah.

He looked like a tall glass of lemonade. Sitting on his forearm, which was bent to make a toddler-sized seat, was Waverly, wearing a cute pink sundress and little pink bows in her hair. She looked adorable and he looked like Dad of the Year.

He was there. She hadn't asked him to come, didn't even know how he found out about the LoveByte interview, but he was there. For her.

"Hey, sunshine," he said with a wink, full of conspiracy and humor.

"Hey," she said, sounding very honeymoon-phase breathless.

"Sorry I'm late," he said, coming up beside her, then slowly lowered his head and an unexpected trill of excitement tingled her lips.

She didn't want to examine her body's response too closely, because she wasn't sure she'd like the conclusion she'd come to. Or why it felt like that bouquet of balloons was now in her belly floating up toward her chest at the mere thought of contact.

He was clearly en route for a brush of the cheek, but somehow her wires got crossed because he zigged as she zagged and before she knew it, they'd made contact.

Houston, we have a problem. Because when his mouth brushed hers, it felt as if her clothes were melting right off her body. He smiled knowingly against her lips before he pulled back.

"I can almost hear the sizzle from the heat," Tasha's voice broke the moment. "It just goes to prove that finding love doesn't have to follow a conventional path. For more on Evie and Jonah's journey be sure to follow her @You'veGotMale."

Tasha stopped recording and Evie said, "Thank you for the, uh, shout-out. That was nice of you."

"My pleasure," Tasha said. "You let me interrupt your day, it was the least I can do."

Tasha blew her adoring audience a kiss, which was met with cheers, then packed up her things. When she was gone, Evie turned to Jonah and Waverly immediately held out her arms.

"Uppie VeVe," she said in her sweet little voice.

Evie pulled Waverly into her arms and gave her a big smack to the cheek, then blew a raspberry there. Waverly erupted into giggles.

"Cookie." It wasn't a question. She was issuing an order, which made Evie laugh.

"It's up to your dad." She glanced over at Jonah, who was looking back with the strangest expression on his face. He just kept silently looking at her. "Jonah?"

"What?" He blinked.

"Can she have a cookie?"

He flashed a flirty smile as if something deeper hadn't just passed between them. "Only one."

They walked to the counter and Jonah followed. She grabbed a cookie from the jar and handed it to Waverly, who mashed it into her mouth, spilling crumbs all over Evie. She didn't care, the little girl was too cute to care about a few crumbs on her uniform.

"What are you doing here?" she asked Jonah.

"Fulfilling my beardly duties," he said with a smile. But Evie's smile turned brittle.

He hadn't come for her—he'd come because of their arrangement. Tit for tat. Even steven. Which was what she wanted. Right?

"How did you even know about it?"

"Your mom may have called me this morning to tell me about the interview," he said. "But the real question is, why didn't you tell me?"

"I know you're busy looking for a new job, working on your yard, and with your family."

"Okay. Now for the real reason."

Evie sighed. They'd agreed that being straightforward was the best route. "I wasn't sure what to say about last week and so I've been avoiding you."

"I noticed," he said. "Do you want to talk about it?"

No. No she did not.

He must have seen the horror on her face because his expression flashed with disappointment. Something in her stomach pinched painfully.

"We have to talk about it sometime," he said quietly.

"Maybe when we're not in public."

"Then we'll have to find some private time that's just the two of us."

That sounded even more dangerous than talking about it in an environment where *it* couldn't happen again. "I guess I just wanted to make sure that we're still on the same page."

"I don't know if we were ever on the same page," he said cryptically, and before she could further question what he meant, Waverly said, "More cookie."

From the mouths of babes.

"More cookie, sunshine?" Jonah said with an amused brow.

"I've had my fill," she said, then closed her eyes. "I mean, no, I'm good."

"You were more than good, if I remember," he said, and she had to laugh. He was lightening the mood, even if it was with innuendos.

Evie's phone buzzed in her pocket so she handed Waverly back to her dad and answered.

"Hey, Cami."

"Mom." Camila sounded panicked. "Where are you?"

"At the shop. Why? What's wrong?"

She felt Jonah go on alert with concern.

"The team is supposed to meet at Darby's Diner for burgers before we head out. All the girls are here and we're ready to leave. Only you're not here."

"We were supposed to *leave* at four thirty."

"No. We're supposed to *be there* at four thirty."

Evie looked at the clock. It was nearly three. Surely, she could leave one of her baristas in charge for an hour until Julie got there. It wasn't ideal, and she'd never done it before, but what choice did she have?

It was a big deal that Camila had made varsity as a sophomore, so she already felt like she had something to prove. Missing the team dinner, especially when Evie would be making other girls miss the dinner, too, would start Camila off on the wrong foot.

She was already taking off her apron. "I can be there in ten minutes."

"Hurry."

They disconnected and Jonah was right there, standing in front of her. "What's wrong?"

"I'm supposed to take Evie and her teammates to cheer camp and I got the time wrong. I need to go and—" She looked out the window at her car. "Shit."

"Shit," Waverly repeated.

"I have a flat tire and the guys who are going to change it aren't here yet."

He held out Waverly. "Take her and I can change it."

"Thank you," she said, beyond touched. "But I still won't make it in time."

"Then let me drive you."

Evie had to blink twice to process what he'd just said. "You are offering to drive a car full of screaming teens to Grand Junction?"

"It can't be worse than the BO stench and farts that fill the car when I drive Ryan and his teammates to games."

Evie looked back at the car and at her phone. "You don't have to do this. Plus, what will you do with Waverly? She's potty training. Long car rides can be tricky."

"So I put the Tot-Pot in the back and when she has to go we pull over."

"This isn't part of the deal."

"It's part of being friends," he said quietly. "And we're friends, right?" Afraid to speak for fear of crying, she nodded her head. "Then let me help."

And for the first time that day, Evie didn't feel alone.

Chapter Twenty-Seven

Jonah

Jonah didn't think through how it would feel to be crammed into his eight-seater Pathfinder with half a handful of cheerleaders, Ryan, two of Ryan's friends, Waverly in the car seat, and Evie riding copilot.

Domestic was the word that came to mind. And if he were hard-pressed to pick a second word it would be comfortable. Not that he'd mention either of those things to Evie—she seemed to be struggling enough with the idea of being friends who'd seen each other naked, and he didn't want to add friends who had more than friendly feelings to the mix.

Only that's what his feelings had become—more than friendly. He still liked feuding with her. She was adorable when she was pissy. And he liked flirting with her because she got frazzled. But most of all, he liked being with her.

He wasn't so sure how she felt about the rate at which things were transpiring, but she couldn't seem to stop sneaking glances at him as they drove. Kind of like how he could see Camila and Ryan sneaking peeks every time they thought the other wasn't looking.

In fact, the two teens, who usually couldn't stop talking on car trips, were suspiciously avoiding each other. Dexter, on the other hand, had no problem chatting up Camila—who was chatting back.

Every time Dexter would say something to Camila, Ryan would grit his teeth. In fact, he seemed so ticked at the unfolding of events that he'd changed seats with another kid who was a row between him and the lovebirds.

Poor kid.

"So are you two going to get married?" one of Camila's friends, Kira, asked while poking her head between the two front seats.

Evie gasped. "What?"

"Moira told my grandma who told my mom, that you and Mr. Stark were marriage material. So are you going to get married?"

Evie looked at him, her eyes big and pleading.

"We're just taking things day by day," he said, then placed a hand on Evie's thigh. She nearly jumped right out of her seat. "Right, babe?"

Evie's eyes narrowed as she took his hand and squeezed— hard. "Right, babe."

"Gross," Camila said from the back of the car. "Can you not?"

"Yeah," Ryan jumped in. "Seriously, Dad?"

Jonah gave Evie's hand a gentle *got-ya* squeeze, then let go. She rolled her eyes. Kira sat back, looking disappointed that the fanfare was over. She wasn't the only one disappointed.

• • •

Evie sat on the bleachers of the university's basketball court, surrounded by the sound of several hundred cheerleaders, a rowdy crowd, and Jonah's yummy male scent and realized that, for a woman who was so adamant about keeping things friendly, this was the closest she'd come to a real date in years. Well, besides dinner.

But like the garden center, this was spontaneous, genuine, and did not fall under the definition of fake.

Because of the packed stands, their thighs were pressed against each other, and their arms brushed every time one of them so much as breathed. And she was breathing a lot—hard and heavy. Because every time they brushed her body zinged and her brain misfired. And she was in her barista uniform. A ridiculous "Get Your Grind On" tank, with coffee cups on her leggings, while Jonah looked dashing in his button-down shirt that pulled taut at the shoulders as he wrapped his arms around Waverly.

His other arm rested on his thigh, placing his hand within holding range. All she'd have to do was move hers a fraction of an inch to the left and their pinkies would touch. And the thought of that had more than her hormones buzzing, it had something deep down, something warm yet unfamiliar, blooming. Something that if nurtured could grow and blossom.

Her dad had once told her that romance was the everyday nurturing of love. And Jonah saving her day was the most romantic thing anyone had ever done for her. Not that she loved him, but she was starting to love their time together.

"What's got you blushing?" he asked.

"What?" She looked up at him and felt her cheeks. They were burning up. "Oh, just the sun."

"We're indoors."

"Then maybe it's the crush of people. We're packed in like

sardines," she said.

"I thought it was because you were debating holding my hand," he said with so much amusement in his voice she wanted to punch him—or hold his hand. The jury was out.

"Just excited for Camila to take the floor."

"Uh-huh. Well, that's what I've been debating."

Her eyes went wide. "You have?"

"And it's driving me insane," he said and rested his hand over hers. "Is that okay?"

"What if people see?"

"Isn't that the point?"

A feeling deep inside her said that wasn't the entire truth. "Is that why you're here and holding my hand? For people to see?"

No hesitation. No pause. Just one concrete word that punched her in the chest. "No."

"Then why?"

"Because I want to. How about you, Evie? Do you want to?"

Surprisingly, she did. And it would be so easy. All she'd have to do was flip over her hand and they'd be connected in a way that was more than pretend. Which was why she took a moment to really think through the ramifications of her decision.

Holding hands was such an innocent gesture, but that's what made it so dangerous. What they'd done the other day was raw lust. This would fall into the affection category.

When was the last time she'd been affectionate with a man? And since when did she want to be affectionate with this man?

Since he came to your rescue.

Evie wasn't in the market for a prince, but he'd made her feel like a princess today. And she wanted to keep that fantasy going—just for another few moments. Then she'd go back to Rational Evie whose diet did not allow sweet gestures, sexy seductions, or knights in shining armor.

"Just for show," she lied and flipped over her hand, and when his fingers laced between hers it not only felt natural—it also felt somewhat right.

"Until it isn't," he said, tightening his fingers around hers.

Evie didn't pull away.

Chapter Twenty-Eight

Jonah

What the hell?

One minute they were holding hands, sharing secret smiles, and he was even gently grazing the underside of her wrist, loving how she shivered. The next, she practically jumped out of her skin, jerking back like she'd come in contact with a viper, then twisted toward him.

Her face was red and her eyes sparkled with unchecked panic. "I didn't think this through," she said over the chatter bouncing off the walls of the arena.

"Think what through?" he asked, afraid she was retreating back a step, undoing the one they'd advanced a moment ago.

"Today. This." She gestured to the arena.

They were in the University of Colorado Boulder's basketball gymnasium. One side of the stands was packed with spirited-colored parents and the other was a mosaic of teens in cheer uniforms that were way too short in his opinion.

Note to self: enroll Waverly in fencing.

"When you offered to be my beard, I was desperate, so I agreed." Not the reason he wanted to hear for what he thought was a pretty amazing afternoon. "But I didn't think of how this would all play out."

"Hey." He took her hands again. "Whatever it is, I got you."

Her expression became even more pinched. "That makes it even worse." She took a deep breath. "First, I want to start by saying I'm sorry. Second, I want to tell you that if you want to leave, I understand. You see, my parents just—"

"We've arrived," her dad sang.

Jonah looked at the bottom of the steps where he immediately spotted Lenard. He was dressed in camel-colored boat shoes, mint green skinny jeans, and a silky shirt with palm trees on it. His face was painted with silver-and-pink sparkles, making him look like a silver fox gone club kid, and he was waving like he was part of the royal family.

"Why are you so worried? Does your dad pack a shotgun under those skinny jeans?" Jonah teased, nudging her shoulder with his.

She cracked the tiniest of smiles. "No, but he has been known to deliver glitter bombs to men who don't treat me right."

He leaned in to whisper in her ear, "Good thing I know how to treat a woman right."

And he wanted to do right by Evie. No matter how this thing started, he was finding himself more and more protective over her.

"I know. But you didn't sign up for the chaos that's about to ensue."

"Look, I've lived next door to your parents for almost a decade. Nothing can shock me."

And that was the truth. He'd accidentally seen Moira

watering her roses naked—he shivered at the horrific memory. Had Lenard tell him that he had the right "equipment" to wear tighter jeans. Then there was the time Camila puked up pizza and ice cream all over him at Ryan's tenth birthday party after jumping in the blowup tent too long—lesson learned, jump house *then* junk food.

"Yes. But you've never seen them at a competition. They are loud, combative, yell at the judges, and boo the other teams. Plus, they try to be funny, but it always comes out perverse. Look."

Evie pointed at Moira, who was in second-skin jeans, an animal-print shirt that said "Resident Cheer Cougar," and matching cougar-print stilettos. In her hands was a bright poster that read, "Nail That Dirty Bird, Cami."

"What's a dirty bird?" Jonah asked to lighten the mood.

"It's a stunt. And this isn't a part of the deal."

"Neither was the other day," he said. Evie kept her eyes forward but the beating pulse at the hollow of her neck was a dead giveaway.

He thought about that day often. It was becoming his favorite pastime. More like an obsession. Now that he knew the taste of her lips, the way her nipples puckered against his tongue, the way her breasts felt in his palms. The way she came apart on his mouth.

Oh no. Jonah was starting to get a sick, strange feeling. He didn't want this. And by this, he didn't want to pretend anymore with her. He wanted it to be real.

"Oh God! Here they come." She spun to face him. "We can hold hands." She grabbed his, but it felt more like middle schoolers trying to figure out how dating worked. "Be prepared. We have to pull this off. Make it believable."

That wouldn't be a problem for him, so the way she was reacting, all panicked and embarrassed, crushed something inside him. All right. She wanted him to play along, he'd play along. He slung his arm around her and pulled her snug against his body.

"What are you doing?"

"Making this believable. So bring your best, sunshine. Because I will."

She seemed flustered, right where he wanted her. She'd thrown him for a loop, so he was going to do the same. Tit for tat. Which pissed him off.

"Do we have to sit so close?"

"Believable, remember?"

Her face crumbled a little bit, and she said, "Right. Now get ready. They will grill you. Bombard you with questions that include, but are not limited to, your sex life, your breakfast cereal choices, boxers or briefs—"

"Boxer-briefs, so I have both covered."

"If you're a ladies-first kind of man."

He leaned in to whisper, "I'll let you answer that one."

She gulped down a gallon of air. "You shouldn't be looking at me like that."

"Like what?"

"Like you're going to slide your hand down my pants," she whispered thickly.

"Do you want me to slide my hand down your pants, sunshine?"

God, say yes. Not that he would right there in the middle of the cheer competition. But knowing that she wanted him to would be enough. His body's response at even the possibility was like a chemical reaction.

She turned to him, those beautiful brown pools connected with his and he was certain she was going to answer, but instead she plastered a fake-as-shit smile on her face and said, "Fun fact.

Did you know that my dad was the cheerleader of the family?" she said, avoiding the topic.

He'd let her deflect—for now.

"He used to coach at the high school. Now he's Camila's team parent," she went on. "Just about everyone knows him here."

Lenard was walking up and down the bleachers kissing nearly everyone he came across. "I can see that. Was he your coach, too?"

Now that he was picturing Evie in one of those skirts, he decided they were the perfect length. In fact, he wouldn't mind helping her pull it out of the attic and having her teach him more about this dirty bird.

"I didn't have time for cheer. My parents had just expanded the shop so I spent my time after school making lattes and cappuccinos."

It was said with a casualness that he knew was a front. And some of that anger dissipated at her openness. At her selflessness. "That must have been hard."

"Why do you say that?"

"You're just so social, it must have been hard watching your peers have the teen experience while you were working." Didn't she say that she'd had a key to her parents' shop by the time she was fifteen? He hadn't thought about what that meant then. But he was sure thinking about it now. Thinking about how he'd just reacted to her uncertainty about the situation and that made him a dick.

"That's why I went away for college."

Only I got pregnant and had to come home was left unsaid.

"It was what it was," she said. "Plus, I liked helping my family."

He noticed she used the past tense. "Do you still like it?"

She opened her mouth and closed it as if debating on whether to tell him the truth or deflect. She let out a big breath and he watched as her body deflated. "Does it make me a terrible person if I told you no?"

He cupped her cheek. "I think you're an incredibly unselfish person who does more than most would."

She leaned into his palm. "My family gave up a lot for me when I was pregnant. They put their retirement years on hold to help me raise Camila."

"That doesn't mean you have to give up your dream."

"I didn't give up on it, I just put it on hold."

"Is that why you want to go back to school?"

"I loved school, but it was too hard raising a kid as a teenager and keeping up my grades. I know other people do it. I just couldn't give one hundred percent to a million different things."

She'd given other people all one hundred of her percent until there was nothing left over for herself. "And if you couldn't do it perfectly then you didn't want to do it at all?" he guessed.

"More like, I was sick seven months of my pregnancy and then I had to work full-time to support Camila."

He ran a thumb down her jawline. "That must have been hard, too. Didn't Mateo help?"

"He's never missed a payment, but in those early years he was just an intern at a law firm, and it took him a while to work his way up. As for emotional involvement, he's pretty much hit or miss. Mostly miss, actually."

"I can't imagine not being in my kid's life."

"Me either. Even though it's been hard at times, I wouldn't change it for anything."

A dreamy smile overtook the exhaustion and his heart rolled over. This was the most she'd opened up to him, and all he could think was he wanted to know every little thing about her. Even if this was pretend for her, it felt real to him.

He took her hand again and she didn't pull away. "What are you studying?" he asked.

"I want to reopen my own organizing business."

"So you can terrorize your clients?" he teased.

She shot him a prim glare. "I like to think I have a velvet glove."

"Not when it comes to me. But you're softening up."

"Maybe a little. Tell me something about you. Wait, let me guess, you were one of those popular jock types."

"Why do you say that?" She reached up and squeezed his bicep. He laughed. "I may have been the captain of a few teams in my day."

"Was your dad your team parent, too?"

After all these years, questions about his dad still hit like a sledgehammer to the chest, cracking his foundation and knocking off chunks of confusion, guilt, and disappointment.

She must have seen something in his expression because she quickly said, "You don't have to tell me, if you don't want."

"My dad committed suicide when I was ten," he said quietly.

Her hands jumped to her throat. "Jonah," she breathed. "I am so sorry. I had no idea. Amber never said a word."

"Because she knew I didn't like people to know. To think of my dad like that, you know? When people hear suicide, especially when attached to someone who's a parent, they think it makes the person selfish or weak. My dad was haunted. He went to Kuwait my hero and came home a shadow."

"That sounds like mature logic for a ten-year-old."

"Oh, I was confused, devastated, angry at the world. At him. I wanted to rage, but the suicide broke my mom, so I had to be the strong one. I got all the aggression out on the field."

"Did your mom remarry?"

He was quiet for a moment. He didn't usually talk about

this with people but now that he'd started he couldn't seem to stop. "She never even dated." He looked over at Evie, and those beautiful eyes of hers were filled with pain and a fierce protectiveness—for him. "Not even once. I think it was the shock of it all that knocked her so off axis she was never able to realign.

"You know, when he was deployed, she'd always have me set him a place at the dinner table. After he died, she started doing it again. She still does. Every night, there it is, the giant reminder that we weren't enough for him to stick around."

"It had nothing to do with you. You know that, right?"

"Oh, *I* know that. But ten-year-old Jonah still wonders what he did wrong. Or what he didn't do that could have made a difference."

She kissed his fingertips. And instead of saying how sorry she was or some other empty platitude, she said, "I'm angry for the boy who lost his dad and even angrier for the man who carries those scars."

"Sometimes I'm angry, too. Like when I graduated college, when Waverly was born, when Amber was diagnosed. And all the small, in-between moments when a decision makes you a boy or a man. I had to figure it all out on my own. For a while I had Amber and now..." He shrugged.

"You have me," she said earnestly. "I know I'm not family, and this is an arrangement, but I'm a good listener and I give great advice."

There it was. The reminder that this was short-term. Something to be endured for her until they both accomplished their goals.

"You also give great orders."

She laughed. "I might also be an I-told-you-so kind of person, but it's because I'm usually right. And if people just listened to me the first time it would save everyone a lot of frustration."

He couldn't help but smile. That's what she did to him—made him want to push past the pain and be in the here and now. "That explains the personal organizer dream."

"I never told you it was my dream."

"You didn't have to. I could tell by the way you talked about it how much you loved your job."

She smiled and shifted the focus. "What about you? Where do you see a new job taking you?"

He saw it taking him to a place that was full of possibilities. "I want to help people like me, who was so buried in grief it was hard to get up, let alone manage Amber's life insurance payout."

She blinked. Twice. "That's very sweet."

"Don't sound so surprised."

"I'm not surprised so much as touched." She went quiet. "Are you still buried?"

"Asking for a friend?" he said without a trace of humor.

"Maybe," was all she said, but the organ in his chest reacted like she'd just admitted that she, too, saw possibilities. But he wanted to be honest. She deserved honesty.

"I think a part of me will always be. But it's easier to breathe now."

"What changed?"

He wanted to say that she was the change but he knew that would scare her. Hell, it scared him.

"Hello, darling," someone interrupted, and they looked up to find Moira looking back, a conspiratorial smile on her face. She looked at their intertwined hands. "Aren't you two cozy?"

He felt Evie fight the urge to pull away. "I got a flat and Jonah gave me a ride."

"I bet he did." Moira lifted a naughty brow. "You do look more relaxed, honey."

"Mom," Evie scolded, then turned to Jonah. "I am so sorry."

"Nothing to apologize for, sweetie," Lenard said. "Your mother's just proud of you. I guess the sex-tervention worked."

"Sex-tervention?" Jonah asked Evie, who rolled her eyes.

"You can still leave if you want. It's not too late."

"And miss this?" He laughed. "Not on your life."

"You want to watch me be utterly humiliated?" She stopped and slapped a hand to her mouth. "Oh my God. Is this how I make Camila feel?" She looked at Jonah. "I've become my mom!"

"Who is standing right here," Moira said. "And if that child is even a tenth as happy as you look then the embarrassment is worth it."

Chapter Twenty-Nine

Evie

Evie's one and only experience in Shoot Your Shot was a blind date that Moira had guilted her into. Chad had been a sweet, good-looking, professional snowboarder who was barely old enough to legally rent a car.

He'd made her laugh, and they'd even shared a kiss, but when he'd invited her back to his place she'd declined. There was only room for one cougar in the Granger house. But tonight felt different. She'd taken care with her hair, picked out a stunning silky top with spaghetti straps and a plunging neckline, dark jeans, and strappy heels. Most would think she'd dressed to impress, but the only person she wanted to impress was herself.

It was a test, to see if she could tap into a side of her that had been extinguished. The part that socialized with friends, tossed back a few fruity cocktails, and laughed like she meant it. Although that part of her, the laughing part, had already made several appearances in the past few weeks. But she wanted to prove to herself that she didn't need a man to laugh, she could come out of her shell on her own.

Julie opened the bar door, and a blast of temperature-controlled chilled air, expensive cologne, and ear-piercing chatter smacked her around. The place was packed fuller than a free Taylor Swift concert—only instead of teens this was a sausage fest.

Suits ran the entire length of the bar, with a few hipsters in the mix. The average age was mid-twenties—then again Evie had a good five to seven years on most of the You've Got Male-Mamas. Whereas Evie had a teenager, these other women had elementary school-aged kids and younger.

Evie's too-high-to-be-anything-but-an-invitation heels dug into the ground on their own accord. What was she doing? This wasn't her. The lipstick, the low-cut top, the extra-mascaraed lashes. The bar scene had never been her. Even the new her didn't like the scent of cigar smell that lingered in the air, or the way the group of men standing at a round top near the front of the bar was sizing them up—like their sausage was looking for a blue-topped bun.

Just turn around, call an Uber, and you can be in sweats with a pint of mint chip in under ten minutes. You don't have to talk to a single one.

"Why would you when you've already got one at home?" Julie asked.

"I said that out loud?"

"Along with the list of other reasons why you're a chicken."

She looked at the men, over her shoulder at the exit, then back to Julie. "I'm not ashamed to flap my wings and *bak bak bak* all the way home."

"And leave me here with all these straight people? I haven't seen this many loafers since I walked into my accountant's firm last April."

"Who wants to be in a place that reminds them of taxes? Am I right?" She turned to make a beeline for the exit when Julie slid her arm through Evie's and locked Evie to her side.

"I take back what I said. This actually reminds me of the night I was drowning my sorrows in a pint of rocky road after I found out Zoe was engaged," Julie said, referring to her ex-girlfriend who claimed she didn't want to be a stepmom, then turned around and married a woman who had three kids. "You showed up to my house with an emergency Girls' Night Out kit, which included a little black dress, enough makeup to cover up a zebra's stripes, and those Doc Martens I'd had on my wish list for two Christmases."

"The pink camo ones with the platform bottoms," Evie remembered. Julie had worn those boots until the soles wore out. They were the perfect juxtaposition of her feminine side with a twist of bad-assery.

"You dragged me to Pandora's Box," Julie said, nostalgia lacing every word. "Do you remember what you told me?"

"That Vera Wang and Doc Martens are a bold fashion choice?"

"That my person was out there, and it wasn't Zoe. But I'd never find my person if I kept metaphorically dragging Zoe with me everywhere I went. So you asked me to leave her in the car, for just the night, and see what happens." She rested her head on Evie's shoulder. "I did and I met my wife that night." Julie lifted her head and looked Evie right in the eyes. "Leave all the baggage in the car. Just for tonight, and see what happens."

Evie jerked back. "Well, I can tell you what's not going to happen. I'm not going to find my person, because I'm not looking for one."

"So you say." Julie took Evie's arm again. "Look, I told you

I was sorry for posting that video of you and Jonah. I crossed the line there. Let me make it up to you by giving you an excellent Girls' Night Out where we aren't leaving until at least one of us is shit-faced."

"Well, *you* dragged *me* here, so you might as well buy me a drink," Evie reminded her.

"Oh. You're right. I did. But only because I love you and you need to get out and have some fun." Julie pulled them through the noisy bar.

Evie was relieved to see the You've Got Male-Mamas in a booth at the back, waving her over. Julie waved back, then took Evie's hand and waved it like this was a scene from *Weekend at Bernie's*.

"Just a reminder, I'm a hilarious drunk."

Julie snorted. "You're an obnoxious drunk. But you're cute when you're obnoxious. Now, here we go."

They waded through the busiest part of the bar toward the back, where all six of the ladies who'd made girls' night stood and swarmed Evie. Before she knew what was happening, she and Julie were in the middle of a GNO huddle, with arms hugging her from every direction.

"We are so glad you made it," Alex said. The young mom had her blond hair twisted up at the base of her neck and was wearing a cute red-and-white polka-dotted 1940s-style pinup dress. "The first round is on us."

"Oh." Evie waved a hand. "You don't have to—"

"Thanks," Julie said, shoving Evie into the nearest seat. "I'll have a whiskey neat and Dr. Ruth here will have a vodka and tonic, heavy on the vodka."

"Dr. Ruth?" Evie asked as one of the ladies headed to the bar.

"You didn't think they invited you here to talk about

cross-stitch, did you? They want to know about sex after single motherhood," Julie said, sliding into the booth next to Evie and blocking her exit.

Evie looked around the table, all the women looking back with rapt attention. "Did you?"

All five heads nodded.

"Only if you want. There is no pressure," Alex said.

"If you want, Evie." Julie nudged Evie's elbow gently.

Alex clapped. "It's just this is the first time for all of us venturing out into the world of dating and sex. Who better to ask than the original You've Got Male girl?"

Evie looked over her shoulder and found the woman returning from the bar with a tray full of drinks. "I'm going to need this first." Evie grabbed hers and downed it in one shot. She coughed at the cold liquid stinging her throat, then set the tumbler down on the table—hard.

While it tickled her nose and she enjoyed the bubbles stinging her throat, it was not nearly enough to get her comfortable talking about sex—especially since she hadn't officially had sex. And it was her intention to keep it that way.

As the other women grabbed their own drinks, Evie leaned into Julie and whispered, "Dr. Ruth is like a million years old. There is no way she'd still be getting her tank filled regularly, if you know what I mean. But she still gives advice, right?"

Julie lifted a brow. "Have you and Jonah not had sex—"

She slapped a hand over Julie's mouth. "No."

"Seriously?" Julie mumbled through Evie's fingers. "Plus, that kiss looked too hot for two people who hadn't seen each other naked." When Evie didn't respond, except to flush, her friend licked Evie's palm.

She jerked her hand back. "Gross."

"If you don't want tongue action then keep your hands to

yourself," Julie said. "Unless you want action, just the right man isn't here." Julie looked Evie up and down, then gave a Cheshire smile. "Interesting. You know that stick that's always wedged up your ass? Well, it isn't as noticeable, like maybe you've had a recent orgasm that wasn't battery operated."

Heat licked up Evie's neck to her face and she groaned. "Fine, we haven't done the deed, but I can attest to the fact that he has a magical mouth."

"Magical?" Alex said and waggled a brow. "Do tell?"

Evie opened her mouth, but nothing came out. Even though this was part of the plan, a surefire way to cement the story that she and Jonah were an item, she didn't want to share any of the details from that day. Not even with Julie—and she told Julie everything. While the other things had been for show—she wanted to keep that day between them.

Between *them,* she snorted, as if there was an official "them." It wasn't like they shared inside jokes about lemonade, or knew each other's quirks and favorite colors, or held hands like a real couple would do. Nope, Evie and Jonah were nothing but a fake couple pretending to have fake feelings.

Sadly, for her, fake was the new real.

Oh boy, was she in trouble.

"I need another drink for this."

"Coming right up," one said, and walked off into the crowd.

"Okay, what's going on?" Julie pulled Evie close and asked quietly. "And don't bother lying, your face is like a living lie detector test."

Evie worked hard to school her features, which only made her look more guilty. "What makes you say something is going on?"

"You have that *I just ate a gallon of ice cream and I'm going to deny it* look." She leaned forward on her elbows until she was within whispering distance. "Is it about the shop? Am I losing my job?"

"No. Your job is fine." Evie turned to address everyone. "It's just that everything with Jonah is still so new. I don't want to jinx it." And she didn't want to add another lie to her already growing pile.

"That's a smart idea," Laura said, approaching the table. Her shoulders were drawn, her eyes were two angry slits, and she had a tray filled with—apparently another round. "Because the Jinx is alive and well tonight, ladies."

"Your date is already over? What happened?" Alex asked, shifting over so Laura could sit.

Laura handed out the drinks, then plopped down. She gave Evie a welcoming but discouraged smile. "He was a creep."

"He's a children's book illustrator. How big of a creep can he be?" one of the other Mamas asked.

"He wanted to know if we could go into the bathroom so he could illustrate me—naked," Laura said.

"Total creep," Alex said, then held her glass up. "One creep closer to Charming."

"One creep closer to Charming," the group repeated like it was their mantra, then *tinked* rims and—down the hatch went round two.

Evie was starting to feel a little loose around the shoulders and her neck felt a little wobbly. Her lips were tingling and her body buzzing. It had been a while since she'd been tipsy, but it felt good to let go a little. Which was the only reason she could account for her affirmative response when Laura said, "Never Have I Ever tequila version."

And that was when Evie went from tipsy to obnoxious and how, six rounds of Never Have I Ever and shots later, she found herself in a dark corner texting her faux toy-friend. Her brain told her to put the phone away and call it a night—her tequila told her to live like she was that fun, extroverted, outgoing woman of years past. So she hit send. Then immediately regretted it.

Evie: Guess what color I'm wearing?

Her words popped up on her screen and she groaned with regret. Maybe if she stuck her phone in her pocket and turned it on silent then the text never happened. Only his response was too fast for her to put her plan into action.

Jonah: You do know it's after midnight.

She looked at her watch.

Shit. It was nearly one.

Evie: It's five o'clock somewhere.

Jonah: Where are you?

Evie: Shot Your Shoot.

Evie: I mean Shoot Your Shot

Jonah: Are you drunk?

Evie: Define drunk?

Jonah: Texting me to tell me you're wearing blue.

Evie: I didn't say blue.

Jonah: You didn't have to. I can sense these things.

Evie: It must be another one of your magical abilities.

Jonah: What was my first one?

Evie: First what?

Jonah: Magical ability. You said another one, which means there is already one.

Evie: I can't tell you. It will go right to your head.

Jonah: Which head are we talking?

Evie rolled her eyes so hard that she nearly toppled off her stool.

Evie: You just proved my point.

Jonah: You're the one who wore blue.

Evie: Maybe I wore it for me.

Jonah: Even through text you're a terrible liar.

She got worse when she was drunk, which was why texting him had been a bad idea to begin with. So then why did she?

Because you're surrounded by a sea of handsome men, yet you keep thinking about one man. And his magic mouth.

Lord, what a mess she'd made of things.

Evie: Am not.

Jonah: Is this our first argument?

Evie: I'm not the arguing type.

Jonah: Then why are you aggressively swiping?

Evie went to punch in a reply and sucked in a breath. How did he know?

She glanced quickly around the room to make sure that she hadn't manifested him. But there was no grumpy neighbor to be seen. A pang of disappointment pushed through her.

Jonah: Got ya.

Jonah: Back to my magical ability.

Evie's lady town started buzzing so she squeezed her thighs tighter, but that only made things worse. She closed her eyes to get her hormones under control when an image of his magical ability popped into her mind.

Jonah: Don't go shy on me now.

Evie: Not shy. Smart.

Jonah: I like smart almost as much as I like blue. I also like knowing that I'm winning this argument.

Evie: We aren't arguing.

Jonah: Good, then tell me a secret.

Evie typed her response, then deleted it letter by letter. Then retyped it again, only to erase it.

"You came here to be bold, so be bold, Evie Granger," she mumbled to herself and retyped the message and quickly hit send.

Evie: Your mouth. Kind of like Magic Mike, only Magic Mouth.

She didn't wait for a response because Bold Evie would leave him with that parting message. Bold Evie would take to the dance floor with her new friends and twirl like she didn't have a care in the world. Bold Evie wouldn't think about her fake toy-friend once. Not when some suit asked her to dance and she declined, not when she ordered a lemon drop—which was essentially adult lemonade—and especially not when she caught a glimpse of herself in the mirror and liked the woman she saw smiling back.

Nope, she didn't think about Jonah once.

Chapter Thirty

Jonah

Jonah stood at the entrance of Shoot Your Shot with a smile on his face as he watched Evie in the middle of the bar, dancing with a circle of her friends.

She had her arms over her head, a grin as bright as the sun on those beautiful lips, her hips relaxed and swaying back and forth in a rhythm that made his mouth go dry.

She was beautiful. And captivating. And a bunch of other amazing things that inspired feelings that scared him as much as they excited him. He couldn't look away. Neither could half of the men in the bar. The group of women was attracting a lot of attention, but his attention was locked on one woman. And one woman only.

Jonah wasn't a fan of dancing, but he was a fan of Evie. Which was why he wove his way through the crowd to the middle of the bar where the women had taken up residence. He pulled up a bar stool and took a seat.

He wasn't there more than two seconds when she happened to turn his way. A flash of confusion furrowed her brow, but it was quickly replaced with surprise—pleasant surprise.

Seemed Evie was as big a fan of him as he was of her. Not that she'd admit it if she weren't shit-faced. Which she clearly was because she gave him a big wave.

The entire group of women turned toward him and followed suit, until the gaggle was wiggling fingers in his direction. Then Jonah found himself doing something that would have the Man Card gods descending upon him and revoking his membership— he wiggled back.

Evie burst out laughing—loud enough to turn the remaining heads in the bar. Then he was the one who was pleasantly surprised, because she whispered something to her friends before walking over to him.

More like strutted. And man, those pants fit her like a glove and when paired with mile-high heels she was a walking wet dream. Then there was her top. Blue, and fitted enough to cling to her curves, with a neckline designed to scramble a man's mind. Christ, her top had these tiny little straps of silk that with a single tug would drop down her shoulders.

Damn, he had it bad. This was quickly moving past infatuation into something more dangerous. An emotion he wasn't sure how to define—one he hadn't experienced before. With Amber it had been a slow burn, starting off as friends, and gradually moving to love. It had been sweet and safe and something he'd desperately needed back then.

This thing with Evie was as fast as a bullet train and headed toward nowhere. She'd made it clear that there was an expiration date. Plus, she could call this off at any moment to go back to her regularly scheduled life—or she could follow the dreams she'd put on hold for so long. Whichever way, her departure would leave him reeling.

Wasn't that a terrifying thought? Even more terrifying was how much it terrified him. Not that he had time to dwell on the anxiousness pumping through his chest because she was standing in front of him. And in those sexy heels, with him sitting, he had a pretty inspiring view of just how low-cut her top was.

"My eyes are up here," she said, thoroughly amused.

He looked up at her, but he took his time getting there, lingering on the sweet curve of her neck, where he knew she loved to be kissed, her lower lip that he loved to nip, and then those big brown pools that a man could fall into and never come out again.

"I was getting there."

"Uh-huh," she said, scooting closer. "What are you doing here?"

"You can't text a guy like that and expect him to sit in bed wondering what happens when he uses his magical abilities."

"You read that?"

"I read that."

"I was hoping that the text would somehow disappear between now and when you woke up to read it." A frown folded on her forehead. "Wait. Why aren't you home asleep?"

"When a man gets a text about his magic mouth, he's going to want to see what happens when he uses it."

"It can melt a woman's clothes right off," she informed him as if she were the reigning expert on magical mouths. Correction. As if she were the reigning expert on *his* magical mouth. A title he was damn happy to give her.

"Shall we test it?"

Her gaze landed on his lips. "It would be odd for my boyfriend to greet me without a kiss. We are in the honeymoon phase after all."

She wobbled a little and had to put her hands on his chest to steady herself. He pulled her closer—telling himself that he was just helping stabilize her. "How drunk are you?"

"Not so shit-faced that I don't know what I'm doing, but tipsy enough to admit I want you to kiss me. Not because of the people in the bar, but because you want to kiss me." Her lashes fluttered. "Do you want to kiss me, Jonah?"

"Desperately."

"Then let's see just how magic that mouth of yours is."

Jonah was, hands down, a blessed man because he didn't get the chance to kiss Evie—she was kissing him. He didn't grab her or take control, he just stood there with his hands casually resting on the curve of her lower back, letting her set the pace. He thought she was going to give him a chaste kiss, but one brush turned into two, and finally, by the time she worked her way into kiss number five, a round of hoots and catcalls went up.

He pulled back slowly, savoring the way she chased his lips, trying to fill the growing distance between them. She blinked at him and the dazed expression was from more than a few drinks.

"Your clothes are still on. Maybe I'm doing it wrong," he said.

"Oh, you're doing it right," she said. "But just for experiment's sake, maybe we should try again. In your car."

He groaned. She was killing him. "There is nothing more I want than to melt your clothes off, but I don't want you to regret it come tomorrow."

She cupped his cheek. "I won't," she promised.

"Let's circle back to that when you're sober," he said. "But until then, how about you let me drive you home so I know you get there safely."

"You came here to make sure I get home safely?"

"Sunshine, I came here to see you in that blue top."

Chapter Thirty-One

Evie

It was well past two and instead of being in bed, trying to sleep off what was sure to be a doozie of a hangover, Evie was lying on her patio lounger gazing at the sliver of moon hanging over the Rockies in the distance, sipping on a hot cup of coffee. The stars were brighter than normal, twinkling in the sky like millions of fairy lights.

The events of the night had her tied into an emotional pretzel. The more time they spent together, the more natural their interaction became, until the beginnings of a bond began to form—a bond she would be crazy to explore. But it was there and impossible to ignore.

Should she have played her cards differently—stuck to the plan?

For one, she never should have invited him inside the house. She should have told him to get his own glass of lemonade in his own damn house. Also, the moment he got within kissing distance, she and her blue panties should have headed for the hills. Maybe climbing the Rockies would have burned off some of that sexual frustration. But instead she'd drunk-texted him, then propositioned him for a quickie in the back seat of his soccer-dad SUV, which housed a booster seat and goldfish-cracker crumbs.

Lord help her. He'd kissed her on the cheek and sent her inside, a perfect gentleman, but Evie had to face facts. In the span of a few weeks, she and Jonah had gone from feuding, to flirting, to faking, to fuc—

A rustling sounded in the distance. Evie sat straight up as a shadow appeared from the side yard, so fast coffee sloshed over the rim, burning her skin. But she was too busy going through all the reasons there would be that kind of foot-on-leaves rustling.

Heart ricocheting off her ribs, she strained her eyes, wondering if maybe she'd manifested Jonah out of high-altitude-thin air. Had he come to melt the clothes off her body? And if so, would she let him know that she was mostly sober?

She watched as the shadow got larger and finally stepped into the center of the yard and the floodlights went on. Her heart gave a little sad tap dance. Instead of a deliciously addictive master of the man-made *O* sneaking through her yard, a brunette teenager wearing wedged heels, a slip of a sundress, and enough apprehension to advertise she was up to no good froze like a deer in the headlights.

"For future reference," Evie said. "You might want to sneak back in on the side of the house that doesn't have motion-activated lights."

Her daughter slowly met her gaze. Instead of being filled with guilt, Camila cocked a hip and sent Evie a bored-AF expression. "I wasn't sneaking. I forgot my key."

"Sorry, try again."

"Fine, maybe I didn't want to be left out in the sneaking

around department. It seems to be a Granger way of life lately. If you know what I mean."

Oh, Evie knew all too well. She hadn't just been sneaking, she'd been lying—to the people she loved the most on this planet. And if Camila was feeling even a tenth as guilty as Evie right then, maybe they needed to have a girl-to-girl talk.

She leaned back and sipped her coffee. "Then maybe we both come clean."

"You mean, like I tell you where I was, and you rat out who I was with?"

"Or you tell me why you felt the need to sneak out in the first place." Even though the light flickered off, plunging them into the darkness, Evie could practically see Camila roll her eyes. "Or we can both go to bed and you can lose all privileges for a month."

"Fine. I was with Ryan," Camila said, walking over and taking a seat on the lounger next to Evie. The light flickered back on at her movements.

Evie grabbed her cell off the patio table and the screen came to life.

"Let me guess, you're calling your *boyfriend* to rat out Ryan."

"I'm turning off the patio lights from my phone. As for Jonah, I'm not telling him anything."

"Thank you," Camila said, sounding relieved.

"You're going to tell him that you were in his house without his knowledge."

"Why?"

"Because he has a right to know that Ryan is sneaking in after-hours friends."

Camila let out a huge sigh and slunk down in the chair. "He didn't know I was coming. I just kind of knocked on his window. It wasn't his fault."

"If you wanted to go to Ryan's, you just needed to ask, I would have let you go over," Evie said. "At an appropriate time."

"You weren't home."

Whatever guilt Camila was trying to ignite in Evie never came. Yes, she was out. And it was about damn time she started living a little. "Not a valid excuse. You could have texted."

"Honestly?" Camila huffed. "I didn't want to talk to you."

Evie's heart painfully tightened at the realization of just how big of a divide her lie had caused between her and Camila. Her daughter might not know the extent of the lie, but instinctually she obviously knew Evie was hiding something. That was not the kind of behavior she wanted to model.

"Do you mind if I ask why?"

Camila shrugged the shrug of a little girl. Gone was the brooding sixteen-year-old and in her place was Evie's precious daughter—who was obviously hurting.

"Because it's about Dad and I didn't want to talk to you about him."

Evie's heart sank. She'd worked tirelessly to make sure she never talked negatively about Mateo in front of Camila. Even when things had been at their worst, Evie always tried to put a positive spin on things. And when that wasn't possible, she'd just hug Camila until the pain subsided.

"I'm sorry you feel like you can't come to me about your dad."

Again with the weighted shrug. "Why would I when you keep things from me and lie to me? Here you're lecturing me about sneaking out and you've been blaming not going to Dad's wedding on the cheer competition."

Panic and disappointment made a complicated knot in her gut. Panic over what her daughter knew and disappointment that she lied to cover up for her ex once again and lied to her daughter, breaking their truth code.

"Even worse, Heather is pregnant. And it's a girl. And he didn't even tell me. I had to find out from his Insta page."

Evie was going to kill him.

"Oh my God!" Camila said. "You knew, didn't you? You knew and kept it from me!"

"Yes, I knew. And yes, I kept it from you." The betrayal in her daughter's eyes was nothing compared to the absolute heart-crushing uncertainty crumpling her petite frame.

"I hate you," she whispered, tears rolling down her face. "More than Dad, I hate you."

Those four letters were like an arrow to Evie's heart.

"Why didn't you just tell me the truth?" Camila's voice was thread thin, emotions sucking the air from her chest.

Evie set her mug on the table and scootched to the edge of the lounger, so she was closer to Camila. "It was Dad's news to share, and I wanted to give him a chance to tell you first."

Camila snorted. "Dad never tells me anything. But you and I are supposed to talk about everything. At least we did before you started dating Jonah."

She cupped Camila's cheek. "This has nothing to do with Jonah. In fact, I found out before we started dating."

Camila rolled off the support. "Were you ever going to tell me?"

"Yes. I just didn't know how without hurting you."

"Letting me believe that you were the one who didn't want me to go to the wedding hurt worse. You always said we're a team and that wasn't very team-like."

"You're right. I shouldn't have lied," she said. "I was giving your dad till the end of his honeymoon and then I was going to talk to you if he hadn't. But I should have come to you straight away." Evie wiped away one of Camila's tears that were streaming down her face. "How do you feel about having a baby brother or sister?"

"I guess that part will be kind of cool. I mean, I love Waverly, and she and Ryan are super close." Camila looked down at her hands, which were nervously smoothing over the crease of her dress.

"But?"

"But they live in the same house. Dad and Heather live in Boulder, and I barely see them as it is. Once they have the baby, they'll be even busier."

"And you're afraid that it will affect your and Mateo's relationship?" she asked, even though they both knew the answer to that question.

Chasing bright, shiny objects was Mateo's MO. He changed directions like a compass in the Bermuda Triangle. And while Evie hoped that his new baby was a wake-up call that would make him step up as a father for both his kids, history warned her to be cautious with her optimism. To not give Camila false expectations for something that might never happen.

"He's already changing," Camila said. "I mean he threw a kid-free wedding. He said it was because Heather has a large family with a lot of nieces and nephews, but I'm not a kid."

"No, you're not." And while Camila was referring to being closer to college-bound than construction paper collages, the subtext was screaming, *"I'm his kid!"*

"Do you love Jonah?" Camila asked and Evie choked on oxygen, which was a miracle since she couldn't seem to get any to her lungs.

Love? No way. Like? Absolutely. *Like-like*? She was afraid to answer that. But she didn't want to rack up another secret, especially with someone who'd been on the receiving end of too many secrets lately.

"I'm not sure," she said honestly. "When we started this relationship, it was because we both needed help from the other. He promised to be my beard to get everyone off my back about dating and put a stop to the ClickByte insanity. In exchange, I agreed to help him get his life together so he could start his new job."

Camila's mouth was open as if poised to swallow a fly. "So you aren't even really dating?"

"A few days ago, I would have said no. But now I'm not so sure."

Camila's shoulders sank. "I'm happy that you're dating, but why did it have to be Ryan's dad?"

"Convenience," she said, but was that really the truth? She could have picked a handful of men from the PTA or even one of the many suitors, like Ernie. Stable, sensitive, single-dad Ernie, who was about as threatening as a gnat.

Instead, she'd gone for a man whose life was a bigger mess than hers. He was the most uncertain, unavailable, and un-dateable man she knew and yet there they were—dating.

The term "fake dating" no longer seemed to apply. The moment they'd had almost-sex all bets were off. Now it was her mission to get them back on. She didn't need any more dependents in her life, and Jonah came with a minivan full of them.

"Does Grandma know?"

"No, and I'd like to keep it that way. But I would never ask you to lie or keep something from her. So if you need to tell her, I support you."

Camila tugged her earlobe. "Nah. I get wanting to have something all to yourself."

"Like Ryan," Evie probed.

Camila's face went slack with surprise. "How did you know?"

Evie nudged her daughter's shoulder with her own. "Just a guess."

"If I tell you something, do you promise not to make a big deal out of it? Because it's not a big deal."

Evie hooked her pinkie around Camila's. "Promise."

"Well, he kissed me tonight," Camila said and Evie squealed. Camila put her hand over Evie's mouth. "Not a big deal, remember?"

Evie zipped her lips. "Right. Can I ask how it was?"

"It was weird." Camila's face took on a shy blush. "But nice."

She slung her arm over Camila's shoulder and pulled her daughter against her side. "I'm glad it was nice, but you know this means no more closed door get-togethers when he's over. And no more after-hours talks."

"So much for not making this a big deal, Mom!"

Chapter Thirty-Two

Jonah

Jonah pulled into the office complex ten minutes before his meeting. Out of the blue his old buddy had called him and asked if he was still looking for a job. Jonah had played it cool and said he was weighing his options but would love to meet and see what Curt had to say.

He damn near strutted into the office in his new suit that Evie had picked out and felt invincible. He was going to nail this meeting and be the kind of provider his family deserved. Damn it felt good.

He felt good.

He hadn't really had the bandwidth to absorb how much of himself he'd lost when Amber had been diagnosed. Parts of himself he was excited to explore again—like helping people manage their futures. He was even exploring what it was like to be a present father, how to show up for the people in his life. And it was working.

Ryan's grades were slowly improving. Waverly was sleeping in her own bed and was a four-out-of-five potty champion. And his mom no longer called him ten times a day to check in on him. Then there was the way his friends treated him—like he was back and better than ever.

Plus, he had a magical mouth.

The thought made him grin.

Evie had been beyond adorable the other night. From the time he tucked her into his car until they arrived home, she had talked nonstop about her night. Even called herself the new Dr. Ruth of ClickByte.

He'd walked her to her door and, a testament to just how good his mama raised him, he gave her a goodnight kiss on the cheek and waited until she went inside her own house where she crawled into her own bed. Then he walked into his own house and climbed into his own bed with nothing but a hard-on and the imprint of her lips on his to keep him company.

That had been three long days ago and he hadn't had a chance to see her since. Between football games, dad duties, and attempting to tame his garden affordably, he'd been beyond busy. And based on how rarely her car was in her drive, he imagined Evie's schedule had been equally as hectic.

She'd been more than upfront about how crazy her life was when she'd approached with her proposition. He'd just never paid enough attention to her comings and goings to see just how stretched thin she was. Yet she seemed to manage juggling all her hats with ease.

At least that's what he used to think. Now that she'd cracked open that door and shown him parts of herself that she kept hidden from the rest of the world—including her family—he knew that in order to keep everyone else's lives spinning she'd had to give up her own. Another thing she'd been upfront with him about. It was the reason behind their relationship.

Jonah's reasons had shifted. He was no longer interested in an easy fix. He was interested in seeing where this thing with Evie could go. Now he just had to get her to admit that there was more to this thing between them than a short-lived, contrived honeymoon phase.

Jonah told the receptionist he was there to meet with Curt, who immediately came out to meet him.

"Man, it's great to see you." Curt greeted him with a side hug and a slap to the back. "Come on in." He followed Curt into the office and took a seat across from his old boss.

"How have you been?" Curt asked with an edge of concern to his voice.

"Really good," Jonah said, and for the first time he really meant it.

"Yeah, I've seen the ClickByte videos. My wife is obsessed. Evie looks good on you."

She really did, he thought, and he wanted to tell her but he didn't want to blow up what they had going. He knew how he felt, but it was in direct conflict with her last rule. And he knew how much she liked her rules. So for now he'd keep things to himself.

He knew she liked him, but it was like a game of chicken, both of them waiting for the other to crack and admit their feelings first, but too afraid in case they weren't reciprocated.

"I even heard that you were practicing again."

"Just taking on a few clients," he fibbed. He had exactly one client. Mrs. Gomez was it and that was more of a favor.

"Heard you took on Frank and lived to tell the story." Curt barked out a laugh.

"He was going to fire some poor new dad to give me a seat at the table. Not my kind of life anymore. You know?" Jonah said, wanting to be upfront. Because while he needed a job, he didn't want the kind of job he'd had before. His family deserved more.

"What are you looking for?"

That was a question he had finally stopped to ask himself. "I want to be challenged, work hard, help my clients ensure their loved ones will be taken care of, and be a present dad."

"What if I can offer you that?"

Jonah waited for the suffocating feeling to swamp him but instead of wanting to hide, Jonah wanted to lean into a new chapter. Working with Mrs. Gomez had really helped him see that he could parent and jumpstart his professional life without sacrificing the things that were important. Sure, shirts would get stained, and there would be more misses than potty-hits, but the love and support was there.

"That would be great."

"It will take a ton of sweat equity, but my partner is retiring and we're looking for someone to manage some of his client portfolios."

"How many clients are we talking?"

"How many can you handle?" Curt looked at Jonah's suit, his eyes zeroing in on the smear of peanut butter he hadn't noticed on his tie, and Jonah could see doubt creeping in. But he wasn't scared of a little peanut butter anymore.

He shrugged. "Kids. They'll get you every time. Yesterday it was frosting from a cupcake. Tomorrow it will probably be something else. Nothing a dry cleaner or spare shirt and tie in the car won't fix."

"Are you at a place to get back in the game?"

Not only was he ready, it was time. If he wanted his family to find peace and move forward, he needed to set an example. And while it would be rough at first, he'd make it work. Hell, he used to be one of the best investment brokers in Denver, he could do it again.

"I'm ready."

"My partner comes back in two weeks, let's schedule an appointment here at the office. I'll introduce you to him. He'll want to see your mind at work, so come prepared with a hypothetical on a widow in her fifties whose husband left her a two-million-dollar life insurance policy. The house is worth a million, but she owns a little over three hundred K with a seventy-five K equity line. She has another mil in an IRA. She's fifty-three with three teens, two of them almost college-aged. We'll see how you do and take it from there."

"Here are some references." Jonah took out a crisp piece of paper and slid it across the table. "Frank's reference will be shit, but you know what I can do."

"I do. That's why I agreed to meet. But know that I need someone I can really rely on. You used to be that guy. I just want to make sure you're that guy again."

"I am."

"My partner has been grooming his son-in-law, but we don't gel. He gave me a month to find someone else. I need to get this nailed down in the next few weeks."

Which meant Jonah had to nail this.

He looked back at Curt. "I'm your guy."

"Good to hear."

. . .

Jonah was an hour late by the time he got home but he was on cloud nine, riding the high of the interview. He had it. He knew it in his gut. He could come up with the perfect hypothetical, he knew it.

He opened the door and walked inside whistling. The shoes by the door were in a straight line, jackets hung on their respective hooks. Even the rug had been vacuumed and not a single toy littered the entry.

Huh.

Jonah kicked off his loafers and walked into the family room, which had a direct line of sight to the kitchen that, save for the two pizza boxes on the counter, was as immaculate as the rest of the house.

Sitting on the couch was Ryan. And instead of being engrossed in a video game, he was watching some kind of rom-com on the flatscreen. Jonah had a strong inkling that the reason for his shift in hobbies was the petite brunette snuggled up next to him.

Camila was pressed against his side and they were sharing a blanket—strange, since it was over eighty degrees today. Jonah held back a chuckle and, instead, in his best dad voice said, "Hands where I can see them."

The two teens parted faster than a set of repelling magnets. Camila straightened her hair, using it as a blanket to cover her bright red face. Ryan's face was red, too, but not for the same reason.

"We were just watching a movie," Ryan defended.

"Waverly was the product of just watching a movie."

"Gross, Dad." Ryan stood and walked toward Jonah, pulling him by the arm into the kitchen. In a low voice he said, "I'm going to ask Camila to homecoming and you're totally blowing the vibe. Can you go someplace else?"

He took in the spotless house. "The vibe I'm getting goes way past a homecoming invite."

"Seriously, how much trouble can we get into while babysitting the lil' monster?"

He looked at Waverly, who was sitting on the floor in her big-girl underwear, and felt a lightness that he hadn't felt since the diagnosis.

"Can't you just go next door? I promise we won't do anything."

Jonah didn't have a problem going next door but *he* did have a problem promising not to do anything. But he said, "One hour and then I'm back. Lights stay on, bedroom is off-limits, and be sure this isn't a Netflix and Chill moment."

Ryan gave him a scout's salute. Not that it made Jonah any less hesitant to leave them alone. Ryan was never a scout.

Jonah ran upstairs to change and then whistled as he walked across the lawn to next door.

Chapter Thirty-Three

Evie

If Evie could sum up her day in one word, it would be glorious. Sun shining, birds singing glorious.

Julie had offered to cover her shift at the shop. Moira was on a date. Her dad had gone to his bridge game at the senior center. And Camila had gone to Ryan's for dinner—after they'd had a chat and ground rules were set.

What had Evie done? Absolutely nothing. She'd spent her day lounging in the sun, while reading a romance book she'd been dying to get to. Okay, she did put in a few hours of studying for her upcoming placement exam, but even that had been fun. Exciting.

Now it was nearing dinnertime and she was still sitting on the lounger on her back porch sipping wine from the good glasses when her phone rang. She looked at the screen and groaned. It was Mateo.

Normally, Evie would drop whatever she was doing to

answer his call, in case it had something to do with Camila. But tonight she was empowered to do things that had to do with her happiness.

"Tonight is all about me," she said and sent him to voicemail.

"You must be reading my mind."

At the sound of Jonah's voice, Evie's head spun around, and her heart leaped into her throat. Jonah stood at the base of her back deck.

Dressed in a pair of low-slung jeans, a light gray T-shirt, and a well-worn ballcap, along with a blast of easy confidence, he was a sight to behold. He was also, *Lord bless him*, holding a pizza box.

For a woman who'd propositioned him just a few nights ago, she was suddenly frozen in place. Tongue-tied and, *whoops,* staring at his lips. Then his other parts, parts that had a zing shooting right through her.

She ripped her gaze up. "I was wondering if you were going to come." With a barely there smile, he lifted an amused brow. "Over. I was wondering if you were going to come over."

"I was wondering, too. I don't want to interrupt your me time, but my house is full and I heard that yours is empty."

"Did Camila offer up that information willingly?"

"Ryan did. It was to get me out of the house so he could have some alone time with Camila."

"How do you feel about that?"

"Alone time?" He walked up the steps, set the pizza on the patio table, and perched himself on the edge of her seat. "I've been thinking about it ever since"—his gaze dropped to her mouth—"learning about my superpower."

"I said magical, not superpower."

He rested a palm on either side of her thighs, then leaned close, caging her in. "You sure about that?"

She pushed up onto her elbows until her chest was brushing his. She felt his gaze drop lower. Grateful that she'd pulled on a fitted tank that made her girls look good, she held her position and let him look.

When his gaze met hers, she lifted a brow in challenge, and she felt as if she'd summoned a beast. Jonah's eye contact never wavered, holding steady—and she held back. She knew she was playing with trouble, but trouble had never felt so exhilarating.

What they'd done last week in her kitchen had been risky. Not because she was afraid of being caught, but because being caught didn't even register. Then there was that kiss in the bar. It wasn't for show, it was for her.

"I'm not sure about anything anymore," she said.

Still leaning over her, he cupped her cheek. "I need you to be sure, Evie, because I'm pretty sure we'll melt more than just your clothes."

Her nipples went on standby as a wave of lust-driven fire surged through her veins. Her heart wasn't sure what she wanted, but her body sure as hell knew—and it seemed to be running the show.

"What do you want?" she asked quietly.

"You." He slid his fingers into the hair at the base of her neck. "Clothed. Naked. On top of me. Under me. Whatever way I can have you. I'm a pretty simple man, Evie."

Her mouth went dry, her core went wet, and her body went deliciously warm.

"This isn't a simple situation."

His eyes went soft. "No. It's not. But we don't have to make it more complicated than what happens next."

"What about Camila and Ryan?"

"I'm okay with leaving them alone if you are."

"We have to trust them sometime, and Camila has really stepped up to the plate lately."

"So has Ryan. He cleaned the entire downstairs without me asking."

Evie smiled. "Actually, your new cleaning lady came today. I walked her through what needed to be done while you were at your meeting."

"Thank you," he whispered and she shivered.

"You're welcome, but I wasn't talking about that." She was worried about how this all would affect their families. She'd come clean with Camila, but it was clear that their relationship was making it awkward for Camila and Ryan. And what did Ryan think about them? Did he know the truth?

"I know, but you said tonight was about you. Maybe it can be as simple as tonight being about you and me."

"And after tonight?"

"What do you want to happen after tonight?"

"For no one to get hurt," she said honestly.

"Then we make a pact. If it looks like someone is going to get hurt, we go back to being friends."

"Friends who fight over property lines or friends who share the occasional coffee?"

"Both," he said with a smile and she laughed, expelling all the heaviness that she'd put on the moment. And when that pressure disappeared it gave way to something simpler. Something warm and comforting. Something that was *theirs*.

"Then I think it's time to test that theory. Superpower or magical ability?"

"How about if it's a superpower, you get to have sex with me. And if it's magical, I get to have sex with you."

"And if it's both?"

"Then you get to have sex with me first. And I get to have sex with you second."

She smiled and he smiled back. He made her feel as giddy as a teen and as desirable as a woman. "That sounds like a deal."

"Shall we seal it with a kiss?"

Chapter Thirty-Four

Jonah

Jonah Stark: luckiest SOB to walk the earth. If he was ever going to get another tattoo that's what it would say. Because never in a million years would he have imagined a reality in which he'd get a second chance with Evie. Not when he'd blown it so epically a few months back.

That day in her kitchen had been the outcome of unexpected, spontaneous combustion. A spur-of-the-moment, drowning-in-sexual-tension decision. But this? This was premeditated foreplay on both accounts.

It took about three seconds, and a swing of those mile-long legs, for it to register that—while Jonah sat on the edge of a patio lounger beneath the sinking sun—Evelyn Granger, queen of public protocol, was straddling him and delivering a wild, open-mouthed, hands-fisted-in-his-hair, real fireworks and fuck-yeah variety of a kiss. It was a kiss to end all kisses, a kiss that left no question of exactly where this night would lead.

And Jonah decided right then, on her back porch, that when it came to this woman, she could lead him wherever the hell she wanted. No questions asked. This wasn't a gentle courtship. This was like a wildfire, blazing hot and fast with limitless acres to scorch.

Man, he couldn't think of anything in this moment that could be better than this.

Scratch that, he thought as she locked her legs behind his back, there was one thing. But he was pretty sure by the way her fingers danced down his chest to tangle in the hem of his shirt, yanking him flush with her chest, that this was just the opening ceremony. The big event, the one with the fireworks and fanfare he'd been fantasizing about for months, was on the evening's itinerary.

"Do you want to take me inside?" she breathed against his mouth.

"I want to take you outside, then inside, then up against the side of every wall in your house."

Locking her fingers behind his neck, she leaned back. "Why don't we start in my bedroom behind a locked door and away from prying eyes."

"That means I have to let go of you." Which, now that he had his hands on her ass, he didn't want to do. But he saw her point. "Your parents?"

"Gone. And Camila said she'd be home by curfew, which is ten. Waverly?"

"Ryan is babysitting."

Evie's eyes skittered away briefly—shyly. "Do you have condoms?"

He tugged her, so their cores lined up. "Several."

She let out a breath of laughter. "You seem pretty sure of yourself."

A younger Jonah would have played it off as confidence, but he was too old for games. And Evie was too special for them.

"The opposite," he admitted. "I'm afraid the first lap might be a sprint, and I want to make sure you cross that finish line."

She smiled a real and radiant smile. "How thoughtful of you."

"I'm a very thoughtful man."

"I'm learning that about you." She went to climb off him, but he tightened his hold. A frown creased her forehead. "What?"

"I've thought of you every step of the way. Not just tonight. But every night. I can't stop thinking about you."

Those big brown eyes widened in shock as she sucked in a breath, and he heard a hint of panic when she exhaled.

"You don't have to say anything back," he said. "I just believe that for this to work we need to be honest. And that was me being honest."

"I don't want to lose sight of what this is," she said quietly.

He ran a hand up her arm to cup her cheek. "Just because this started as a ruse doesn't mean that it can't grow into something more." He didn't want to elaborate how much more this was becoming for him. He didn't want to scare her off, which was why he'd avoided this conversation, but he also didn't want her to think tonight was just about sex. "I like you, Evie."

She released a whoosh of air. "I like you, too. But I'm just scared that this will become too much for both of us. Between you looking for a new job and me starting school, we have a lot resting on our ability to focus on what matters. I don't want to lose sight of that."

"What if we make each other a promise that this won't interfere with our goals. And if it does, then we reassess the situation."

"I like the sound of that," she said and pressed the gentlest of kisses to his lips, then unwound her legs and stood. She slid her fingers through his, tugged him up, going on her toes to whisper against his lips, "Now, are you going to take me inside? Or is it my turn to take you?"

Without waiting to respond, *she* took *him*. In the house, upstairs, down the hallway and, *thank God*, to her bed, which they both fell onto in a tangle of arms and legs—their mouths never parting. They didn't even come up for air. Jonah was surprised that neither one of them passed out along the way from hyperventilation.

He never knew that talking it out could be such a turn-on. Hell, after this talk he was going to become a master communicator—maybe even buy a few books on the topic. The kind that you dog-ear and use a highlighter on—because this was, by far, the best conversation he'd ever had. Deep, intense, passionate, a real give-and-take kind of situation.

There was also heat—enough heat to cause a backdraft the second they came in contact with common sense. Because beneath the fire was a whole hell of a lot of emotion. And it wasn't an unreciprocated kind of thing. Oh no, Evie was eating up the air between them as if she, too, couldn't stand the distance.

Her pulse pounded beneath his lips as he kissed his way down her neck, to the gentle slope that had her back arching off the bed.

Her favorite spot, he'd come to learn. Well, her second favorite spot. Her first favorite was—he ran his hands down her torso and lower and—*jackpot*.

"Jonah," she moaned, and rolled her hips so that they pushed against his hand. Even through the thin cotton of her shorts he could feel how wet she was.

"Lift up, baby," he said and when she did, her shorts—these flimsy little cotton things with a drawstring and nothing else holding them on—slid down her legs. Just like he knew they would.

Today's thong wasn't blue, but a soft pink and was the sexiest thing he'd ever seen. He'd bet it would look great between her ass cheeks.

"Roll over, sunshine."

"Like this?" She turned until she was on her knees and her back was to him. Looking over her shoulder, she gave a little shimmy of the hips. Yeah, it looked magnificent.

"Pink is my new favorite color," he said.

"You might want to see what's beneath door number two. It could just become your new favorite."

His gaze lifted, and his mouth immediately watered. Could he be so lucky? How had he not noticed before? Her shirt was fitted and white and did little to disguise the gentle curve of her glorious breasts. Her bra-less breasts begged to be admired, leaving him with a one-track mind.

Her tits.

The shape, the weight, the way they'd feel as he worshipped them, toyed with them, sucked them into his mouth, nipped at her peaked nipples.

He had several entry options.

Pray for X-ray vision so he could see them right then. Then again, he already had a superpower, and it was his mouth—he didn't want to be greedy.

Secondly, he could dispose of her shirt as efficiently as possible—one, two, over the head and sailing across the room, leaving her breathtakingly bare. Thirdly, he could slowly lift it, exposing every inch of silky skin between her belly button and collarbone. That option led to two more. Leave it tucked beneath her arms, trapping her with it—like they didn't have the time to go any further. Or—and he was kind of partial to this one—lifting it over her head and tying it around her hands and securing them to her headboard.

Then again, he could also pour water all over her glorious body and let the thin fabric do what it was created to do.

"You okay?" She chuckled.

"You got any water?"

"The shower."

He ran a hand down his face. "Too far."

"I have a glass on the nightstand." He followed her gaze but shook his head.

"Not enough."

"You want me to do it?"

"I'm just a little flustered. I need a minute."

But a minute was too long because she crawled off the bed and stood just out of reach. Gripping the hem of her tank, she started to pull.

Yeah, this was what he wanted, to watch her watching him so she could see just how badly he needed her.

"Slower," he said and, *Lord help him*, she actually listened.

She took her time, stopping right beneath the undersides of what he already knew were perfect tens, and lifted a brow. "Ready?"

"Come here." He cupped the back of her thighs and pulled her toward him, and when she was standing between his legs he pressed kisses up her stomach to right beneath her breasts, then looked up at her. "Now I'm ready."

With a smile she lifted the shirt the rest of the way and dropped it to the floor, gifting him the view of a lifetime. And yes, camo was his new favorite color. And yes, this was exactly how he wanted to uncover them, with her taking the lead and setting the pace.

"Like that?" she asked.

"Just like that."

He put his mouth to her, loving how her nipple went hard

against the flat of his tongue. He worshipped it before moving to the other, back and forth until her hands were fisted tightly in his hair and she was moaning.

He ran his palms up the curve of her ass, letting the strip of lace slide between his fingers. Then that lace was sliding down her legs, leaving her, head to toe, in his new favorite color.

"Come here." He tugged her onto his lap and laid back, urging her to scoot up and up until she was practically sitting on his face.

"Jonah, what are you—?" She tried to squirm away, but he held her firm. "Oh, I don't think—"

His answer was to lick her up the center. And it seemed to be an answer she liked because the moan she let out could have been heard from the other side of the Rockies.

Their conversation quickly picked up speed and intensity. He used his tongue, teeth, and his mouth to work her, until he felt her knees buckling and he was pretty sure she was going to suffocate him. But what a way to go.

"Jonah, I'm going to collapse if you keep that up," she whispered on a ragged breath.

He laced her fingers through his, then brought them to rest on the mattress above his head so that she was bent at the waist and in a position he'd love to further explore. It took her a minute to acclimate, but that didn't stop her from bucking against his tongue, pressing down on his mouth, riding his face until she was crying out.

He felt the tremors shake her body, rode out her orgasm with her until she was spent and collapsed on her side. He came up on his elbow and looked down at her sex-dazed expression.

Slowly her eyes opened. "I guess you took me first."

"I am a ladies-first kind of guy."

"How about a mutually-beneficial kind of guy?"

"I am, if nothing, an equal-opportunity lover."

"Good." She yanked his shirt off. "Because I want to get to some of the mutual beneficiation parts. And that starts with you naked and beneath me."

He didn't need any more encouragement. He was taking his shorts off and she was doing her best to help—which was more stroking and groping than anything—and then they were both naked and twisted up like a pretzel on the bed, arms and legs interwoven, their mouths fused together, their hands everywhere all at once.

She kissed her way across his jawline and nibbled on his earlobe, running her tongue around the shell of his ear, before whispering, "Let me touch you, Jonah."

Mind. Blown. He went ballistic, trying to reconcile all the emotions and pent-up tension from the past week that had twisted into a really fucking complicated hot ball that settled right in his groin. Especially when her hands smoothed down his chest, teased across his stomach, and—*bingo*—it was go time.

Two strokes had his eyes rolling to the back of his head. Her hands were something of a legend, a fact that was confirmed as she moved from base to tip, tightening a little more every time the motion was repeated, driving him closer to the edge with each pass.

"Evie," he said, taking her hands and locking them above her head, because even though a part of him cried at the thought of her stopping, another part of him knew that he was one good jerk from done.

"Sunshine," she whispered, her mouth wet and her hair a beautiful mess. "I like it when you call me sunshine."

Yeah. He liked it when he called her that, too.

"Sunshine," he said, "I need to be inside you when I come."

She nodded and he reached for his shorts, grabbing the

condoms out of the back pocket. Without any further fanfare he was wrapped and inside, sinking as deep as he could. The pressure nearly had him exploding then and there.

He'd found the Holy Grail.

Giving himself a moment to gain control, he slowly started to move and, *damn*, it was spectacular. She was spectacular. Giving what he needed and taking what she wanted. And she took him on the ride of a lifetime. Swirling her hips in this rhythm that was beyond erotic. It was like that sexy sway she had the other night in the bar—confident and hypnotic.

Seductive.

The pace accelerated rapidly—all gas and no brakes—like there was no slowing down. It was almost too much and not enough at the same time.

"Jonah," she moaned.

"I know, baby," he said and reached between them to press on her pleasure button.

"I'm almost there."

Embarrassingly, he was too. All it would take was a little more friction, a little more speed and he'd—

He never got to finish the thought because he felt her coil and then burst seconds before he let himself dive headfirst over that edge, tumbling at a rate that ensured he was going to crash land—or stroke out, whichever got him first.

He pumped his way through the orgasm, back arched, head back, loving the way she felt around him. Or maybe it was loving the way he felt around her. Either way he knew he was in trouble because he never wanted this conversation to end.

· · ·

More than an hour later they both lay in her bed breathing heavy and holding tightly to each other as if they didn't want the night to end. Jonah was bursting at the seams to tell her the good news but he was in such a languid state he didn't want to ruin the moment.

As if reading his mind, she asked, "How did the interview go?"

"We can talk about it later. Right now I want to enjoy this."

She rolled over and put her hands beneath her cheek. "There is no way I can wait until tomorrow to find out what happened."

His smile nearly broke his jaw. "I was just offered a partnership in a boutique brokerage firm in Boulder. Well, offered the chance to earn a partnership."

Her face lit with genuine excitement. "Oh my God, Jonah! That's amazing."

He ran a hand down his face in disbelief. "It's terrifying. I have two weeks to get my shit together or it goes to someone else."

"You can do this. Look how far you've come. And when you need help, know that I'm here."

And Jonah's heart rolled over.

Chapter Thirty-Five

Jonah

"Deeper," Evie said, a bead of sweat trickling between her shoulder blades.

"Like this?" Jonah asked.

"Deeper. Really put your back into it."

"Christ." Jonah wiped his brow with the cuff of his shirt. "How many of these do we have to plant?"

"The design your landscape architect came up with says that these shrubs line the length of the fence."

He looked at her beneath the bill of his ballcap. And even in the shadow it cast she could see the intensity of those cobalt-blue eyes that never failed to get her body strumming. "*You* are my landscape architect."

She lifted her chin. "And a damn fine one."

"How many, Evelyn?"

Even when he said her full name in exasperation, she liked it. Her nipples, on the other hand, loved it. It was a thrilling little secret that belonged to the two of them. A secret that was starting to debunk their other little secret.

"Just a few more," she said.

Jonah eyed the army of the potted shrubs that had been delivered that morning and were sitting on the bottom step of his deck. "A few?"

"Okay, eight."

"Eight?" He rested his boot on the head of the shovel and his elbow on the top of the pole, then looked up at the sky and blew out a breath. "Maybe I should have hired someone else to do it, money be damned."

"And miss out on the opportunity to get parched?" She walked closer, swinging her hips like she meant it. She stopped when she was but a breath away. "Not on your life."

His gaze dropped to her lips. "And are you parched, sunshine?"

"Like I've spent a millennium in the Sahara."

"We can't have that, now, can we?" he asked as he slowly lowered his head, flipping his ballcap backward right as his mouth brushed against hers.

"It's a problem," she whispered against his lips.

"Oh, it's a big problem," he whispered back. "It's been a problem ever since you came prancing out of your house in those wet-dream denim cutoffs and that white top that gapes every time you lean over, gifting me a view of the promised land. And I noticed you've been leaning over every chance you get. Is that for my benefit?"

"What do you think?" she said and ran her tongue along his lower lip.

He kissed his way up her jawline to her earlobe, where he sank his teeth in. "I think you're playing with fire."

Something about the word *playing* rubbed her the wrong

way. After the other night—*God,* the other night!—something inside her had shifted. Opened up. Become more vulnerable.

She pulled back so she could search his eyes when she said, "What if I'm not playing?"

His expression went soft. He tossed the shovel aside so he could get his hands on her hips. They were so large that they spanned all the way around her. "Sunshine, this has never been a game to me."

Her brain tried to figure out the significance of his words, because her heart knew what he was saying was vital to how the rest of—well, she didn't know how long—but the two parts of her couldn't agree on the translation. "What does that mean?"

"That I like you, Evelyn. I like you a lot," he said sincerely.

"I think I like you, too," she admitted shyly.

He lifted a brow. "You think or you know? Because I've learned from history that if two people aren't open and honest about where they are, both parties will get hurt." Leaning in so his forehead was against hers, he whispered quietly, "Sometimes very, very badly."

His voice was so heartbreakingly sad Evie's chest ached. "Your dad?"

"My dad. My mom, even though she tried her best." He looked away, as if ashamed over what he was about to say. "Amber." It was barely a whisper, filled with guilt and that anger he'd told her about last week at the cheer camp.

She slid her arms through his until she was embracing him, her head tilted back so she could see his expression when she asked, "You weren't on the same page?"

"Nah. She was accepted into this trial," he said, unbearably low. "I thought, this is it, you know? It wasn't a cure, but it was extending lives up to five years. Five years. She could have seen Waverly go off to kindergarten, Ryan graduate high school and start college…"

"And you'd get five more years with the love of your life," she said, and even though the words shouldn't hurt, they slammed a door deep inside that she'd been slowly opening up.

"She went to one treatment, and it drained her. The regimen was four hours a day, three times a week, in addition to chemo. Saying it now, it sounds like an awful way to spend the rest of your life when you knew it would end anyway, but at the time I just felt like she was leaving me."

Evie wondered if she were in the same position what she'd do. *No,* she thought, *she wouldn't have the luxury of opting out.* In reality, Camila had but one parent and Evie would do whatever it took to be there for her daughter.

She wasn't judging Amber. Everyone was affected by life-changing news differently and their reaction to it varied, but she felt for Amber's family and what that kind of aftermath must have been like. Especially for a man who'd had so many people leave him behind.

Was Evie going to be one of those people when their time was up? Was he going to create a mental place setting for her in his life? Would she?

Unsure how to respond to such a vulnerable moment, she went up on her toes and gave him a gentle kiss that expressed all the sorrow and heartache she felt for him and his family. He must have understood the gesture, because his hands tightened and ran up her back to thread in her hair.

She couldn't ever fully understand what he'd gone through, but she did understand how the loss of a parent could change a child's outlook on the world and where they belonged in it. She saw the struggle in Camila daily.

"I thought I was parched," Jonah said. "More like dehydrated for you."

"I know the feeling."

"Once wasn't enough," he said against the gentle slope of her neck.

"I believe it was three times."

"Three hundred wouldn't be enough," he said and something inside her stilled. What they had between them was good. So good. Too good to be true.

Which meant she was going to enjoy every moment of it.

"Your car is bigger than my bed," she said. "We could just take a little trip to the lookout over Denver."

He pulled back with a wicked grin. "Sunshine, are you asking me to go to Make-Out Point?"

She took both of his hands and led him backward toward the driveway. "I was hoping we'd do more than make out."

Chapter Thirty-Six

Evie

Lenard was having a good day. So good, in fact, that he wanted to pull a shift at Grinder—which meant that Moira would run things while Lenard chatted up the customers. And so Evie had the full day to herself.

A day free of frizzy hair from the frother, intrusive loved ones wanting to know how her sex life was, and nosey customers wanting to take a ClickByte video with her. It also left her free to obsess over the past week.

And what a glorious week it had been.

Nearly every night after the lights went out at their respective houses they found a way to quench their ever-growing thirst. The more time she spent with him—in and out of clothes—the thirstier she became and not just for the sex-tacular benefits, but for their friendship and connection. It was nice to have someone to share her day with, to unpack the good and the bad.

It wasn't just a one-way conversation, either. Jonah's floodgate had been breached and he was more transparent and open with her than any man she'd ever been with. He was in touch with his emotions, mature in the things that mattered, and playful in the ways that counted.

Like just that morning, after Camila left for school, she'd found a note taped to her back door.

You and me, paint the town blue today?
(Clothes optional)

[ ] Yes

[ ] No

She'd checked yes immediately and taped it to his back door, gave a little tap and then raced back to her kitchen, where she was standing by the window like some teenager, waiting for the cute boy next door to write back.

Then he appeared, and a tingle started at the apex of her thighs, fizzing all the way up her stomach until she felt like a champagne bottle about to pop.

Dressed in a blue button-down that was rolled at the sleeves, his hair styled to devastating, and a smile that made her nether region sing, that boy next door was all man. He was a tall drink of water on a hot summer day. And she didn't just want a sip, she wanted a lick and a nip and a whole lot more.

She grabbed her notepad and scribbled a message, then held it up.

Are you asking me to the school dance or a trip to Make-out Point?

He waggled his brow and then went to work on his response.

Why choose when it can be both?

SHOULD I BRING A BOUTONNIERE?

[ ] YES

[ ] No

She held the notebook to the window and her heart leaped as he laughed. She couldn't hear it through the window, but she felt it in her chest. He didn't answer the question, but wrote:

WEAR SOMETHING PRETTY. I'LL BE AT YOUR DOOR IN AN HOUR.

An hour? Evie hadn't had an hour to get ready for anything in over a decade. It wasn't often that she had a family-free house and the luxury of primping. She didn't just want to look pretty, she wanted to look sexy and sophisticated—like the kind of woman who had her own personal Prince Charming.

And he was. Charming and thoughtful and had this assurance about him that made her feel safe. He wasn't like the other people in her life who needed her to hold their world together. Over the past few weeks he'd proven that he had his own world under control. And sure, she'd helped him get there, but he'd helped her equally as much.

She'd been afraid that anything more than their arrangement would be one more obstacle between her and her goals. Instead, he'd been supportive, someone in her corner who respected her choices and her dream to finish her school, and a huge part of the reason why the shop was doing better.

Not only had Evie taken his advice to expand their menu to include more edible items, she'd renegotiated with some of their vendors and moved to some new ones as well. If things kept up like this, she'd be able to hire a second manager and enroll full-time in school. Maybe even have the freedom to open her professional organizer business. Juggling the café, school, and her own dreams didn't seem so chaotic. She could practically feel herself walking across that graduation stage and receiving her diploma.

Her world consisted of her, her family, and a lot of worry—about finances, business, her parents' health, Camila's happiness. She deserved to live in the now and enjoy every single moment of what today and the next few weeks brought. So instead of the safe jeans and silky top that she'd normally choose, Evie reached into the back of her closet and pulled out a flirty, more-fitted-than-not sundress, which may or may not make her bustline look like J. Lo's. She also slid on a thong. Gentleman's choice of royal blue.

She caught a glimpse of herself in the mirrored closet door and her hand crept up to touch her cheek. She was glowing. One of those glows that initiated from the inside and bubbled its way up to tickle the chest, sparking all kinds of happy tingles. Every time she thought about Jonah, she felt this foreign happiness overtaking her.

She was just finishing her makeup when there came a knock at the door. And that glow turned radiant. One look and Jonah would know that she wasn't going to be able to keep this a casual, for-however-long-it-lasts, situationship.

Oh, who was she kidding? This thing between them might have started out as a situationship but had turned into something to cherish—something to hold on to. He'd said that they'd see where this led until it got in the way of their lives. But history told her to progress with caution.

"Don't get too attached," she told herself. "Because honeymoons always come to an end. The excitement eventually fades and life crashes down around you."

It was inevitable.

"Which is why you're enjoying the ride while it lasts," she told herself with a stern look in the mirror. She slid on a pair of strappy heels and rushed down the steps. She was breathless when she opened the door—and it had little to do with her sprint down the hallway.

Not only had he added a tie to his shirt, but he was also holding a corsage. A blue peony with baby's breath and a white ribbon fastened around it. She couldn't remember the last time a man, other than her dad, had brought her flowers. And she wasn't talking about the You've Got Male roses she'd been inundated with since she'd become ClickByte famous.

Suddenly she remembered her comment about the boutonniere. "I was joking. I didn't really have a boutonniere."

"I know," he said, his eyes drinking her in. "But it got me thinking that a proper date required the proper kind of wooing."

She smiled. "Are you wooing me, Jonah?"

"Do you want to be wooed, sunshine?"

"Depends on who's doing the wooing."

He stepped into her and ever so slowly lowered his head, then planted a kiss on her that made her head spin. "Are you still wondering?"

"It's becoming clearer."

He slid his fingers into her hair and cradled the back of her head—and this kiss made her heart spin right out of her chest. "How about now?"

"I'm pretty clear on the topic," she breathed.

"Good." He took her hand and brought it up to kiss her fingers, then he slid the corsage on. "It might be a little old-fashioned, but—"

"It's beautiful." She nervously toyed with the ribbon.

"You're beautiful." He held her hands out to the sides and looked her up and down and everywhere in between. "So fucking beautiful that if we didn't have plans I'd take you right here against the door."

Her legs trembled. "I'm sure a few minutes won't hurt."

His eyes darkened with interest, turning the color of waves crashing against sea cliffs. "What I want to do to you will take a hell of a lot longer than a few minutes." He kissed her roughly. "Plus, I'm wooing you, remember?"

"What comes next in this wooing, if it's not me?"

• • •

"I didn't think wooing involved coming to work," Evie said as they pulled up outside Grinder.

"I just have to run in and grab something really quick," he said, but he sounded nervous. Not the uncertain kind but the excited kind—the kind that turned her inside out.

Before she could argue he hopped out of the driver's side and she watched him walk his very fine ass around the front of the car and then he was at her door, holding it open. He reached in and took her hand, slowly easing her out and into his arms where he kissed her again. It was chaste and short—but it had passion. Toe-curling passion.

"I figured we'd start the day with one of those famous lattes I've heard about on LoveByte."

"You watch LoveByte?"

"Every episode where they talk about you," he said.

"You mean us," she corrected. "Remember I dragged you and your very private life into the spotlight."

"I remember," he said. "Have I thanked you for that?"

She tried to listen for any trace of sarcasm but couldn't find any. He was being serious. He was thanking her for bringing them together. At least that's what she thought he was saying. Before she could gain any further clarification on the subject, he led her into the shop—

Where everyone she knew stood looking at her with anticipation. And by everyone, she meant *everyone*. Her friends, her family, regulars, the You've Got Male-Mamas and You've Got Male-lorettes—even Tasha Hart, who was rolling tape as the event unfolded.

"Surprise!" they yelled in unison.

It was such a shock that Evie stepped back—right into a strong, supportive wall of muscle and yummy man. She looked at him over her shoulder. "What is this?"

"A celebration for all that you do for everyone," he said, and her eyes grew moist.

"You did this?"

"It was a team effort," he said modestly, downplaying his involvement like it was no big deal. But to her it was a gigantic deal.

"Thank you," she said quietly.

"Can I tell her?" Camila asked, and before she was given an answer, said, "We've made it to the top three of Denver's Best!"

"What?" Evie looked at her parents for confirmation. "Is it true?"

"I just got the email yesterday," Lenard said.

"You put this all together in a day?" she asked Jonah, who winked down at her.

"We're the first LGBTQ-owned coffeehouse ever nominated," Lenard added, and the crowd erupted into claps.

Evie walked over and gave him a hug. He held her tightly. "Dad, I'm so happy for you."

"Me?" He pulled back. "Sweetie, this is all because of you."

Evie was one word away from crying. This could be their saving grace. Their long shot. Business was already booming and they were finally making more than they were spending, and a good part of that was thanks to Jonah for helping her streamline the back end of the business and encouraging her to look at different options to really leverage the shop's name. Camila's ClickByte posts were getting traction, and even Moira's Get Grinding cards were helping to introduce new customers to their specialty coffee and beverages.

Then there were the You've Got Male groups who had grown into book clubs and lunch meetups, which had doubled the food side of the business. Grinder was, once again, the place to be.

"We *all* did this," Evie said, a little choked up.

"Your father and I know how much you've sacrificed to help us this past year," Moira said, tucking Evie's hair behind her ear like she used to when Evie was little.

"That's what family does," Evie said.

"Not all families," a man in his early thirties who could double as a Gap model said. Then he reached out a hand. "Abe. I'm with Moira."

Evie looked at her mom, who shrugged. "He's thirty-six, so technically he's over the age limit. And he's right. Very few people would give up what you have for their family. Which is why we're promoting Julie to general manager and hiring a new assistant manager."

She choked. "We can't afford that." She'd worked tirelessly to get them in the black and in one swoop her parents were going to land them back in trouble.

"We can now," Lenard said and looked at Jonah. "Seems your man here once managed the investments of the food and beverage buyer for the University of Colorado. Your mom and I met with him after the cheer competition and guess who is the new supplier for all the U of C campuses?"

Evie looked around the room and back at Jonah. "You did that for us?" she asked him.

"I did that for you," he clarified.

Her heart's response to that single word was to roll over and show its soft underbelly. "Why?"

He cupped her cheek. "Because you do a lot for the people in your life and I wanted someone to do something for you."

Her knees turned to vapor. "And that someone was you?"

"That someone was me," he whispered.

Chapter Thirty-Seven

Jonah

Jonah hadn't felt this right, this content in years. Watching Evie work the crowd, seeing how happy she was made by the outpouring of support had him wanting to make her happy every day. And if he played his cards right, that could be a reality.

But was he ready for that kind of reality? Evie's life was as full as a Thanksgiving plate at a buffet, which meant she could call it quits at any moment. Every person in his life had called it quits and it was a gut-hollowing feeling he never wanted to experience again. He should be protecting his heart instead of putting it on a silver platter for her to carve up.

But it was too late for that. Jonah was in too deep to find his way back. He just wasn't sure how deep Evie's feelings were. Oh, he knew she liked him, but did she think about him in terms of forever—like he did her?

Did you just say forever, man?

Tension crept up his spine, but he wasn't sure where it

originated from. Was he more afraid that they'd end things after their usefulness for each other came to a close, or that if she did bail he might not be able to come back from the loss?

"Hey," a sweet voice said as a gentle hand rested on his arm and all that tension evaporated at the feeling of her warm skin on his. Yeah, he had it bad.

"Hey," he said back, and without even thinking about it he pulled her in for a hug. A long cheek-rested-on-her-head, hands-spanning-as-much-of-her-back-as-possible kind of hug that was filled with equal parts question and promise.

She must have sensed the knot of emotions roiling in his stomach, because she tightened her arms around his back, locking her hands behind and pulling him flush to her so that not even air could penetrate their bond. That simple gesture was all the clarity he needed.

He didn't know when it happened or how it happened, but he loved her. The heart-and-soul kind of love that tied every string he had around this beautiful woman's heart. He was hers to save or destroy.

"Jonah?" she whispered, concern in her voice.

"I'm good," he said. So good he pulled back and gave her a kiss to prove it.

She smiled up at him. "Can you help me in the office? I need to get something really quick," Evie asked. "I can't seem to reach it."

Without letting him respond, which would have been a *hell yes*, she took his hand and led him through the crowd. They reached the back office and she rested back against the closed door.

"What do you need?" he asked.

He heard the lock engage, and when he turned there was a look in her eyes that made his dick twitch.

"I need to get lucky," she said. "We don't have long so this will have to be quick."

Heart strumming deep in his chest, he stalked toward her like she was prey. "Sunshine, there's nothing quick about it. It's going to be slow and long and so hard you'll collapse while screaming out my name."

"Screaming might attract attention and I don't want attention. I just want you."

"Just you and me?" he asked roughly.

"Just you and me."

She was killing him.

"Then I change my mind."

"What?" she whispered, uncertainty quivering in her voice.

"I don't want this hard. I want to worship you with my hands"—he cupped her cheek—"my tongue"—he gave her a long, languid kiss—"and my mouth," he whispered against her earlobe and felt her shiver. "I want to show you how you deserve to be cherished." He kissed down her jawline until they were eye to eye. "And I want to show you I'm the guy who can do that."

Her gaze never left his, but he could tell his statement scared her.

She swallowed. "What do you want from me?"

"Whatever you have to give."

"Even if I don't know what I can commit to yet?"

"I'd rather have ten minutes a week with you than nothing at all."

She licked her lips. "Okay."

That tension that had been pressing down between his shoulders released, and he let out a big breath. "Yeah?"

"Yeah. Now kiss me."

"I'm going to do more than that."

It took point-one seconds for him to get his mouth on hers.

As promised, he kept it languid and light, one kiss bleeding into the other until he didn't have a clue as to how much time had passed. All he knew was that when she wrapped her arms around him and pressed that soft body against his he felt like he'd finally come home.

"I like soft but right now I want hard and consuming."

"Let the consuming commence."

Jonah gripped her hips and walked her backward until she bumped into the edge of the desk. She put her hands on the ledge as if to boost herself up but he stopped her.

Instead, he spun her so she was pressed with her stomach to the desk and her ass nestled against his dick. "You want hard, then lift up that pretty dress of yours."

Her answer was to bend over the desk and look at him over her shoulder, which was sexy as hell. Always one to pull his weight, Jonah slid his hands up her thighs, under the hem of her dress, over her globes, until her ass was uncovered and all that was between them was a thin strap of—you guessed it—blue lace.

He ran his thumbs beneath the waistband and debated how he wanted to handle this. "We said 'Paint the town blue,' so the lace stays on." That didn't mean he wanted them all the way on. Oh no, his little seductress wanted to get dirty, so dirty he'd give.

He pulled the thong down to her ankles, and when she went to step out of them he stopped her. "Leave them there."

She didn't move. "Good girl. Now widen your stance until the lace is biting into your skin a little."

He kicked her feet out to the side and she gasped. "Now it's time to get lucky."

Jonah reached around and palmed her, using the heel of his palm to put pressure, then slid one finger inside her and... "Damn, baby, have you been like this the whole time?"

"Ever since I found your note."

"I've been rock hard ever since I saw you in those Gnope panties." He ran his fingers down her center and she was so slick he became impossibly harder. "Put your hands on the desk."

Even before her hands made contact, he slid two fingers inside her, and she gasped. He didn't waste time adding a third and she was so primed it didn't take long for her to start pushing back against his hand, riding it hard and fast.

"I'm almost there," she said, sounding surprised at the speed at which he'd driven her to the breaking point. "Yeah. I'm right—"

Jonah pulled out.

"What are you doing?"

"Sunshine, when you come, I'm going to be consuming you."

While he was talking he pulled a condom from his pocket and undid his pants. He was wrapped in seconds and, with one hand around her waist, the other protectively placed between her and the sharp edge of the desk, he positioned himself and drove forward.

"Fuck," he groaned.

He didn't mean to give such a deep first pump but she pushed back right as he was moving forward. When he hit full tilt, she moaned out his name and he stilled.

"Is that too hard?" he asked.

She looked at him over her shoulder. "Not hard enough."

With a grunt of approval, Jonah pulled back and thrust forward, deeper than he'd ever been. He didn't just want to consume her, he wanted to own her—body, heart, and soul.

He bucked again and again until her head fell to rest against the desk, allowing him to go even deeper. He was surrounded by her heated scent, her silky curves, and the softness that could only be described as feminine.

He moved in and out, loving how she kept trying to spread her legs farther but her panties were acting as a rope. The image she created was so sexy he was about to get off before her—and that was not acceptable.

Moving his thumb, he found her pleasure button and pressed down hard, then made soothing circular motions. She let out this sexy little sound, so he did it again.

He could feel her tighten around him, coiling and drenching him. His thumb pushed harder, then feather soft, bringing her right to the edge and then backing off. He paid attention to her as she moved, when she moaned, cataloging every little thing she liked, and what she loved.

And she was loving on his erection as if it were hers to conquer.

"I'm there. Oh God, I'm so there," she said in this raspy voice that did him in.

Her hips moved, raw and hungry, and when she parted her legs even more, he moaned a sigh of rightness. He took a moment to soak her in, breathe her air, taste her skin.

He was as desperate for release as she was, so he picked up the pace, pumping into her and swirling his thumb over her tender spot, going deeper until, just like that, she flew apart around him. Her body trembled with her release and her hips jerked back against him, and he lost it.

He pushed into her so deep that she had to dig her hands into the desk to support herself, and he could hear her thighs slapping against his with every thrust. The sound and the pressure were so right, so perfect, he detonated, moaning her name and pumping into her until he reached his last tremor.

He practically collapsed on top of her, putting his hands out to catch himself, but his chest was flush against her back, both of them slick with sweat. After some long gasps of breath, he straightened and lifted her up and sat her on the desk.

God, she was beautiful. Cheeks flushed, lips wet from his,

eyes sex-dazed, and her hair tousled like someone had their fist tangled in it. *His fist,* he realized with a grin.

Her thong slipped off her feet and fell to the floor. He picked it up and, after refastening his slacks, tucked it into his pocket. She lifted an amused brow.

"I want to know that you're naked and wet from me when we go back out there. Like our little secret."

At the word, she went quiet as if it didn't settle right. It didn't settle right with him, either. He was tired of their secret. He was tired of pretending that what was happening between them was nothing but a fling.

"What are we doing?" she asked quietly.

He rested his palms on either side of her thighs, bending over so that they were sharing space. "The truth?"

"That's what we promised each other."

His eyes fell to her lips and back up. "I think we're falling in love, sunshine."

He braced himself for her to throw those walls back up and hide from what he knew was the truth. Afraid that she wasn't ready to acknowledge it.

She cupped his face between her hands. "I think so, too."

Chapter Thirty-Eight

Evie

A new doubt popped into her mind for every flashcard she turned over.

Today was test day and Evie was a mess. So much rested on the outcome of a single test. It would decide where in her academic career she would start. As a junior or forced to take 101 classes to refresh before she could move on. It would determine how long it would take to earn that diploma and walk across that stage.

It would also determine how love was going to fit in her life. She hadn't meant to fall, she hadn't meant to even care, but she cared so much it was a physical ache when she wasn't with him. But feeling it and saying it were two different things. One scared her, the other terrified her—made something that was supposed to be straightforward into something that had so many strings it was a gigantic knot of emotion in her belly.

What have you done? Traded in every ounce of common

sense for complete chaos, that's what.

"Whoa, I know that look. What's going on in that head of yours?"

Evie looked up to find her parents standing at the counter, both looking concerned.

Moira was dressed in a silk robe with cream feathers down the trim and matching kitten heels that doubled as slippers. Her face was made up, her hair perfectly coifed, and her eyes were luminous. This was Moira in the morning.

Lenard was in rainbow-striped pajama bottoms and a shirt that read "GLAM-PA NOUN: /GLA`M/PAW. A REGULAR GRANDPA, JUST MORE FABULOUS."

Evie, on the other hand, was in the sweats and oversize T-shirt she'd slept in. Her hair a riot of curls and a hint of toothpaste on the corner of her mouth. But it was the bowling ball wedged in her gut that was the most obnoxious thing in the room.

Evie could play this one of two ways: pretend everything was fine—like she always did—or actually let the two people who loved her most in the world help. Between them they had thirty-five years of love. Perhaps strictly platonic and not the conventional. But her parents' relationship was one of the healthiest she knew. Maybe it was time she absorbed some of that knowledge that came from decades of wisdom.

Evie walked to the counter and sat on the stool. Dropping her notecards to the table, she said, "I think I blew it last night."

Moira snorted. "I bet Jonah woke up a very happy man."

"You knew?" Evie felt embarrassment creep up her cheeks.

"Honey, anyone who was a hundred yards from the office knew," Lenard said. "So, do I need to sterilize the desk?"

"Dad. Seriously?"

"Lenard," Moira chafed and Evie was happy to have at least one parent on her side. "Back to you and blowing."

Or not.

"I think I told Jonah that I was falling in love with him."

"You think, or you did?" Moira asked.

Moira's smile racked up some serious wattage and Lenard clapped his hands in front of his mouth. Evie covered her face. "I so did. I ruined it."

Moira placed a hand on Evie's. "Honey, the only way you can ruin love is if you aren't honest. With yourself or your partner."

She looked up. "I don't have time to take care of anyone else."

"Who are you taking care of?" Lenard asked. "Because from my point of view Jonah is a big, strapping, responsible man who can take care of himself."

Moira cupped her chin. "He isn't Mateo."

"I know. But I'm still me and I'm a control freak."

"That's another thing about love," Moira said. "You can't control it. It just happens."

"My whole life has been a series of 'just happeneds'."

"Honey, the best things in life come from love, but people try to control it to avoid a broken heart. A broken heart just leaves room for more love."

Was that what she was doing? Using Mateo as an excuse to avoid future heartache? But who's to say that heartache was the end result? Plus, her heart hurt even thinking about ending things with Jonah.

"Then why are you dating all of these incompatible men?" Evie asked.

Moira sighed. "I'm not looking for love."

"Mom, you have more capacity for love than anyone I know. Maybe it's time you let someone love you back."

"How did you get so smart?" Lenard asked.

Evie smiled. "I have these really amazing parents."

. . .

Anxiety set in with every passing moment. Every time a new student took a seat her heart thumped. Three people had mistaken her for the professor and, while she was dressed to impress, the others were dressed like they'd just rolled out of bed.

Then the professor walked in and— *Wait, was he old enough to be a professor?*

Evie had a good decade on him. Great, she was going to be judged by a guy who looked like a gamer and didn't know a world without the internet.

None of that matters! she reminded herself, pulling her shoulders back.

What mattered was she was taking that leap toward reaching her goals. And she'd leaped—in more ways than one. It was as terrifying as it was exhilarating. So what if she was older than everyone? Her life experience would give her an advantage. She'd been preparing for this day since she was forced to drop out of school sixteen years ago.

This was *her* time. *Her* chance to put herself first and accomplish her dreams.

It started with a test—which she could ace with her eyes closed. A test that would open the doors to a future she chose— instead of one that chose her. Not that she'd regretted a single decision over the past sixteen years, but she'd missed being a priority in her own life. And today was the first day in this new chapter—a chapter that was all hers. A chapter she never would have had the confidence to start if it hadn't been for Jonah's encouragement and support.

Jonah. Another thing in her life that was as terrifying as it was exhilarating because she was pretty sure she was, for the first time in her life, in love.

"Please take a test and Scantron and pass the rest back," the professor said, walking toward each row and handing Evie a package—because of course she was in the front. Gold-star, serious students sat in the front and she was serious as hell about getting off on the right foot.

Evie took one and handed the rest to the kid behind her who—

Are you freaking kidding me?

"Dexter?"

"Hey, Mrs. G," he said, like she was the team parent who brought the orange slices to the game. "What are you doing here?"

"Taking the placement exam. Same as you."

"Cool." Dexter looked around, then lowered his voice. "It's an invite only, but this frat I'm rushing is having a day-ger."

"A day-ger?"

"Yeah, like a rager, but during the day. Anyway, you should come. Just tell them Dex sent you."

"Um, thanks."

"Sure thing, Mrs. G."

Evie turned back around, wondering what kind of quantum-realm nightmare she'd just entered. She didn't have time to process the moment because the professor said, "Calculators, cell phones, laptops, and any other kind of device need to stay in your bags at all times. If I see one, you fail. If I see you talking, you fail. If I see you looking at your neighbor's papers, you fail. Understood?"

"Yes," Evie said brightly, then realized the question must have been rhetorical because no one else spoke up.

"You have three hours to finish the exam. When you are done, set them on the podium and quietly exit. Your scores will be on your University Portal next week. Begin."

Evie licked the tip of her finger, then opened to the first page. It was the English section—which was her strongest skill. She breezed through the first part of the test, no problem. Then she got to the math section and felt a sigh of relief. They didn't have to show their work, which meant she could use logical math, not this fancy new math Camila's generation invented.

She'd just answered her first equation when her phone vibrated in her purse. She looked around to make sure no one heard it, and the professor pointed to his eyes, then hers. Evie swallowed hard and put her eyes back on her own paper.

It vibrated again. And again.

Six times in a row the phone went off.

The professor locked gazes with her. "Can you please turn off your phone?"

"Will I fail?"

"You will if you don't stop the disturbance. A quick in and out, no looking at the screen."

Evie gave a decisive nod and took her phone out. She didn't mean to look at the screen, she really didn't but Waverly's preschool's number flashed and her heart went triple rhythm.

"I am so sorry." Evie took her phone and approached the podium. "I just need to get this."

"The rules were clear."

"Can you make an exception? This might be an emergency."

"No phones. No exceptions. If you're going to answer you need to do it outside."

Evie nodded. "I'll be right back."

"Once the tests are handed out no one is to leave the room."

The phone blew up again.

"What if I have to use the restroom?" she asked.

"Then you may go, but all devices must stay in your bag. And your bag must stay in this room."

"But it might be—"

"No exceptions, ma'am."

"Did you just *ma'am* me?"

For the first time the professor looked uncertain. That smug entitlement vanished and what was left behind was likely a teacher's aide.

"One day, you are going to be in this same situation and I hope the gatekeeper to your dreams isn't a raging asshole."

Evie picked up her purse and exited the room. Her palms were sweating, her heart heavy with disappointment. But if this was an emergency, she couldn't ignore it. It rang again and Evie swiped to answer.

"Hello?"

"Evie Granger?" a frantic voice said.

She cupped her phone to her ear and started toward her car. "This is her."

"Hi, I'm calling from Waverly's school. She is running a fever and has been throwing up. We can't seem to get ahold of her father and you are listed as her emergency contact. We need you to come in right now."

Chapter Thirty-Nine

Jonah

It was after three by the time Jonah pulled into his driveway. Evie's car was nowhere to be seen but he knew she was home. Well, at his home. The four unanswered calls and texts from her explained as much—not to mention the messages from the preschool. The high from signing on as a partner at the new firm was squashed under the guilt thumping in his chest.

He'd been so caught up in playing the big man that he'd let the important things slip through the cracks. Evie assured him in her message that Waverly was okay, just a little tummy bug, but he could tell by the defeat in her voice that everything was not okay. In fact, it was as far from okay as things could get.

Today was her placement exam. He knew this. Knew that Waverly was a little fussy when he'd dropped her at school but had chalked it up to typical two-year-old crankiness. He hadn't even checked her forehead for a fever—which she'd apparently had.

The drive home was, unquestionably, the worst half-hour of his life.

Wanting to appear like he had it all together, Jonah had put his phone on silent for the duration of the meeting. What kind of single dad does that? One who was pretending to have his shit together when in reality his world was still tilted far off axis—and it was derailing the lives of the people he cared about.

Grabbing his phone and briefcase, he strode up the walkway and into the house.

"Evie?" he called out.

He heard the television coming from the back of the house and followed it to the family room. This time his chest thumped for a different reason all together.

Evie was curled up on the couch in a pair of fitted jeans and no shoes, looking adorable and comfy, like a safe harbor in the midst of a storm. Nestled in her arms, fast asleep, was his baby girl. Cheeks flushed while clutching her favorite bear, Waverly looked comfortable, content—safe.

Remarkable, considering what a day they both must have had. Even more remarkable was Evie, managing her world in a way that he'd never achieved on even his best days. She was calm and capable, her confident energy giving Waverly the security she craved.

Hell, seeing her like this, with his daughter in her arms, gave Jonah the security he craved. Something inside him rolled over as a wealth of relief took hold. It had been a while since someone had his back. Only his relief had come at someone else's expense.

Shit.

Today only added to his greatest fear: that he wasn't enough on his own.

Evie had yet to notice him, so he stood silently in the threshold, breathing in the moment as she smoothed back

Waverly's baby-fine hair and brushed a kiss over her forehead. Watching the motherly gesture tugged at the core of his heart.

Jonah realized that, while he'd worked hard to be part of his kids' lives, when Amber had been alive he'd been on the periphery. As the working parent in his marriage, he'd struggled to find a balance between being breadwinner and parent. When he'd become a single dad the pendulum had swung in the opposite direction. Either way he couldn't cut it and came up short. But that wasn't an option anymore. His kids needed stability and structure, and it was up to him to provide those.

Kicking off his shoes, he padded over to the couch. Evie looked up and damn she was beautiful. The kind of beautiful that had a heart-rending tenderness taking over his body.

"Hey," he whispered, sitting on the coffee table in front of her so that he could read every emotion on her face. Unfortunately, she was carefully schooled.

"Hey," she said. Her tone was hard to decipher, but her body language spoke volumes. It reminded him of the way strangers looked at him when Waverly had a meltdown in public.

He reached out and ran a hand over his baby's cheek. It was sticky and warm. "How is she?"

"She'll be okay. I'm pretty sure it's just a tummy bug."

"Thank you for today." He took Evie's hand but she didn't hold his back. In fact, she just let it hang there loosely. Not a good sign. "I'm so sorry this fell on you."

"Can we talk," she said, then situated Waverly on the couch and stood. They walked to the kitchen.

"First, let me tell you how sorry I am for how this all went down."

"You already apologized."

"Well, I need to do it again," he said.

She wrapped her arms around her stomach as if it hurt.

"What happened?"

"I had the meeting with Curt and his partner, and I put my phone on silent and left it in my briefcase. I didn't even hear it buzz." He searched her eyes. "How was the test?"

"I wouldn't know, I got a call in the middle of it and had to leave."

"Will they let you make it up?"

"Sure. Next year."

"Jesus, Evie. I really fucked up. If I'd known this would happen, I would have left my phone on. This day was really important for me."

That was the wrong thing to say because any openness she had vanished and all those walls snapped into place. "Today was important for me."

"I know." He reached for her hand but she backed away.

"Do you? Because they only offer this test in the fall, which means I have to put off school for another year."

"Maybe I can call them, explain that there was a family emergency—"

"There aren't any do-overs, Jonah," she said, sounding weary. Up close he could see how tired she was, how the creases around her eyes were deep with discouragement and resignation. "This is just the reality. My reality. You made a decision that suited you and it blew up my plan."

NO. The guilt hit him like a punch to the stomach. She'd had so many people derail her life. How could he have let this happen? He hated that he was just another in a long line of people who'd put her last.

"I don't know how to fix this," he said, cupping her cheek. "Tell me how to fix this."

"You can't. I get why you did it. But the end result is the same. I can't carry any more weight, Jonah."

"You don't have to carry me, sunshine."

"Today tells me I do. I've been carrying people my whole life, and for once I wanted someone to carry me."

"Then let me," he said quietly.

That's when the first tear lined her lash and his gut hollowed out. "I'd rather do it alone than risk being dropped again."

"What are you saying?"

She shook her head and that tear fell. Followed by another and another. "I can't do this anymore."

He had to take a moment to decipher what she was saying. Yesterday, she'd told him she was falling in love and today she was suddenly done.

"That's it?" he asked roughly. "One mistake and you're calling it quits?" It was as if he were right back in that moment when Amber told him she didn't want to be part of the medical trial. She chose to leave him rather than fight. And Evie was doing the same thing.

"Both of us knew that this was never going to last."

"That's bullshit and you know it."

She wiped angrily at her cheeks. "Maybe at one point I believed that it could be more, but more can't exist when there isn't any room left. There's no room for you in my world, Jonah."

"Then let's try to make some room."

"I'm tired of waiting for something to change. The only way I'm going to make my life better is to change how I'm going about it. Plus, this was never real, remember?"

And that was the stake through his heart that he'd been dreading. "This is as real as it gets for me," he said. "I love you, Evie."

She shook her head and stepped back. "Love shouldn't mean giving up parts of yourself for it to work." She went up on her toes and gave him a gentle kiss on the cheek. "I can't do that anymore, and we both agreed that if it wasn't working we'd reassess."

"Yeah, reassess how to make it work."

"It can't work, and the longer we ignore the truth the worse it will be when we finally do."

The air vacated his lungs and filled him with panic. He was losing her. He could feel it in his soul. "So what are you saying? We go back to being neighbors separated by a fence who argue over a fucking tree that overlaps some invisible easement?"

She blinked and fresh tears fell. Each one like a lance to his heart. "Trees that are growing and thriving and shadowing my life. Trees that bring rodents to my yard and mess up my efforts to grow and nurture and cultivate. Trees that leave lasting marks on the sidewalk that even a power washer can't fix. My life has so many marks, most days I can't even see the light, let alone get enough to bloom," she whispered. "I love your family, and I loved you so much that I was willing to walk away from myself again."

He took her hands. "Love, sunshine. Present tense. Please say it's present tense."

"Love isn't always enough, Jonah. Not the kind of love that makes you choose between yourself and everyone else."

"I choose you." His plea barely pushed through the emotion clogging his throat. "I'll choose you every moment of every day if you'll let me."

"But you can't," she whispered hoarsely. "We both have a long list of people who have to come first, and they deserve to come first."

"What about us? What about what we deserve?"

Her fingers slipped from his and no matter how fast his hands chased them it wasn't fast enough. "We deserve to spread our wings as far as they can go. I need to spread my wings." She took a baby step closer and went up on her toes. "And you need to spread yours."

The pain in this moment was like a living thing, consuming the air between them.

He regarded her silently. "So that's it. You tell me you love me and the minute we hit a speed bump you want me to pull the car over so you can get out?"

"Would you rather me get out now while we can still walk away in one piece, or wait until we crash into a brick wall?"

She watched the roll of his throat as he swallowed. "So I don't get a say? That's not how love works."

"But that's how our agreement works."

"Agreement? Are you even hearing what you're saying?" he asked, and it felt like his hands were gripping the bottom of her heart. "This isn't some project you can compartmentalize, someone's life you can organize and stick in a closet. This is real life, and real life is messy and complicated and exciting and alive. You make me feel alive."

"So do you, but eventually our obligations will kill whatever we have, and I'd rather have you in my life than not have you at all."

He expelled a short, humorless laugh. "Don't do this, sunshine."

"I don't know what else to do to protect us both."

The air between them was filled with hurt and disappointment. And worst of all, betrayal. She'd betrayed his trust and his heart. "I'm not going to stand here and beg for you to choose me. I can't do that again."

"But I am choosing you, and one day you'll understand. I just hope until then you don't hate me." She gave him a kiss that shattered what was left of the organ in his chest. Ripped it out and let it crash to the ground. Just like what his life felt like. A giant puzzle with pieces that would forever be missing.

Chapter Forty

Evie

Evie was back in her work uniform but for some reason it felt heavier today—suffocating. Similar to what was happening inside her chest. She hadn't been able to take a deep breath for three days—ever since the breakup.

If breaking up was even a thing when they were never officially together—not really. What had started out as a ruse quickly turned into an experiment of compatibility, and eventually companionship—a sweet and tender companionship unlike anything she'd ever experienced. But in the end their lives were as compatible as orange juice and toothpaste. Their schedules clashed, they were in different phases of parenthood, they couldn't agree on the same wine—even their yards were at war.

The most heart-wrenching of all? There was no way to fix it. It wasn't like he could stop being a dad or she could stop taking care of a family that was always on the brink of chaos.

They didn't fit. And she should have seen it from the

beginning. It would have saved them both a lot of hurt. And she'd hurt Jonah, it had been in every inch of his expression. The way his forehead had caved with confusion, his brows sunken with sadness, and his jaw had clenched hard with heartache. Then there were his eyes, pleading and full of pain and promise. So much promise that she had nearly given in, but then she'd thought of how much pain would come when one of those promises was, yet again, broken. And there would be many. It was inevitable.

The end had been inevitable from the very start. A hard fact she needed to accept.

But she couldn't think about that today. Today was the final vote for Denver's Best official announcement. The winner would be in the paper, on local television, even Tasha Hart was coming out in support to help spread the news of, what had been nicknamed, Cupid's Official Coffee House. And rumor had it that Grinder was a serious contender. She just had to charm the judges with their signature drinks, family-like atmosphere, and supportive community.

If you believed ClickByte, rumor also had it that Jonah was going to either: 1) ask her to go to Paris with him, 2) ask her to move in, or 3) ask her to be his wife. Little did they know Jonah wasn't even going to be there. And by rumors, she meant polls. There were actual ongoing polls, which she was certain Moira was behind.

What a mess she'd made. No one knew about the breakup, and she hoped to keep it that way, at least until after the ribbon cutting tomorrow. Then she'd come clean, not about the ruse, but about the breakup. If people found out she'd lied it could ruin everything—including Grinder's standing in the community.

Terrifying as it was, she was going to fess up to her family. She was talking the truth, the whole truth, and nothing but the truth. They deserved that. But she'd never let her lapse in judgment endanger her parents' shop.

Evie was parked in the alleyway that paralleled the side of Grinder, and through the side window of the coffee shop, Evie could see her family and the staff zipping about in preparation for Denver's Best judges, who were supposed to arrive between eight and ten. Refilling sugar dispensers, setting out fresh cream, stocking the pastry cabinet. She should be in there helping, but instead she'd been in her car trying to cover up her dark circles and bloodshot eyes with makeup and eyedrops.

She glanced in the rearview mirror and groaned. "I give up."

It would take a cargo van full of product to make her look presentable, which was why she'd taken the last three days off, claiming she was sick. And she was sick—lovesick for a man with whom there was no future.

She snapped her compact closed and thought about turning tail and heading home, where she'd crawl back into bed and hide under the comforter with a container of her mom's snickerdoodles. The amount of energy it was going to take to fool everyone into believing her heart wasn't torn in two seemed insurmountable. But it was all hands on deck, and people were counting on her. She wasn't about to let them down because she'd chosen the easy way out.

That wasn't the Evie way.

She laid her head back against the headrest and stared out the sunroof. October was flexing, with rustling yellow and red leaves, bright blue skies dotted with a few scattered clouds drizzling down on the town that was slowly coming to life. One last time she allowed herself to fall into the past few weeks, remember the deep conversations and even deeper connection, the kissing, the flirty notepad exchanges, that first time they'd made love.

Every memory was fueled with emotion and affection—so much affection it spilled over into other parts of her life. Scratch that. It had spilled over into every part of her life, leaving marks that would never disappear. They might fade over time, but they'd always be there.

There was a tap on her window and she nearly jumped out of the sunroof. Hand to her heart, she turned her head and her stomach sank. A tiny part of her had hoped it was Jonah, there to tell her that he couldn't let her walk. That he'd miraculously found a way for this all to work—for Evie to chase her dreams, be there for her family, and still have time to devote to their relationship. And love.

But love, she'd learned from distant and not-so-distant history, didn't seem to fit into her schedule. So when she saw Julie's nose-pierced face pressed against the window, she let out a sigh of equal parts relief and disappointment.

Evie rolled down the window.

"You want to tell me why you're sitting out in your car looking like someone shit in your best handbag?"

Before Evie knew what was happening, tears that she thought had long ago dried up resurfaced, leaving her blurry and uncertain of what was in front of her.

"Okay, scoot over," Julie said, opening the door and shoving Evie over until they were sharing the same seat. She slammed the door shut and the console shanked Evie in the ribs. "I knew you weren't sick."

"How?" Evie asked through a few stray sniffles.

"Best friends know these things. Plus, you have never called in sick. Not even to play hooky, which is a damn waste of the general manager title if you ask me."

"Or it's the responsible thing to do."

Julie rolled her eyes. "Responsible is something sad people say."

"Or something successful people say."

Julie looked at Evie's shirt and snorted. "You're wearing a shirt that says 'Good Morning,' I Whisper to My Latte. It doesn't quite have that cover of *Time* magazine vibe. Plus, I saw Jonah at the market last night."

At the sound of his name, adrenaline jump-started her pulse, kicking her brain into hyper speed. "You saw Jonah?"

"In the flesh."

"Did he say anything?" Evie asked, going for unaffected, although her body was affected as hell by the mere mention of his name.

"Didn't have to. He looked like roadkill."

Evie didn't know if that made her feel better or worse, that he was as messed up as she was. "But did he say anything?"

"Yeah, like, I said, 'Good to see you,' to which he grunted. I said, 'How's it hanging.' He said, 'South.' Then he said something about screwing up and needing to make it right."

"He can't make it right," Evie heard herself say.

"Why not?"

"Because the only way for this to work would mean one or both of us giving up our dreams," she said, although she felt like she'd already given up on one. "This is all your fault, by the way." She poked Julie in the arm.

"Ow." Julie poked back. "And how am I the dream stealer?"

"Because"—she emphasized with another poke—"you"—poke, poke—"just couldn't stay out of my dating life." Poke, poke, poke.

"Before me you didn't have a dating life."

"Exactly! And I was fine. Now I'm in the same spot, just miserable."

Julie's expression softened. "You dumped Jonah?"

"How do you know I broke it off? Who's to say he didn't do the dumping?"

"The fact that he's looking for solutions and you're sticking to the whole martyr complex."

"I might have a superhero complex but I'm not a martyr."

Evie had never complained to her family about the sacrifices she'd made. Ever. She just kept her head down and pushed forward. In fact, the only person she'd been completely honest with about being stretched thin was Jonah.

"Nah, superheroes are brave in the face of fear. When it comes to yourself, you're fearful of anything remotely brave."

"Are you saying I'm a coward?"

Julie pulled a brush out of the glove box, which meant she had to lean across Evie, elbowing her in the boob. "I'm saying that you've gone through some rough experiences that would make any sane person afraid to dip their toes into the love lagoon. But love doesn't have to end badly."

"He made me miss my placement exam, Jules," Evie whispered. "He made an irresponsible choice and, mistake or not, it derailed my life. And I'm tired of other people skidding into my lane and then saying, 'Whoops, sorry about totaling your car, but I was on the phone.'"

"What if he had the blinker on the whole time and was trying to merge, but you were so busy keeping your eyes forward that you missed the signals?"

Oh, she'd missed them all right. Maybe that's why they had collided instead of merging, because she was in the carpool lane with a family who refused to put on their safety belts. And Jonah's car wasn't any safer. In fact, even with his third row they couldn't fit both their families into a single vehicle.

"Do you want it to work?" Julie asked quietly.

"Yes, but I can't see it happening right now. I just don't have enough to give and I'm not willing to let my life slip through the cracks for a man again."

"Too bad," Julie said.

Evie blinked. "That's it? Too bad? That's your advice?"

"If he made you choose between your own needs and his,

then you did the right thing."

"Then why does it hurt so bad?" Evie whispered.

"Because you love him," Julie said, pulling her into a hug. "I saw it at the bar."

"Do you think everyone saw it?" And by "everyone" she wondered if that included Jonah. Yes, she'd told him she loved him, then she'd walked away as if her heart wasn't breaking. But did he see it, feel it like she did?

"I think the people who mattered saw it."

Julie ran the brush through Evie's hair and began styling it.

"What are you doing?"

"You've got a hundred or so people who are waiting to see the famous You've Got Male girl, who are here to cast their final vote for Denver's Best. There's already a crowd of people who have gathered inside. And there are even people waiting outside, since the fire marshal threatened to come out if we allowed more than our maximum capacity in today."

"Seriously?" Evie squinted and peered through the side window of Grinder and looked through the shop. She caught a glimpse of a herd of brightly colored umbrellas huddled near the front door, which was around the corner on Main Street.

"They've been there since six. Asking for you."

Evie craned her neck farther. "But it's raining."

"Not even Zeus could take on Cupid at this point."

"Until everyone finds out that we broke up. Then the Greek Goddess Pheme will have her way and people will be talking about the poor broken-hearted sap who gave love a try only to have her life hijacked."

"Well, then let's reclaim it. And when people talk, and they will, you just keep your chin up and say it wasn't meant to be but you're still open to finding love."

"Even if I'm not?"

"Especially then. Otherwise everyone will know you've still got it bad for the irresponsible prince next door." Julie pinched Evie's cheeks. "Fake it till you make it, babe."

Fake it till you make it. That was going to be Evie's new motto.

Julie gave Evie's hair a final fluff, then sat back and looked at her handiwork. "That will have to do." She opened the door and stepped out, then yanked Evie to her feet. Her hair immediately frizzed on contact with the drizzle.

"What are we doing?"

"We're going to greet your waiting fans, celebrate how well Grinder is doing, and blow those judges' cocks off."

"You mean socks off?"

"Tom*ay*to. Tom*ah*to. Now let's go show them what a woman who is taking charge of her destiny looks like."

For the first time since the breakup, Evie felt something other than debilitating pain. In fact, she felt powerful. Like her future was hers to define. The closer she got to the shop, the higher her shoulders rose until that martyr was replaced with a superhero.

Too bad it only lasted ten seconds.

"Mom." Camila came rushing over, her face pale and her eyes watery. "I didn't mean to. I mean, I didn't think... Kira saw Ryan and me holding hands and the team made a big deal about how he could be my stepbrother so I told them..." She broke off in a sob. "I told them..."

"Hey." Evie took her daughter by the shoulders. "Whatever it is, we can fix it."

"We can't fix this. I told them you and Jonah were a lie."

It was as if the entire world slowed to a halt, so suddenly Evie lost her balance and nearly fell flat on her face. Her lungs stopped working and her skin felt too tight to contain all the emotions racing through her body. Panic being the biggest offender.

"It wasn't true?" Julie asked, her voice so confused Evie had to work hard to swallow. "You lied to me?"

"I didn't want to, it just kind of happened and—"

"We're here with Evie from You've Got Male," Tasha Hart said, rushing down the street and shoving her phone in Evie's face. "LoveByte Nation and ClickByte subscribers want to know if it's true."

A bad feeling started in the pit of her belly. "Is what true?"

"Did you fabricate a relationship as a publicity stunt to win Denver's Best?"

The blood left her face and she felt lightheaded. "What?"

"A source close to the family went on record saying that you and Jonah were never dating. It was all a big ruse."

Evie looked at Camila, who was crying. Julie, who looked betrayed. And the crowd of "supporters," who now looked like an angry mob. Then there were her parents, holding on to each other as if they needed the support.

"It wasn't a publicity stunt." But now that she viewed it from an outsider's perspective, that's exactly what it looked like.

"But was it real?" Tasha pressed.

Evie could keep the lie going, which would make Camila look like the liar. And then when they found out that Jonah and Evie ended their relationship the day of the judging it would look staged. What had she gotten herself into?

She found her parents, standing at the front door of the shop, their eyes locked on Evie's, so much betrayal and disappointment in their expressions it was too hard to look at them. But she knew what they were thinking. Not only had she lied to them, her lie could cost them the shop. And lying would only make things worse.

"Yes. It started as a partnership to get everyone off my back about dating, but—"

"So you admit you were playing us all?"

"That wasn't my intention, but I can see how that would…"

Go for honest, Evie. "Yes, I was playing everyone."

A collective gasp went up and Evie felt those once-again high shoulders sink with regret and a good dose of shame.

"Well, you heard it here folks, You've Got Male was a marketing hoax—"

"I never said that—"

"Preying on the innocent romantics of the world. Cupid's Coffee House doesn't sell love. It sells lies. And I can assure you that this is one unsatisfied customer who will be taking my caffeine needs elsewhere."

"Tasha," she called out, but Tasha was already packing up her things and heading toward the parking lot, taking with her the crowd that had turned out to see if true love was real. And left heavy hearted.

Join the club.

"Evie," a pain-filled voice said from behind. Evie turned and it was Alex from the You've Got Male-Mamas. She had a baby popped on one hip and a toddler by the hand. "Is it really true? You didn't find your prince?"

"It looks like I didn't," Evie said, but something in her heart wanted to argue.

"You know, we all looked up to you. Believed that if it could happen for a single mom like you then maybe it could happen for us, too."

"And it still can," Evie said encouragingly. "Just because I shortcut the system doesn't mean that you did. You and Ernie seem like a really good match."

"Excuse me," a man in a suit holding a clipboard said. "I'm David from Denver's Best and we're here to check out the famous Cupid's Coffee."

Fuck. Her lie hadn't just hurt the people around her. It had the power to destroy her parents' shop.

Chapter Forty-One

Evie

The next day, Evie woke with the strangest feeling that she was being watched. The hairs on the back of her neck registered that it was more than one set of eyes staring at her.

"Did I sleep through my alarm?" she asked, her voice scratchy—the product of a night spent sobbing. Not only had Tasha taken the crowd with her, not a single customer had walked through Grinder's doors for the rest of the day.

Okay, that was an exaggeration. A few people had walked in wanting to know if it was true and when Evie confirmed that it was, they left sans coffee. Then there were her parents, who were avoiding her—or was she avoiding them? Didn't matter, the end result was the same: they hadn't had the conversation that was like a giant weather balloon filling the house, ready to pop at the first sharp word.

"Nope," Lenard said. "Figured you were already awake."

She hadn't gotten a wink of sleep last night, but it upped the guilt factor that her parents hadn't, either. She knew the talk needed to be had, but she couldn't face it until after the sun came up.

"Can we talk about this after I have some coffee?" she asked.

The light flicked on—answer enough.

Evie groaned and put the pillow over her face. It was immediately snatched away. Then she smelled the warm aroma of caffeine wafting beneath her nose.

"Coffee for one," Moira said.

Evie opened her eyes to find her parents sitting on the edge of her bed like they used to when she was a teen and got caught sneaking out. She'd considered just that scenario last night. Packing her backpack and climbing through the window, hitchhiking to California and starting a new life under an assumed name. But her dad would be able to smell the guilt from a thousand miles away.

With a groan, she sat up. Her head throbbed, her lids were scratchy when she blinked, and that cold, empty feeling that had settled in her bones now felt like frostbite.

"I'm so sorry," she began. "So, so sorry about what happened yesterday. I never meant for things to go this far, and now I've put the shop in even more trouble. And that I put our chances of Denver's Best in jeopardy."

Lenard and Moira exchanged looks, then Moira took her hand. "Honey, we don't care about some stupid contest."

"I do," Evie said and, again, there were exchanged looks. "I promised you guys that I would make Grinder a success again and I blew it."

Moira held one hand and Lenard the other, but it was Moira who spoke first. "The day you were born we made a promise as parents to take care of you, but lately we've been letting you take care of us."

"I don't mind. It's my turn," Evie said and meant it from the depths of her soul. "You guys took care of me when I got pregnant, then Camila when she was born. You're still her biggest champions."

"That's because we're her grandparents, not because you two are some kind of obligation. Love could never be an obligation."

At the word love, Evie's chest went on hiatus and refused to take in oxygen. It was as if the mile-high kite had reached new elevations and the air was too thin to breathe. She knew she'd made the responsible choice, but it didn't mean that she didn't feel the loss with every breath.

"Love isn't always easy, but it should be treasured and protected, no matter the circumstances." Lenard leaned down and kissed her on the forehead. "And we should protect the ones we love, and we didn't protect you. We took advantage of your generous spirit. You have always been so happy to do for others that you rarely let people do for you."

"But you needed me," she assured them.

"Now, you need us."

"I'm okay," she whispered.

"If you were, you wouldn't have spent the past few days locked in your room crying," Moira said.

"And you wouldn't have felt the need to lie to us," Lenard said.

"I shouldn't have lied but—"

"We weren't listening," Moira said. "In our quest to make you happy, you got your heart broken."

"It just wasn't my time."

"Oh baby," Moira whispered. "Time isn't ever ours unless we take it. You deserve to be happy, and I think Jonah made you happy."

He had. He really had. Until he hadn't. In her head she knew

Jonah hadn't set out to sabotage her plans, but her heart was having a hard time getting past being forced to walk away from her dream once again.

But had she been forced? And if the roles were reversed, and it was Camila in trouble, wouldn't he have done the same thing? Undoubtedly yes. Just look at how he'd dropped everything to drive her and her teammates to camp, or how he'd made her dinner for no reason other than to be nice. He listened to her, really heard what she was saying, and then went out of his way to do nice things for her.

Like the corsage and surprise party. And instead of showing her appreciation, at the first hint of complication she had bailed. Just like everyone else in his life.

Wait.

Oh God!

"You want to talk about it?" Lenard asked.

"I told him I loved him and then blamed him when life attacked. Just like Mateo bailed when he realized being a young parent wasn't all about going to Disneyland and bragging rights."

"Sometimes, it seems easier to protect ourselves from the possible fallout of love, when in reality, finding love is what makes it bearable when the bottom falls out," Lenard said.

"Take your dad and I. We were both in so much pain from the divorce that we wouldn't have been able to bounce back. The only reason we did is because we had each other to lean on, had the love and friendship to protect us."

"Your mom could've walked away the minute I told her I was gay, but instead she put the hurt aside and embraced me."

"I think you're forgetting when I burned your Gucci collection."

Lenard winced. "I still think about those vintage ties." He sighed. "The point is, we promised each other that we would always be in each other's lives. No matter how hard life became."

"When you find your soulmate, platonic or otherwise, hold on to it with everything you have because you've only got one," Moira said.

"How could he be the one?" Evie asked, but her heart was suddenly clear on where it stood. "We have nothing in common except for that we have nothing in common. I told myself if I ever got serious with a man again he'd be emotionally mature and available, with a life that meshes with mine, and would have his shit together."

"Sweetie." Lenard laughed. "You work with your gay father, cougar of a mother, boy-crazy teen, and sleep in a room that has boy band stickers on the walls. But you also live surrounded by love and people who would do anything to protect your happiness."

"Even if it means sticking their noses in my dating life?" Evie asked.

"Apparently someone needs to," Moira said. "Left to your own devices you dragged your friend's widower into a fake relationship, lied to your family and friends, pulled one over on America, kept him a secret, then dumped him when your priorities didn't align."

"When you say it like that, I sound like an asshole."

"Everyone is the asshole at one time or another," Lenard said with a waggle of his brow.

Evie smoothed her hands over the comforter. "I just don't want to get further down the road and realize that it could never work."

"Don't let this checklist you've created in your head be a shield between you and love. Because while love takes some sacrifice, the lifetime of joy is worth it. But you've built up these walls that are so thick and high no one could possibly climb them.

And that includes you, dear."

She wanted to argue that Jonah had. He hadn't just scaled them, he'd taken them down brick by brick. Only she didn't have the courage to step across that line. Suddenly, her foundation turned to quicksand.

"What do I do?" she asked as an idea slowly took shape, blurring her vision. "I don't know what to do."

"Do you love him?" Moira asked.

"So much I can't breathe."

"Then let the world know it," Lenard said.

For the first time in days, elation bubbled up in her chest. "I love him," she repeated. "And know just how to tell him. I know how to fix everything. But I'm going to need help. Lots of people's help. Oh, and I think it's time for that blue dress."

Chapter Forty-Two

Jonah

Jonah sat on the back deck, staring off into the distance. He saw none of the freshly planted flowers overflowing in the raised beds, or the new shrubs that lined the fence and side yard. He saw nothing but blurred, empty space—kind of like what was carved into his chest.

He'd been in a zombie-like state since Evie had chosen the easy way, leaving him with the cold hard truth—his love wasn't worth fighting for. He'd been here before—twice—but this time had wrecked him beyond repair. He still felt the marks her words left with every breath he took.

Today was the walk-through with the Beautification Board. She hadn't come. Evie hadn't even shown up to see the finished product of what they'd grown together, making it more than clear that being with him was too much of a sacrifice. That a life without his love was easier to accept than the baggage that came with his world.

He knew he'd messed up—big time. But not big enough to justify her walking away. He'd been tempted to call her a thousand times, but he'd meant what he'd said. He couldn't fight for another person who would rather leave than work things out.

Every word of hers had turned into fists, socking him in the chest, over and over, leaving his heart bruised and battered. Unlike bruises, though, these would never fully heal.

With a growl, he walked down the slate path and out into the front yard to hear the final outcome of the Beautification Board's ruling. He didn't want to hear it. He didn't want to hear anything that reminded him of Evie. It was as if the sun had been extinguished from parts of his soul and they'd never feel the warmth again.

But he needed to get it together. He couldn't put his kids through another downward spiral. They deserved better.

With that last thought, he walked through the gate and came to a full and complete halt. The crowd had doubled. His front lawn had more senior citizens than Thursday night bingo. It smelled like fresh-cut grass, Werther's caramel candy, and Bengay. And they all looked as if they were about to burst with news.

"Do you need to check out the backyard as well?" he asked.

"No," Mrs. Gomez said. "The board only has oversight of what is visible from the street. And what you've done is just lovely, dear. Amber would be so happy to see her flower-lined walkway again and the shrubs are quite the statement. You went above and beyond."

Before he could stop himself, he said, "I had help."

Confusion tinted Mrs. Gomez's expression. "We know. Which is why we're surprised you're here."

Now it was his turn to be confused. "Of course I'd be here. Where else would I be?"

"At the coffee shop," she said, and mumbles of agreement

wafted up from the crowd.

"Why the hell would I be there?" That's the last place on the planet he'd be...unless they didn't know. Secrets were a commodity in their neighborhood, so he'd just assumed that word had traveled of their breakup.

Shit.

He ran a hand down his face. He did not want to explain his personal life to a bunch of busybodies, especially since their fake relationship and subsequent breakup had played out for America to see. "I wanted to be here to hear your decision."

Neighbors turned to each other in quiet conversation, and it was as if everyone was in on the secret but him.

"What's going on?" he asked.

"We're guessing you haven't been following Tasha Hart on LoveByte."

"Why would I?" The only reason he had for logging onto ClickByte was to see Evie. The first thing he'd done after the breakup was to delete the fucking app.

"I think there's something you need to see," Mr. Karlson said, walking over to him. He pulled out his phone, opened the app, and searched for @YouveGotMale, then handed him the device.

His breath caught painfully in his chest when he saw Evie's face on the screen. She was standing in front of Grinder wearing that blue dress he'd seen in her room all those weeks back. Her hair was hanging in long, silky waves, she was worrying her lower lip, and there was this vulnerable expression that got to him. She was so beautiful it hurt just to look at her.

Only, he couldn't explain what was happening, but something a whole hell of a lot like hope flickered in his chest.

"Hi," she began and her voice wobbled. "It's Evie again, and I need your help. Which is huge for me because I have a hard time asking for help, but I'm working on that. Because I'm learning that part of love is being vulnerable and admitting when you're scared. And I was scared. I guess I still am, but I'm not going to let my fear control me.

"When my friend posted that video, she did it because she wanted to see me put myself out there and find some of that happiness I'd lost. But happy is terrifying because once you capture it there's a chance you might lose it. I thought it was safer to avoid finding real love than find it and lose it. But I was wrong."

"Love *is* scary," one of his neighbors said and Jonah shot him a *zip it or I'll zip it for you* look. The guy went palms up as if to say, *Well it is.*

Jonah went back to the video. "I never meant to lie to you," she said, and Jonah knew that she wasn't talking to America anymore. She was talking to him. "We did have a relationship. A beautiful friendship that turned into something more. Something to treasure, something worth fighting for. I thought if I gave into what we had, I'd lose myself. But I realize now that falling for you helped me find parts I thought I'd never get back. It also helped me find some of that happy. A lot of happy, and I want to be happy again."

She took a step closer to the camera and it was as if she were standing in front of him with her heart in her eyes. "You are worth fighting for, and I'm sorry if I ever made you feel like you weren't. You are kind and thoughtful and everything I could want in a partner. But you know how sometimes when things get messy I try to organize them but end up making a bigger mess of things? Well, I messed up."

"So did I, sunshine," he whispered.

"I know how it feels to be walked away from. I know how much it hurts. Just like I know how much I hurt you. But I promise that if you give me another chance, I'll fight for love every day. I'll fight for you every day. Please let me fight," she said, and he could see the emotion well up and line her lashes.

Jonah hadn't thought about that before now. He'd been so fixated on his own hurt and insecurities, he forgot that Evie had been left with a huge responsibility she had to shoulder all on her own at a young age.

He hadn't just made her miss her exam, he'd made her miss out on something she'd already lost once.

"I'm going to be where this all started, where I handed you an invitation that ended up changing my life, with my heart open and yours if you want it. If it's not too late. I'll be standing right here at one forty-three, with my final rose, hoping my prince charming shows up to claim it. Not to save me, but to love me and let me love him back."

God, he wanted her love, almost as much as he wanted to love her.

He looked at the time on the phone and felt his palms sweat and his heart race with panic. It was 1:38 p.m. and the shop was ten blocks away.

"Do you need a ride, son?" Mr. Karlson asked. "I've got my car running and ready to go."

"With traffic there's no way I make it." Jonah didn't even stop to think, he just took off in a dead sprint.

Chapter Forty-Three

Evie

Evie looked at the crowd that had gathered. There were so many people, they were spilling out onto the street. Phones were recording, the air hummed with anticipation, there was even a giant countdown clock someone had strapped to the top of their car.

One forty-one it read and Evie felt sick. What if he didn't come? What if her public apology and plea had only made things worse? And why had she put the stupid timer on it?

She gripped the rose in her hand so tightly that a thorn pressed into her thumb, breaking the skin. But the pain was nothing compared to what she was going to feel if he didn't show.

"He'll be here, Mom," Camila said. "I know he will."

"He will, Mrs. G," Ryan assured her, but she didn't feel reassured. She felt terrified. Terrified that she'd found and lost love all in the same week.

"What if he didn't see it?" Even worse, what if he had and

decided *she* wasn't worth the fight.

"He saw it," Moira said. "Karlson promised me he'd take care of it."

Evie choked on air. "Since when do you and Mr. Karlson team up?"

"Since we're going out on a date tonight. Seems I'm finally ready for a man."

"I'm really happy for you, Mom."

"Can we put a minute on the clock?" Tasha's voice interrupted, and that's when Evie realized that the next sixty seconds were going to define the rest of her life.

"You got this," Julie said, giving Evie's hair a fluff, and then stepped off camera.

"We're coming to you live from Grinder, to see if this coffee shop is really visited by Cupid. And with me is You've Got Male, for part two of our exclusive story on if love over social media works," Tasha said into the camera on her phone. "You all remember Evie, the one who hired a beard to trick America into thinking she was off the market?"

"I didn't hire him, I—"

"Well, she's back on the market and looking for love. Only, she's looking for a specific man's love. Turns out, she needed a little beard in her world because that lie turned into love and she's waiting to see if Cupid is on her side. So who here is team Cupid?"

"Cupid! Cupid!" the crowd chanted.

"And how many of you believe someone deserves a second chance at love?"

Nearly every hand in the audience went up, and Evie felt some of her nerves evaporate. Surely if all these people believed in second chances, then she stood a chance. Right?

"Well, let's see if Evie is one *no* closer to her *yes*, or if she's finally found it," Tasha said. "And it looks like we're about to find out."

Evie went up on her toes to look over the crowd as Mr. Karlson's car pulled up. Her heart started hammering and she felt like she was going to float into the sky and pass out all at the same time.

"Ten, nine, eight," the crowd counted down as it parted, making room for the car to pull up to the curb and Evie's lips curled up into a smile on their own accord. Love, that's what she was feeling. Raw, honest, till-the-end-of-times love.

"Seven, six, five." The words echoed through her ribs like the ball bearing in a pinball machine.

She ran her fingers through her hair, then smoothed down her dress. This was it. This was the first day of the next chapter of her life.

"Three, two..."

Instead of "One" a thick hush rolled over the crowd like fog and Evie's heart plummeted to her gut. Every heartbeat felt like a punch. Every breath felt like swallowing glass.

He wasn't there. Karlson's passenger seat was empty.

Jonah hadn't come.

Hundreds of eyes went soft with pity, like how one would look at the woman at the bar who nursed her drink for two hours after being stood up. Only, she hadn't been stood up. She'd been left. Alone. With her breaking heart for everyone to witness.

The crowd went blurry from the tears gathering, and her hand that was clutching the rose fell to her side. *This* was the first day of the next chapter of her life, and she was the responsible party.

She dropped her head to stare at her shoes, which was easier than facing the onlookers, and watched the first tear drop onto the concrete. It hit the ground and shattered into a million particles of water, like a rain cloud opening up.

Before another could fall, excitement rose from the street. The sound of cheering tore through the air and she slowly lifted her head.

The crowd was once again parting and pushing his way through the middle, like Moses and the Red Sea, was Jonah.

Hope bubbled up in her chest, tickling her throat and the backs of her eyes.

He didn't stop running until he was standing in front of her.

"You came," she whispered.

"I'd never leave you here alone," he said, and the starting of hope fizzled like a flat soda. Had he come there just to save her from the humiliation? Or had he come for love?

"I'm so sorry," she began and he shook his head.

"You have nothing to apologize for," he began. "I ran here today, do you know why?" he said, his voice coming in bursts from his run. He'd run there. In a suit. That had to mean something.

"Because of my video?"

"Because you were right when you said you were making the best choice for us both."

"I was?" she croaked out, barely able to breathe past the pain.

"You were, sunshine," he said. "I don't want you to be with me because of some arrangement made out of desperation."

"No, of course you don't." Evie could no longer look at him so she studied his shirt.

His finger cupped her chin and tilted her head until she was looking at him again. "I want you to be with me because of all the right reasons."

"And what would those be?" she whispered.

"Because you want to be. Because you love me. Because you can't imagine spending another day without me in your life. Because that's how I feel. I love you, Evelyn, the kind of love that doesn't go away over a little speed bump. Hell, I'd be willing to scale a problem as big as the Rockies if it means earning your heart." He gripped her hips and gently tugged her toward him. "Let me earn your love. Prove to you that we can make this work."

"You don't have to prove anything to me." She pressed her palms flat against his chest. "You already have my heart."

"Thank God for that, because I'm pretty sure I've loved you since you offered to toast my balls."

She choked on a laugh. "I'm pretty sure I fell that night over the summer on the back porch when we talked beneath the stars and shared a glass of wine."

"I might not have been ready then, but I am one hundred percent ready now. The question is: Are *you* ready, sunshine?"

"Yes," she said, and before she could get another word out, his mouth came down on hers. And it wasn't just a kiss. It was the kind of fireworks, sweep-you-off-your-feet, famous-World-War-II-in-Times-Square-kiss kind of kiss that went soul deep.

And the kiss went on and on until they slowly became aware of the people around them. Some were chanting, "Cupid! Cupid!" Others were talking feverishly about tossing their pennies into the Lucky in Love tip jar. But it was her heart that Evie was listening to, and it was telling her she'd found her Charming.

Jonah pulled back and there was so much emotion in his eyes she started crying again—the good kind this time. Then he did the unexpected: he took both of her hands in his and got down on one knee.

A bit of panic set in and he must have seen it on her face because he gave her a reassuring squeeze of the hands.

"Evelyn Granger," he began. "Will you do me the honor of becoming my real girlfriend?"

"Does that mean you'll accept my final rose?"

He stood and pulled her into his arms. "Sunshine, I'll accept all your roses."

Epilogue

Evie

Two weeks later...

Kristen Bell didn't have a thing on Evie.

She was about to pull off the greatest surprise in the history of surprise parties. And her mom hadn't a clue what was going down.

Arms slid around her waist from behind and she felt lips nibble her ear. "Beautiful," was all he said.

Evie took in the yard. "It really is beautiful, isn't it?"

Evie stared at the rose-lined walkway, the white tents glowing with fairy lights, and the white mesh draped over the entrance like curtains. Then there was the red carpet that connected the pathway to the party, which was held in the backyard. It looked like some elaborate party from the Golden Age of Hollywood. Then there was Jonah's yard.

He'd worked so hard to make sure it was perfect. And he'd

reached perfection. In fact, everything about him was perfect for her. He'd proved to her over the past few weeks what an incredible support system he could be, and what an incredible man he was.

Their lives still resembled a three-ring circus—a ring for each other's dreams, their respective families, and a ring just for them. And their ring seemed to be growing by the day. Every secret look, every gentle kiss, their romance was blossoming. Because they were each nurturing the love between them.

"I was talking about you." Another gentle kiss pressed against the column of her throat.

Evie turned in his arms and what she saw shining back at her robbed her of oxygen. She'd never had a man look at her like she was his whole world.

"What?" he whispered.

She went up on her toes and gave him a tender kiss. Against his mouth, she said, "I love you."

"Remember the rules?" Camila said. "No PDA. If Ryan and I can't make out then neither can you guys."

With an amused smile, Jonah gave her one last peck and released her. "PDA is over."

"Good, because Grandma just texted and said she's around the corner."

Evie's heart raced with pride. She'd done it. She'd out-sneaked the sneak and she couldn't wait to see the look on her mom's face.

"Everyone, go inside the tent and hide," Evie said, looking at the large group that represented every family member, friend, and loved one. "She's almost here."

There was a flurry of excitement as a hundred partygoers ducked into one of the two tents and waited. A few moments later a car pulled into the driveway, and she could hear the click of Moira's kitten heels as they clapped against the stone pathway.

Then she was there, and everyone jumped out. "Surprise!"

Moira put a hand to her chest and gasped as if she were in complete shock. But a tingle of suspicion crept up Evie's neck. She knew! Evie didn't know how but her mother knew!

Not only was Moira dressed to the nines, looking like she was going to a movie premiere, she also had Mr. Karlson on her arm dressed in a tux.

Mr. Karlson!

Moira smiled and said with as much faux surprise as she could muster, "This is all for little old me?"

Evie narrowed her eyes at Moira, who gave a delicate shrug of a shoulder. But her grin was 100 percent *got ya!*

She waited until Moira made her rounds before she approached. "Who told you?" Evie demanded.

Moira cupped her cheek. "Honey, the second those invites hit inboxes people were abuzz. So it wasn't just any one person. It was everyone. Ducking my calls. Avoiding me in the market. You and Dad sneaking around and whispering behind my back."

"So it wasn't Karlson."

"I kept my mouth shut," Mr. Karlson said.

"Then why are you in a tux?"

"Well, I couldn't show up stag to my own party. And my date needed to look the part."

"He's in a tux and it's eighty degrees out," Evie pointed out.

Mr. Karlson took Moira's hand and kissed her knuckles. "I'd wear this to the Sahara if it meant another date."

"I was thinking today's date would blend into tomorrow," Moira said, wiggling her brows seductively, and Evie held up a hand.

"Camila's right. No PDA at the party."

"If you say so," Moira said as Karlson wove her arm through his and escorted her into the tent.

Jonah approached with two glasses of champagne and took her hand. He led her up to her bedroom and the balcony that overlooked the yard. From there they had a bird's-eye view of the party.

"What are we doing?" she asked.

"I wanted you to see what you did. You brought all these people together, sunshine. That's what you do."

"It's just a party," she said shyly.

"It's more than that. You're more than that. You're like this bright light that seeps into people's hearts. And you've seeped into mine, lighting me up from the inside. I love you, Evie. I am so in love with you."

"I love you, too," she whispered.

Jonah didn't waste any time kissing her. It was slow and tender with an undertone of adoration. The kiss went on for a long moment, so long that her heart felt like it was going to explode with happiness.

Evie had chased happy and finally caught it. And she was never letting go.

Acknowledgments

I would like to thank my fabulous editors Molly Majumder and Jessica Turner for pushing me to make this story the best it could be, and Liz Pelletier for taking a chance on my work. To the rest of the team at Entangled, thank you for all the amazing work and support.

To my agent, Jill Marsal, for guiding me through this industry and always having my back. You are a fairy godmother, savvy agent, and dear friend all wrapped up in one.

And to the readers. Without you none of this would be possible. So thank you for all your continued love and support.

Finally, and most importantly, to my fabulous daughter and husband, for understanding that this is more than just my dream and believing in me no matter how crazy things got.

*Don't miss the exciting new books
Entangled has to offer.*

Follow us!

 @EntangledPublishing

 @Entangled_Publishing

 @EntangledPub

AMARA

an imprint of Entangled Publishing LLC